David of Jerusalem

By LOUIS DE WOHL

DAVID OF JERUSALEM
(translated from the German by Elisabeth Abbott)

FOUNDED ON A ROCK
A History of the Catholic Church

LAY SIEGE TO HEAVEN

CITADEL OF GOD

THE JOYFUL BEGGAR

THE GLORIOUS FOLLY

THE LAST CRUSADER

THE SPEAR

THE SECOND CONQUEST

SET ALL AFIRE

THE GOLDEN THREAD

THE RESTLESS FLAME

THE QUIET LIGHT

THE LIVING WOOD

David of Jerusalem

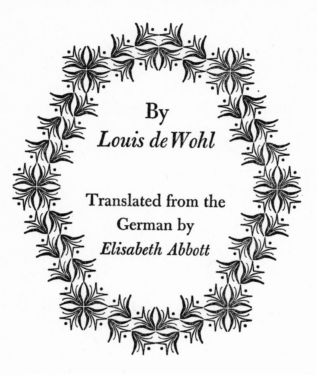

By
Louis de Wohl

Translated from the
German by
Elisabeth Abbott

J. B. Lippincott Company
Philadelphia & New York

This book is published in the original German under
the title *König David*.

LIBRARY OF CONGRESS CATALOG CARD NUMBER: 63–17674
PRINTED IN THE UNITED STATES OF AMERICA

David of Jerusalem

1

SLOWLY, SILENTLY, AND UP THE WIND, like all good hunters, the lion crept over the thin grass. Behind the yellowish-brown mass of rocks around the little depression, he was practically invisible. He stopped and measured the distance to the grazing sheep. Still a little too far. Stealthily he moved forward, two steps, three steps, four. He crouched, stiffened—and sprang.

But the ram had seen his shadow; bleating loudly, he leaped to one side, while the lion sprang into empty space. A short, hoarse growl, and already he was crouching for the next spring. The flock of sheep ran in all directions, but in their panicky fright the animals could not find the narrow exit into the plain.

"So there you are again!" shouted an angry young voice. "Just you wait, I'll show you!" And, placing a smooth stone in his leather sling, the young shepherd swung it, pulled back, and let fly. The stone struck the lion on the temple with such force that he staggered. Roaring, he shook his heavy, matted mane.

Tossing his sling aside, the shepherd ran to the lion, flung his muscular arm around the beast's neck, and pressed with all the strength in his young body. The lion, still half dazed, tried to shake him off, but he could not. Planting his legs firmly on the ground, the shepherd flung back his head and tightened his strangle hold. The lion's jaws opened wide, his tongue hung out over his lips. A trembling shook the mighty limbs. The claws on the hind feet tore convulsively at the ground. But the shepherd's arms did not yield an inch; he seemed to be made of iron. Suddenly the huge cat went limp, his feet gave way, and as he fell, he pulled the strangler with him to the ground. But even now, lying half under the lion, the shepherd did not let go until the lion's eyes rolled upward and blood dripped from the corners in thick, dark drops. Then at last the shepherd relaxed his hold. As the lion's body lay limp and motionless, the victor carefully freed himself and stood up. "There now," he announced, "you won't steal any more of my sheep." But to be on the safe side, he gave the lion a kick. As the animal did not stir, he nodded in satisfaction. Then, frowning, he noticed that the flock was still running wild. "Qui-et!" he sang out, "qui-et, good sheep!" and he strolled leisurely towards them, stopping on the way to pick up his sling and run his hand lovingly over it. This sling was an old friend. It was not the first time it had proved to be reliable.

A tall, gaunt man stepped out from behind a group of rocks. "David," he exclaimed and his voice trembled, "how could you dare . . . ?"

"Caleb!" cried the shepherd in surprise. "What are you doing here?"

The gaunt man shook his head. "To fight a lion with your bare hands," he stammered. "Who ever heard of such a thing?"

"Samson did it," said the shepherd. "I've wanted to try it for a long time. It's not so hard if you get the right grip. But to be on the safe side I shot him on the head with a stone. Last month I had to fight a bear, but he gave me more trouble."

"You aren't hurt?"

"No."

Working together, the man and the young shepherd gradually rounded up the excited sheep and quieted them. The shepherd asked, "What are you doing here, Caleb?"

"Your father sent me. You are to come home at once. The holy man from Ramatha is there."

"Who?"

"The prophet! All Judah and all Israel know him. You don't

mean to say *you* don't know who he is! He speaks in the name of the Lord. Even the king fears him."

"You mean Samuel? He is with my father? But what does he want?"

"He didn't tell me. But if I were you, I wouldn't keep them waiting. Your father, your brothers, and the holy man—they're all waiting for you."

"All right, I'll go. Look after the sheep meantime. And skin the lion for me."

Caleb rubbed his chin and looked around. "I only hope that old fellow wasn't married," he said. "I've no desire to explain this little incident to his widow."

David flung back his head and laughed. "That fellow had no wife. He was an old recluse—like the holy man from Ramatha."

Caleb watched David go. "Samson did it too," he murmured. "But Samson was a giant, with arms as thick as my two thighs put together. Where did the boy get the strength?"

Half an hour later David reached Bethlehem and his father's house on the edge of the town. His mother, as blue-eyed and reddish-blonde as he, was standing in the doorway. Eight sons and two daughters she had borne and she was still a good-looking woman. David was proud of her.

"They are all at the place of sacrifice," she called when he was still a good way off. David nodded to her and pushed on.

The place of sacrifice was a hill to the east of the city. David could see smoke rising in thick clouds from the sacrificial stone, and behind the smoke the group of men on the hill looked unreal, almost ghostly. One of them seemed to be wearing a white veil around his head and chin. No, it wasn't a veil, it was hair, white hair and a white beard; that must be the holy man of Ramatha.

As David climbed the hill, he smelled the odor of the sacrifice, a young heifer. What was being consumed by the fire was the fat over the intestines, the liver, and the fat of the kidneys, with the kidneys themselves as the law prescribed. Now, as he came closer, he could smell the fresh blood on the sacrificial stone.

"Here comes the boy," he heard his father say. "That is David, my youngest."

"Why does Father look so upset?" David wondered. Then he looked at the holy man and his thoughts stopped. He saw a broad face covered with a network of deep lines and wrinkles, and above the short, flat nose, bushy white eyebrows. The eyes . . . David had not feared the lion's gaze, but before the two suns that now burned into him, he had to lower his own eyes.

"He is the one!" said a surprisingly high, throaty voice. "The Lord has chosen him." The forefinger of a hand the color of parchment and covered with age spots pointed directly at David. "Take off your shoes," commanded the terrible old man. "Give him a pitcher of water."

Father Jesse held out the pitcher to his son, and with it a towel. His hand trembled a little.

"What are they going to do to me?" thought David. And suddenly it occurred to him that perhaps he himself was to be the sacrifice. Had not the Lord demanded of Abraham that he sacrifice Isaac? At the last moment He had then been satisfied with a ram. Perhaps this time He would not be satisfied, and the old man would cut his throat with the sacrificial knife. He could run away, of course. None of his brothers could catch him and certainly not the old man. But what if it was the will of God? The holy man from Ramatha was a prophet, as everyone knew. And one could not run away from God. God was everywhere and He alone decided the hour of death.

In silence David completed the ritual washing. Now the old man was fumbling about his girdle. But instead of the sacrificial knife with the broad blade, he drew forth a little horn and carefully removed the silver stopper. A heavy, sweetish scent permeated the air. The old man prayed silently, his head held so high that the white beard pointed sharply upward. Then he said: "Come nearer, David, son of Jesse."

David obeyed.

"Bow your head."

"Balsam," thought David in amazement, as the heavy drops rolled slowly over his hair. It was impossible. He must be dream-

10

ing! When he woke up, there would be a sheep or two missing,
like last week, or a wild beast had come and— But no, he wasn't
dreaming: some of the balsam had run into his eyes and it burned
like fire. So then he really was awake. But the silence around him
was like the silence of death.

The prophet closed the oil horn and carefully tucked it back
into his richly embroidered girdle. "It is good," he said in his
high voice. "For the rest the Lord will provide." He bowed low
before David, so low that several wispy strands of white hair fell
down over his face. For David's father he had a brief nod, for
the brothers only a wave of his hand. Without another word he
turned and strode down the hill.

No one dared to say anything until he was out of earshot. And
even then Father Jesse spoke in a whisper. "May the Lord keep
all evil from us. I do not understand this."

"No one can understand it," agreed Jesse's eldest son, big,
sturdy Eliab. "But he said he had come to sacrifice with us to
the Lord."

"And that is what he did."

Shammah, the third eldest son, grinned. "Of course, Father.
But he himself brought the sacrificial animal with him. It was his
property. Then why did he need you and us? The sacrifice was a
pretext, nothing else. What he really wanted was something very
different."

"Why did he stare so at all of us, one after the other?" asked
Eliab. "He has eyes like—knife blades!"

"He began with you," Shammah nodded, "and I clearly heard
him murmur, 'This is not the one!' "

"That's what he said about you, too," retorted Eliab angrily.
"And about Abinadab and all the others."

"Yes, yes," Shammah agreed. He dearly loved to make big
Eliab angry. "All the others—except the boy. And him, he
anointed."

"But why?" asked Eliab half to himself. "That's just what I
can't understand."

"Father," asked David, "do you know why the prophet
anointed me?"

Jesse shook his head, but did not speak.

"And he bowed before him, too, as if he were a great lord," sneered Eliab. "Are you a great lord, David?"

"For his goats and sheep he certainly is," grinned Shammah.

"Leave the boy alone; we're going home," ordered Father Jesse, and he led the way.

David ran his hand over his forehead. The high, throaty voice was still ringing in his ears. "He is the one. The Lord has chosen him." Chosen? But for what? "I always thought only kings could be anointed," he said thoughtfully.

"King of shepherds," murmured Shammah, and the brothers laughed, all but Eliab, who said grimly, "We have a king. People say he is not very patient. If King Saul hears what the old man has done here, he'll have us all killed."

Father Jesse turned around. "That's enough," he said with unusual violence. "None of us can guess the prophet's thoughts. It is foolish to try. And dangerous."

"It *is* dangerous," continued Eliab. "King Saul has only to hear that—"

"It's always the same with you, brother," Shammah cut him short impatiently. "When you once get your teeth in an idea, you never let go of it. King Saul! He sits up there in his castle and doesn't even know we exist."

"Who knows?" growled Eliab. "They say, too, that the king isn't quite right in his head. And crazy people—" He broke off as his father turned around again and glared at him sharply.

"Keep a better watch on your tongue," said Father Jesse harshly. "First you spoke disrespectfully of the prophet Samuel, and now of the king. The king is the anointed of the Lord. His person is holy. Another such word and I shall make you rue it bitterly."

At home, during the evening meal, David sat silent and lost in thought. His mother watched him with anxious eyes, but said nothing. After supper, however, when she saw him take his harp and slip out into the garden, she sighed with relief. Music always relaxed him.

David went to his favorite retreat under a thick cluster of

palm trees beside the garden wall. Ten feet high that wall was, too high for a hungry panther or jackal to leap over. He could not get the old man from Ramatha out of his mind. "He is the one. The Lord has chosen him." But what had He chosen him for? Gently he ran his hand over the red-gold hair that was usually so unruly but now was smooth and soft through the magic power of balsam. Only kings were anointed. And the anointed of the Lord sat in his palace and his courtiers trembled before his rages. Old Nahum ben Sichar, the town elder, whom King Saul had called to his court, spoke of it once when he had drunk too much wine. That had been last year. He had also told about a curse the holy man was said to have put upon the king. And since then the king was sometimes . . . strange. But a mighty ruler he still was, a victor in battle, a head taller than any of his subjects. To be king—that meant being very close to God, as close as it was possible for a human being to get.

David plucked the strings of his harp and sang to himself. And the words seemed to come of their own accord:

> O Lord our Lord, how admirable is thy name in the whole earth!
> For I will behold thy heavens, the works of thy fingers: the moon and the stars which thou hast founded.
> What is man that thou art mindful of him? or the son of man that thou visitest him?

The clear young voice carried effortlessly to the house, and the mother smiled to herself. It carried over the wall, and in neighboring houses men ceased their toil and stood at their doors to listen. David sang:

> Thou hast crowned him with glory and honour: and hast set him over the works of thy hands. O Lord our Lord, how admirable is thy name in all the earth!

God Himself was the quintessence of kingliness. No one could become king without God's will. That was what sanctified King Saul.

David ran his hand over his hair again. The balsam smelled

strong and at the same time sweet. . . . The prophet had come from Ramatha, a journey of at least two days, long and difficult for an old man like him. Half way between Ramatha and Bethlehem lay Gibeah, the king's castle-fortress with its strong walls and watch towers, high above on a rocky plateau—an eagle's nest. This castle he had had to pass. Perhaps the king's soldiers had seen and recognized him! If so, then there was real danger brewing, not only for the house of Jesse but also for the prophet. Why had he laid himself open to that risk? What did he want from David, son of Jesse the shepherd?

When he went back to the house he found his mother waiting at the door. She kissed him. "No one sings like you," she said. "I killed a lion," he told her. Horrified, she clasped both hands together. "David! Did he . . . are you hurt?"

"No, mother."

She smiled, at once relieved and proud. "What did your father say?"

"I forgot to tell him."

Three days later Nahum ben Sichar, a thin, elderly man with a well-kept gray beard, came to Bethlehem. He rode an ass with a many-colored, richly embroidered saddlecloth, and around his neck he wore a gold chain the king had given him. Father Jesse received him with all the honors due a king's councilor. A lamb was slaughtered for him, and a clay vessel containing the best wine was dug out of the earth where it had rested for years. At table there was talk of an unfortunate military incident in Negev, an encounter between a detachment of Philistines and a few Israelite farmers. There had been men wounded on both sides— fortunately no dead. But the most disagreeable result was that the Philistines had raised the price of metal again. "They take advantage of every opportunity to raise prices," sighed Nahum ben Sichar. "They know only too well that we have no choice but to pay."

Father Jesse nodded. "It's a pity there are no smiths in Judah and Israel." Every knife, every scythe, every ploughshare had to be bought from the Philistine smiths at a high price. Weapons were not allowed to be sold to men from Judah and Israel, and as a result they were forced to rely in battle on bludgeons, sling-shots, and pointed wooden staves—unless they had been lucky in taking spoils of war.

"The king does not think the incident will have serious con-sequences," said the guest in reply to Father Jesse's anxious ques-tions. "At least not yet. The Philistines have clan feuds among themselves. But the king . . ." he broke off. "I have a message from him to you, Jesse." He looked down at the ground.

The master of the house turned pale. "Leave us, my sons," he commanded, "I must be alone with our guest." But Nahum ben Sichar raised his hand. "Let your youngest son stay here," he said.

David turned around. He seemed very calm, but his eyes burned. His brothers also did not move.

"It concerns him," Nahum ben Sichar went on.

"Concerns . . . David?" stammered Jesse. "What does the king know about David?"

Eliab, Shammah, and the others disappeared silently.

"I am ordered to bring him to the king," said Nahum ben Sichar, as he stroked his beard.

Jesse stiffened. "To the king!" he repeated in a hoarse voice. "But why? What has he done?"

"Done?" The councilor smiled. "Nothing. Not yet."

Father Jesse wiped his broad sleeve across his forehead. "I don't understand," he murmured.

The councilor toyed with the gold chain around his neck. "The king listens to me," he said with a touch of pride. "I may say that I enjoy his confidence to a greater extent than many others. The poor king—he has not had an easy time since the—incident between him and the prophet. You know Samuel, don't you?"

"Everyone in Judah and Israel knows him," said Jesse gloomily. Was Nahum ben Sichar playing with him as a cat plays with a mouse?

"No one knows exactly what happened at that time," the coun-cilor went on. "And perhaps it's better not to ask too many ques-tions. But since the incident, since the . . . hm, differences between the king and Samuel, we at court sometimes do not have

15

an easy time." He shrugged his shoulders expressively. "The king is a great man, but he is not happy. He seldom smiles. He worries —he flies into sudden rages—in a word, he suffers. And that is why I thought of your youngest . . ."

"Nahum ben Sichar, I still don't understand you," said Jesse who was worried to death.

"The king is filled with suspicions," explained the councilor. "He sees enemies all around him—intrigues—conspiracies. He knows that people generally come to him only when they want something. So I told him: 'My king, you should have music at your court.'"

"Music?"

"Yes. 'Nothing dispels a bad mood as well as music,' I said. 'And if it is your will, lord, I will bring you a young man who has a voice like no other and who plays the harp so beautifully that all who hear must stop and listen to him. And he plays and sings not only the old songs of our people, but he himself composes new songs and the music to them.' Then the king said, 'Bring him to me. At once.' He did not even ask for his name. And when King Saul says 'at once,' it is not wise to tarry. I therefore mounted an ass, and came here."

"And is that all?" asked Jesse incredulously. "Really all? You're not keeping anything from me?"

"What should I keep from you?" cried the councilor in astonishment. "You don't seem overly pleased by my mission. Is it not a great honor for so young a man to be needed by the king?"

Jesse took a deep breath. "It is an honor," he admitted.

Nahum ben Sichar rose. "You have sons enough to look after your flocks," he said, "and the king's castle is not so far from here that David cannot visit you from time to time." He laughed good-naturedly. "That will comfort his mother."

"Are you leaving now?"

"Yes, to be sure. And I'm taking the young singer with me. 'At once,' King Saul said. He doesn't like to be kept waiting. Bring your harp, David. That is all you need."

But Jesse shook his head. "I can't let him go without a sign of gratitude for the honor the king has shown this house. We are plain folk and can not offer golden chains. But I will give David a kid to take with him, and bread and a bottle of wine."

"Good, good, but make haste."

Half an hour later David rode out of Bethlehem beside the councilor toward Saul's mountain fortress. His mother had wept, and that grieved him. Shammah had advised him to wash his hair quickly before he left. "Your hair still smells of balsam, little brother, and kings have sharp noses."

Eliab had whispered to him, "All that business about the harp and singing is of course only an excuse. We'll never see you alive again." The other brothers had stared at him half anxiously, half curiously—somewhat the way, the year before, they had stared at Eliab when he had black smallpox. Eliab had survived the smallpox. One did not succumb to every danger.

David felt himself strangely light and winged, like the time his father had taken him to Ascalon, to the sea, when for the first time in his life he had been allowed to swim. It had been an entirely new experience, almost a new life. He was suddenly no longer just an earth creature. The water, too, was now a domain in which one could live and disport oneself. A pity a man couldn't imitate the birds too. Had not God set Adam as ruler over the whole earth and all that in it lived? One should be able not only to run and swim, but to fly. When he expressed that thought at the time, his brothers had made fun of him and even his father had shaken his head. Since then he had never mentioned it. But now that strange, intoxicating sense of a great adventure was there again. "I'm going to the king's court," he thought. Purple from Tyre, silk from Sidon, costly cedar woods, men with golden chains around their necks and on their arms, princes, princesses. And the king himself, who needed him to drive away the cares that weighed on him.

He had not answered Eliab and Shammah. It was clear that they were angry, angry and jealous because the prophet had anointed him, the youngest brother, the "little one," and not them. "Little one!" He hated that name. Of course he was not exactly tall, but he could take on any of his brothers, yes, even two of them at a time. And if the king intended to have him

17

killed, it was not necessary to lure him to court under a pretext. He need only send his soldiers after him.

"What does one say to the king?" David asked.

Nahum ben Sichar smiled: "Nothing. You wait until you are spoken to."

David nodded. "But if you are spoken to, how do you answer?"

"Courteously, but briefly. One does not contradict the king— at least, not unless it is absolutely necessary. You do not leave the room or the tent before he gives the sign. You address him as 'lord' or 'my king.' We are not like the Phoenicians or the Assyrians who speak flattering words to their rulers: 'O Brother of the Sun and of the Moon,' 'O Ruler of the World,' 'O Crown of Life.' "

"Those are foolish names because they are lies," said David. "But even if they were true, the king of Israel would be more than that, for he is the anointed of the Lord."

The councilor looked down at him obliquely. "Maybe," he said. "But don't forget, the king is ill. Strangely ill. Perhaps he won't even remember that he ordered me to fetch you. Perhaps he won't like you. He—he can be very angry. I don't want to worry you unnecessarily but—anything is possible. Be prepared for anything."

Gibeah, King Saul's castle, was practically an impregnable fortress. It was laid out in the shape of a hexagon, on a vast, rocky, steeply rising plateau. From each corner a watchtower projected twenty feet beyond the wall. The king's relatives, his councilors, and courtiers lived in a circle of houses on the slope of the hill, but in case of attack, they would draw back into the fortress itself. As the two riders passed the entrance gate, the guard raised his spear briefly in greeting to the councilor.

The royal palace was a long building occupying more than half the space inside the fortress. One side of the flat roof was open to view, but the balustrade around one of the other sides was hung with gaily-colored cloths. "That's where the women live," Nahum ben Sichar explained.

A broad-shouldered officer with rough-hewn, irregular features approached and nodded curtly. He wore a coat of mail made of tiny pieces of metal, very unusual in this part of the country and probably booty from the last war. "Is this the musician?" he asked bluntly.

"Yes," replied the councilor, "this is David, son of Jesse."

"I'll show him to his dwelling. He's to live in the palace behind the royal apartments. When he is needed, I'll send for him." Then he turned to David. "Follow me."

"I have brought gifts from my father."

"Gifts? You?" The officer looked at the heavily laden ass and grinned. "Even without that the king won't go hungry and thirsty. Give the stuff to the servant here, he'll take it over to the storehouse."

"No," said David calmly. "It is a complimentary gift. I must deliver it to the king myself."

The officer put his hands on his hips. "Just look at this young cockalorum!" he jeered. "Because he is to crow before the king, he gives himself airs! What I say goes here, young man! Get that!"

"David," the councilor broke in hastily. "This is Jacob, the captain of the king's bodyguards."

"My father's gift is for the king," declared David, "not for the captain of the guards."

"Now that's enough!" the officer roared at him. "We'll teach you not to be impertinent!" And balling his fist, he strode threateningly towards David. The next moment, however, he cried out, for David had gripped his right shoulder and wrenched it. The pain was so intense that the man's knees began to buckle, and he swayed.

"David, what are you doing!" wailed the councilor, dancing from one foot to the other. "David!"

"What is going on here?" asked a girl's contralto voice. "Is this a wrestling match?"

David looked up. Before him stood the most beautiful girl he had ever seen. Her flowing bright green gown with its jewel-encrusted girdle half revealed a figure as slim as a reed. Beneath her blue-black hair, her slender face was the color of ivory, her lips a burning red. She held her chin high, and in the dark, rather slanting eyes there was a gleam of goodnatured mockery.

Nahum ben Sichar bowed low. "Princess Michol," he whispered to David.

David released the officer's shoulder, and as he did so one of the little metal pieces from the armor came off in his hand. Stooping quickly, he pretended to pick it up from the ground. "How could I dare to wrestle with the captain of the bodyguards?" he asked, holding out the piece of metal to the princess. "I saw that this had come loose from his armor and I tried to keep it from falling, but it slipped through my fingers." And with that he handed the metal piece to the astonished officer.

The princess looked at David and the corners of her mouth twitched with suppressed laughter. "There is a harp fastened to your animal," she said. "That your fingers are strong I have already seen. If they are as quick as your wits, you must be the best harpist in the land."

"The ass is laden with a gift from my father for the king," said David. "I must deliver it to him."

At last the officer was able to speak again. "Princess, this young man insisted upon delivering this stuff to the king himself. I told him—"

"Yes, yes, my good Jacob, I understand. What is your name, harpist?"

"David, son of Jesse."

"Then, David, follow me. I know my father is expecting you. We shall see whether he can receive you at once. But you cannot take an ass with you into the palace." The princess's mocking glance wandered from the ass to Nahum ben Sichar and from the councilor to the captain of the bodyguards. "My women will take the gifts with them," she said, and only now did David notice two plainly clad women behind the princess. "Are you satisfied? Good. Then follow me!"

She led the way through a wide, dark gate into an anteroom where armed soldiers stood guard, then into a second room, where a dozen dignitaries waited for an audience, and from there into a third room, in which there was only one man, a small, thin man with a scroll in his hand.

"Is my father alone, Chusai?" asked the princess.

The young man nodded. "Yes, Princess, but . . ." His ugly, but intelligent face wrinkled slightly and he shrugged. Princess Michol bit her lips. Gliding to the nearest door, she pulled aside the curtain and peered in. David saw that her long, ivory-colored hand trembled.

"She is afraid," he thought. "Even she is afraid." Looking over her shoulder, he saw the king.

2

KING SAUL, SUNK DEEP IN THOUGHT, was seated on a couch of exquisite furs. His arms hung down at his sides, his prematurely gray hair fell over his forehead, and because he held his head down, David could not see his features. He rocked his heavy body continually to and fro.

It was wrong and disrespectful to look at the king—Saul thought he was alone—as wrong and disrespectful as it had been of Ham to look at his father, Noah, when the latter lay drunk and naked on his bed. David stepped back. "Let us go, Princess," he said softly.

"Wait," Princess Michol commanded. Her sensitive lips twitched. "Take your harp. Play! That's what you have been sent for, isn't it?" A sharp little line appeared between her eyes.

David hesitated a second. Then he took his harp and began to play the new melody that had come to him in the garden at home.

Chusai the secretary looked on in astonishment. He was not at all musical, and the sounds this young man with the reddish hair was producing were, to him, merely chirpings, nothing more. But it was strange to see how the harpist's face changed as he played—as though somewhere in the distance he saw something tremendous and indescribably beautiful.

The princess had glanced quickly at her father, but after the first sounds of the harp she turned to David. She, too, noticed the change in him.

"O Lord, our Lord," sang David softly to himself, "how admirable is thy name in the whole earth—"

Suddenly he broke off. The king, tall and pale, with deep, dark shadows under his lusterless eyes, stood in the doorway. He wore an old garment of purple linen, spotted with wine. "Michol," he called.

"Yes, Father?"

"Is that the singer they were going to send me?"

"Yes, Father."

"Let him come in. Alone." The king turned away and shuffled back again.

Michol shrugged her shoulders and smiled mysteriously.

"If you value your life, obey him," she said.

Silently David entered the king's chamber. Saul was seated again on his couch, all in a heap as before. "One of my toadies and lickspittles has brought you here," he said in a hoarse voice. "I don't remember who it was. But that doesn't matter. Go on playing. No. Begin again from the beginning."

David began. He sang softly, and in his singing there was a deep reverence for God and the king whom God had set over Israel and Judah, the poor, sick ruler. After a while Saul raised his head and looked up. The pale, prematurely aged face with the hooked nose and stubborn mouth was sad and noble. The song came to an end.

"That is better than wine," said the king. "I like you, young man. Is your father still alive?"

"Yes, lord. My father Jesse sent you a gift, bread and wine and our best kid. It is all outside."

The shadow of a smile passed over the melancholy face.

"I thank him," murmured the king. "He has sent me more than a gift. I shall—" Suddenly his eyes glittered ominously, like the eyes of a wild animal. He reached behind him and pulled out a short, strong spear. "Who is out there?" he roared.

The curtain was flung back. "Only your servant Chusai, my king," said the little secretary imperturbably.

23

"Chusai . . ." The king laid the spear across his knees. "A messenger goes to Jesse in . . ."

"In Bethlehem, my king," said David.

"In Bethlehem. I thank him for his gift. And his son remains here in my service. I have taken a liking to him. Go, my good Chusai, go."

David's service to the king was easy. Saul usually slept late. In the forenoon he received in audience a series of dignitaries, officers, and city fathers. After the midday meal he rested for an hour. Then came the administration of justice, ranging from adjudication of tribal quarrels to settlement of those disputes between farmers, neighbors, and neighbors' wives which for one reason or another could not be settled by city or village authorities. The administration of justice was one of the king's most important prerogatives. Not so long ago Israel had been governed by judges, but when the people insisted upon having a king, the old prophet Samuel, had given them in the name of God their first king—Saul. And Saul was a just judge, when he was not suddenly seized with an attack of his strange illness. Generally it began with a silent, brooding stare; sometimes also with a sudden outburst of rage. Then he would dismiss the persons around him, withdraw to his bedchamber, and send for David. The soft music of the harp and the singer's clear young voice never failed to have its effect. The king was calmed, and usually after a few minutes. Sometimes he fell asleep and David would steal softly from the room. But even toward the young singer the king behaved strangely. Since their first meeting he had not once addressed him; and as one could not address the king until one was spoken to, there was never any conversation between them. Saul scarcely even looked at David, and when he did, his glance was empty or vaguely surprised, as if he were seeing him for the first time.

Yes, it was an easy task and it left David much free time. Life in the castle was gay and varied; one met the great of the land, one heard all sorts of interesting things and saw even more. And yet David often longed for Bethlehem. Not so much for his brothers as for his father, and even more for his mother; but most of all for the silence, the peaceful solitude of the pastures. Sheep were neither hostile boors like Jacob, the captain of the guards, nor did they love gossip and intrigue like the majority of the courtiers. That his strange position as "soother" of the king should lead to all sorts of talk was inevitable. Some considered him a magician whose duty it was to exorcise the king's demons; others thought he was a secret ambassador of the prophet Samuel. "The old man sent the young one to drive the king completely mad." Still others envied him because he could live in the royal palace. On the other hand, Chusai, the clever, imperturbable little scertary, had become his friend. With him, and with him only, could David occasionally exchange thoughts. Chusai with his broad, flat nose and wide mouth, looked like a monkey, but behind the low, lined forehead was a keen intelligence. "You are a second Orpheus, David," he said one day.

"Orpheus?"

"Yes, an Achaian once told me about Orpheus. He was a singer, and so great was his art that even wild beasts listened to him enthralled instead of tearing him to pieces."

"King Saul is no wild beast, Chusai."

"No," the secretary admitted, "but there is a wild beast in him and it sometimes breaks out. You haven't seen that yet, but we who have known him longer have seen it. Perhaps there's a wild beast in each of us. Only sometimes it is a little one—or perhaps its cage is stronger."

"Where did you say the man who told you about Orpheus came from?"

"From Achaia. It must be a country across the sea."

"Across the sea?" echoed David in wonder. "I thought the world came to an end on the shores of the sea, the land world, that is."

"No. There is an island called Crete. I have talked with people who came from there. They had bronze weapons. I wish we had some. Bronze is not as good as iron, but much better than wood."

"And the Achaian came from Crete?"

25

"No, from much farther off, from another land he called Sparta. Have you heard of the city of Troy?"

"On the pastures you don't hear much about cities."

"It was a very great and powerful city, much, much bigger than Gibeah. The Achaians made war against it and finally captured and destroyed it. It was all because of a beautiful woman, they say. Among the allies of the Trojans were some wild tribes who left the land after the city fell and moved south. You have heard of those tribes, even if not on your pastures. They are the Philistines."

David's eyes shone. "So the Achaians conquered the Philistines! What they could do, we ought to be able to do, too."

Chusai sighed. "If only we had better weapons! The Philistines have an army of professional soldiers, men who from their youth have been trained in warfare. We are farmers and cattle raisers. No wonder they rule, and we—are ruled."

"Chusai! We are no slaves!"

"No." replied the little sceretary bitterly. "The Philistines are too clever to make slaves of us. They know very well that free men work harder and better because they work for themselves. So they let us become prosperous—and then they come and plunder us."

"But we have sometimes won out against them."

"Yes, when Samson was still among us. And King Saul, too, has sometimes won a battle against them, but not against their whole army, only against a few tribes. For a few years now things have been going well with us. Perhaps there will soon be another attack."

"We ought to win over the Achaians as allies," said David thoughtfully.

Chusai laughed. "They went back to their distant homeland long, long ago. But you talk almost like a warrior. Who taught you that? Not Jacob surely—he is not exactly a friend of yours."

"I know."

"And he is a powerful man," Chusai warned. "Look out for yourself. There is not always a princess around to appear at the right moment—"

"I have never seen Princess Michol again," said David.

Chusai loked at him sharply. "She does not come to the king often," he said slowly.

"She is very beautiful."

Chusai smiled wanly. "That is like saying the sun is lukewarm."

David was too young to recognize the deep longing in Chusai's eyes. Carefully controlling his own enthusiasm, he said, "That is the way the woman you told me about must have looked—the one for whose sake the Achaians waged war against Troy."

"Perhaps," murmured Chusai. Then after a pause he added bitterly, "I can't fight in any war. My left leg is too lame. And besides I am not strong. And if a woman who is expecting a child speaks to me, she turns her eyes away so that the child may not be as ugly as I am." And he turned on his heel.

Now at last David understood. He seized Chusai's hand. "A good shepherd must watch the sky," he said. "There he sees and learns many things—for instance, that the stars are too high above us in the sky for mere mortals to touch them."

"The sun," murmured Chusai. "Not the stars, they are cool and clear. The sun is hot and dangerous. He who exposes himself too much to the sun, loses his mind—he who comes too near is burnt."

Then the king called Chusai and the friends had to part.

David was standing at the castle gate when the messenger rode in, a bearded little man with a dead-white face. He had barely passed through the gate when the ass he was riding collapsed under him, kicked the sand with its hoofs, and died. Two guards pulled the man out from under the animal and helped him to his feet. Hanging limply between their arms, he called weakly for the king. An officer ran up. It was Jacob. He leaned over the man, who whispered something to him. Jacob straightened up, motioned to the guard to take the man to the palace, and followed hastily after.

The castle courtyard was soon filled with a throng of curious people. A number of servants ran out of the palace and scattered in all directions. A few minutes later a wiry man with a fox-like face, tanned a leathery brown, entered the palace at the head of a group of officers. It was Abner—after the king himself, the supreme commander of the army. Now it was fairly clear what news the messenger had brought. Another half-hour passed, then came the alarm. Dozens of messengers rode out of the gate, and the castle courtyard rang with commands.

"Hey, you there!"

David saw Jacob's hand beckoning to him and he went over.

"You are from Bethlehem, aren't you?" the captain of the guards asked gruffly. "Have them give you an ass and ride home as fast as you can. Inform the city elders that the Philistines are marching on Shochoh. The reserves are called out. Rallying point, the Valley of Elah. The men must be there by noon of the third day."

"But the king," objected David. "If the king—"

"The king has other things to think about now than your harp thumping," Jacob snapped roughly. "Now he needs men and not singing boys. Go home, deliver your message, and then you can sing to your goats." He turned away abruptly. "A messenger for Hebron," he roared. "I need a messenger for Hebron!"

David took leave of Chusai hastily. "Now it's the same with me as with you," he said bitterly. "I, too, am not allowed to fight in the campaign. You are lame and I am too young."

"Whether we are both in it or not is of no importance," replied Chusai wearily. "We'll be defeated in any case."

"David."

"Yes, father?"

"How long has it been since the reserves were called?"

"Five weeks, father."

Jesse sighed. "Five weeks—and still no news!"

"If something decisive had happened, we would have heard of it," David comforted him. But it did not sound very convincing. He had been obliged to say it so often.

Jesse sighed again. "Eliab," he complained, "Abinadab, and Shammah. Three of my dear sons with the reserve and no news. Your mother cannot stand the uncertainty any longer—and neither can I. Early tomorrow morning I shall have a wagon harnessed for you. Drive to the Valley of Elah and see if all is well with your brothers."

"Gladly, father," said David quickly. "I could even go to-day . . ."

"No, early tomorrow. I will give you three sacks of parched corn and ten loaves of bread. Who knows what they are getting to eat?" Father Jesse brought out a basket that was carefully lined and covered with palm leaves. "Here are ten milk cheeses," he said. "They are for the leader of their section—he is our neighbor, Ezra. He can send my sons to their death. It is just as well to put him in a good mood." The old man sighed again. "One thing more," he added. "The king's tribute is due again soon. Tell your brothers they are to give you their pay to bring to me. Where they are now there is nothing to spend it on and the tribute must be paid; otherwise the king's police will come and collect it the way they did last year with poor Simon."

"Yes, father."

"That is all. And—come back safely!"

The way to the Valley of Elah was not far, but one had to be careful. It was quite possible that the Philistines might try a circling movement or at least send out patrols to test the situation at the front. David kept his eyes open and wherever possible avoided valleys beween groups of rocks or between sand dunes. But not until he caught sight of the Israelite army's barricade of wagons did he know that he need no longer fear an attack. This barricade stood on a wide plateau, forming a fort to which in case of necessity the army could withdraw.

From the barricade David could overlook the whole battle-ground. The Israelite army was drawn up in the formation of a huge fan, occupying a long chain of hills. On the opposite hills, scarcely more than the flight of an arrow distant, glittered and sparkled the metallic mass of the enemy's army. It looked as though they must come to blows at any moment. How was it possible that fighting had not started long before? David looked around the barricade. Not a single wounded man to be seen.

Had the Philistine army just arrived? He put his wagon in the care of a baggage guard.

"Where do you come from?" asked the man curiously.

"From Bethlehem."

"And what have you in your wagon?"

"Bread and parched corn for my brothers who are with the army."

"Bethlehem? That means House of Bread." The man grinned. "You've brought the right thing along."

But David had no time for the guard's humor. "I hold you responsible for my wagon. Where are the reserves from Bethlehem?"

"On the right wing, I think—honored sir."

David hurried to the right wing. He had to pass a number of sections before he saw men from Bethlehem who could tell him where to find Ezra. He reported to him, explained that he had brought him a present from his father, and asked about his brothers.

"They are well," replied Ezra with a shrug. "As far as that can be said of any of us. When you go back to your father, give him my thanks. Haven't seen milk cheeses for a long time. You can't milk Philistines."

The brothers received him with a marked lack of enthusiasm. "What are you doing here?" asked Eliab peevishly. "Don't the goats need you any more?"

"Our parents are worried about you. And father says to tell you—"

"There he comes again," Shammah broke in loudly.

"Where?" asked Eliab.

"Haven't you any eyes in your head? He's certainly big enough, the sevenfold accursed infidel!"

David looked at his brother in amazement. Then he noticed that the entire section had become restless. The men clenched their fists around their spears, a few of them turned pale, and in the eyes of all lay fear and hatred. From the enemy's ranks there now emerged the strangest object David had ever seen; it looked at first like a shimmering metallic bear walking upright on its hind legs. Slowly the monster came nearer. Now David could see that in front of the creature walked a tiny figure, a five-year-old child, perhaps, or a dwarf; it was dragging a round object as big as itself.

In the Israelite ranks there was total silence. Nearer and nearer came the strange pair, and suddenly David knew that the tiny figure was neither a child nor a dwarf, but a man, a normal sized, strongly built man, who looked small only because the creature behind him was so huge. And this creature seemed to be a man too—only he was larger and taller than any man on earth. He wore a brass helmet, and of brass, too, were his buckler and his greaves. The spear in his hand was fully eight yards long and he carried it as if it were a feather. He was a figure out of a nightmare! Now he stood still, raised his spear, and began to shout something—what it was David could not hear at that distance. It sounded like one long, derisive battle cry.

The silence on the Israelite side was oppressive. David could not stand it any longer. "What sort of a creature is that?" he asked.

A soldier from the next section turned and looked at him. "Don't you know? He comes out every day."

"I've just arrived," David explained. "Who is he and what does he want?"

"Who is he? The strongest man among the Philistines," the soldier said sullenly. "And the biggest, as you can see. What he wants you'll soon hear from him. He goes up and down the whole front every day. Here he is now."

The giant had meanwhile come nearer, and he now stood at most thirty paces away. David saw his yellowish-brown face with the broad nose, the brutal mouth, and the malicious little eyes. Most of the rest of his face was covered by a woolly black beard. Again the giant raised his spear. "Here I am," he shouted. "Here stands Goliath of Gath, Goliath the Philistine, Goliath the unconquered! You slaves of Saul, choose a man from among you and let him come down and fight me hand to hand! If he is able to fight with me and kill me, we will be servants to you; but if I prevail against him, you shall be servants, and shall serve us."

Silence! No one spoke or moved. Then the giant began to laugh. "Again nobody? Is there really no man in your army?"

With a scornful gesture he started to move on slowly, clumsy, clattering, a walking tower of flesh, muscle, bones, and metal.

"The king has offered a high reward," said the soldier to David with a bitter smile. "But there has been no one who wants to earn it. No wonder! What good is the finest reward to a man when he is dead? No man in Israel or in Judah can stand up to that monster. The fellow wears armor, too, from head to foot. Of course he knows no one will accept his challenge. He just wants to insult us."

"A reward, you say? What sort of a reward?" asked David. He was still watching the giant. It was probably only the armor that made him walk so stiffly. The muscles of his arms and legs were like enormous coils.

"The reward is truly royal," said the soldier ironically. "Wealth, freedom from tribute for the whole family for life, and the king's daughter to wife. More than that a man can't ask. But the king can promise heaven and earth. No one will come forward, and if anyone were crazy enough to do it, he'd never live to receive his reward. Dead men get nothing out of their riches, they don't have to pay tribute anyway, and what good is the most beautiful girl to a corpse?"

"The king's daughter," David repeated. "Are you sure that is right?"

"Of course it's right," a bearded captain intervened. "The king swore it solemnly."

"And you mean to say no one has come forward?" David exclaimed. "No man was ready to risk his life for such a prize?" The men grinned in embarrassment. "And we let this uncircumcised dog of a Philistine jeer at us day after day?" David was growing more and more angry. "Reward or not—can we take that silently, we, the army of the living God?" In his excitement he did not notice that he had become the center of attention.

Then Eliab turned on him: "What are you doing here anyway, you whippersnapper? Did you come down to see the battle, eh? And meantime who is taking care of your sheep and goats? I know you! You're just trying to make yourself important, that's all!"

"What have I done to you?" cried David angrily. "I only asked a few questions. Anyone in my position—"

"Acting bumptious as usual, you fool! Or do you want to fight the giant yourself?"

"Why not?" said David, now quite calm and self-possessed.

Eliab laughed out loud. "This is my baby brother," he said. "Don't listen to the boy, men. He likes to boast."

The bearded leader chuckled. "If you really want to fight the giant, I'll be glad to take you to the king."

"Do that," answered David to the man's amazement. Eliab, Abinadab, Shammah, and the others laughed. The leader hesitated and did not answer at once.

"What are we waiting for?" asked David sharply.

Now the leader laughed too. "All right. Follow me, you big hero."

"Goliath will die of fright when he sees him, even at a distance," jeered Eliab. However, the three brothers did not feel quite comfortable when a great crowd of men followed the leader and David. Nor were they the only ones to have qualms. Even the leader began to feel that the joke had gone far enough and he gradually slowed his steps.

The little hill on which King Saul stood with Abner, Jacob, and other high-ranking officers was not very far away. Several of the higher-ranking officers had already turned to watch the crowd of men coming toward them.

"Young man," said the leader, "if I were you I'd go home as fast as I could."

"So would I—if I were you," retorted David and strode on. The leader's face flushed scarlet. If this young braggart was so set on making a fool of himself, there was nothing to do about it. Angrily he too stalked on, and the crowd followed, half curious, half worried. But when Saul caught sight of them, they all stood motionless.

"My king," said the leader, "this young man says he wants to fight Goliath." At the same time he raised his eyebrows slightly to show he was well aware that the request was ridiculous but that he had not been able to prevent it. "You have ordered us to bring before you anyone who offered to accept the challenge," he added cautiously.

The king looked at David. "A boy!" he said in amazement.

David looked him straight in the eye. "No one need be afraid of that fellow out there," he said. "Your servant wishes to fight him."

Saul shook his head. "A boy," he repeated. "You don't know what you're doing! Goliath is not only ten times stronger than you, he is an experienced fighter, from youth up. What can you do against one like that?"

"He doesn't recognize me," thought David. Then aloud, "Lord, I am a shepherd," he said, "I have already fought a lion and a bear when they tried to steal my sheep."

There was a slight smile on Saul's face. "And you drove them away?"

"I killed them, lord."

The king looked at him sharply. "How did you do that?"

"I killed the bear with my slingshot." There was a pause.

"And the lion?" asked the king.

"I strangled him," David admitted.

"Of course he's lying," growled the captain of the guards.

"But the little fellow has courage," Abner muttered.

"Bah, he knows the king can't permit the fight."

"Just take a look at his forearms," whispered Abner. "They're as thick as his thigh. Like little clubs."

Unconsciously Jacob rubbed his shoulder. "Against that giant his wrestler's trick won't help him much," he thought grimly. "He doesn't even come up to his shoulder." But he said nothing.

"The Philistine will fare no better than the lion and the bear," declared David. "Especially not that one. For he does not fight against me alone."

"What do you mean?" asked Saul attentively.

"He has scorned the army of the living God," cried David. "The Lord himself will give him into my hands."

The king's dark, heavily shadowed eyes flickered. More than

34

any other man he had suffered under the disgrace that among all the thousands of men from Israel and from Judah no one dared to accept the Philistine's challenge. That was bad enough, but to have to face the shame day after day. . . . Gladly would he have ordered an attack on the enemy's army, but his generals were against it, even Abner, the best and bravest of all. The troops' morale was not high enough to attack an enemy that so far outnumbered them and was so much better equipped. Yet the position here between Shochoh and Azekah was the best in the whole land for fending off an invasion by the Philistines. Abner had chosen it carefully. This was the gate to the mountainous land of Judah. However, if the Philistines did break through, the road through the valleys to Hebron and Bethlehem would be open to them.

But they had to come through here. The king could not understand why they had not already attacked. Abner was worried; he was afraid they were waiting for further reinforcements or, even worse, that they had sent out troops from Gath or from Accaron to make an attempt at encirclement. But in spite of this danger—unfortunately all too imminent—Abner did not want to risk an attack.

Most of all, Saul would have liked to accept Goliath's challenge himself. If only he were twenty—even ten years younger—but his arms and legs no longer obeyed his will as before, his eye was not sharp enough, and above all, only the Lord could grant victory, and he, Saul, had forfeited the Lord's help. The terrible old prophet had made that quite clear . . . that time . . .

And now here came this boy, this young man. The courage he showed might stem from a desire for revenge, or it might be foolhardiness, or sheer madness. That he had taken on a lion and a bear was the first glimmer of hope. But that he counted on the help of the Lord, that Israel's cause was sacred to him—he had that unshakable belief in his eyes, in his voice—those were the decisive factors.

"Go and fight," said the king, and his voice was hoarse. "And the Lord be with you. Achab! Give him my own armor and my weapon." But he had to grit his teeth when the two armorbearers

35

took off his helmet and sword, his coat of mail, and the greaves from his legs in order to put them on the young daredevil. It was—almost—an abdication.

David was not happy either. He had never worn a coat of mail. The armor—leather with metal plates—did not leave his arms free to move, and the greaves on his legs made fast running impossible. But the king's sword pleased him. He weighed it in his hand, made a few passes in the air, a few thrusts. It was a weapon a man could become fond of. But that took time; swordplay was an art. There were, undoubtedly, hundreds of fine points, tricks, and feints one must first learn and then practice. Goliath knew them all, of course, and had practiced them for years and years. There was no point in fighting him with weapons in which he, David, was unskilled, a beginner, and Goliath a master. David thought about the giant's slow, awkward movements; the heavy armor hindered even him. He shut his eyes and thought about it. At that moment he heard a gentle splashing. Opening his eyes, he saw a little brook flowing near the hill, and his face lighted up. He stood before the king. "This will not work, lord," he said. "I am not accustomed to this sort of armor. I can scarcely walk in it. Allow me to fight in my own way." And he began to take off the armor. Saul was about to protest, then he thought better of it and motioned to the armorbearers to help David.

Freed from the heavy splendor, David picked up his shepherd's crook—it was a thick, gnarled stick with a curve at the end not unlike a bludgeon—and went to the brook. Stooping, he searched and pulled out a stone. Exactly the right size, but not smooth enough. This one was better—and that one—and this one, too. All the stones that met his approval he flung behind him on the ground. When he had collected about a dozen, he picked out the best, five beautiful, smooth stones, exactly the right weight, and put them in his shepherd's bag, first taking out his leather sling. Satisfied at last, he returned to the hill, raised his staff in salute to the king, and went with leisurely steps down the slope.

The Israelite warriors stepped back to right and to left to let him pass. Now he stood alone on the plain the distance of an arrow shot between the two fronts. A light breeze ruffled and played with his reddish-blond hair.

Scornful laughter rose from the ranks of the Philistines.

The giant, now far away, was just about to repeat his challenge before another section of the Israelite army, and he did not hear the gibes at his unexpected opponent. But his armorbearer heard them and looked over at David, and as he bent double with laughter he called something to his master.

Goliath turned and stared incredulously at the tiny figure waiting there alone for him. Slowly he moved forward, clumsy, clanking, a walking fortress.

3

DAVID WAITED AND LET THE GIANT come to him. His sharp
eyes noted that as Goliath walked he held his head down almost
continually, looking at the ground. Big, heavy men often did that
to be sure that the ground was even, for such men could not
afford to stumble.

The armorbearer still walked in front of him, and only when
he was about thirty steps away from David did he stop, hand his
master the gigantic shield, and withdraw. Goliath calmly straightened the shield and then looked up.

"A little boy!" he shouted, indignantly. "Is that the best you
could send against me, you slaves of Saul? And where are your
weapons, midget? Am I a dog that you would fight me with your
stave?" The veins on his broad forehead swelled with rage. "By
Dagon the Mighty," he roared. "By Beelzebub, the lord of terror,
cursed shall you be for your boldness! Come nearer to me that
I may give your bit of flesh to the birds and the beasts of the fields
to eat!"

The answer came sharp and clear. "You come to me encased
in armor, and you swear by your heathen gods. I, however, come
to you in the name of the Lord of Lords, whose people we are.
You have mocked the army of the living God. Therefore will the
Lord give you into my hands. I will slay you and cut off your

head. Not only your dead body will I hand over to the birds and the beasts of the field, but also the dead of your army."

"What does he say? What does he say?" excitedly asked a young officer who stood close beside the king.

"Quiet, Prince Jonathan," growled Abner. "He speaks in the name of God."

The king stood motionless, his hands gripped around the hilt of his sword. "Where does this young man come from, Abner?"

"By your life, lord, I do not know."

"Find out."

". . . Sword and spear do not grant the victory," cried David, "but the Lord, and the Lord gives you into our hands."

Snorting with rage, Goliath lumbered heavily forward, holding the upper edge of his shield as high as his chin, his spear raised and ready either to throw or to strike. He had had time enough to look over the ground that separated him from his enemy, and he kept his eyes sharply on David.

David dodged him in slanting curves, doubled like a hare, and, as he ran, pulled one of the five smooth stones out of his shepherd's bag. Then, doubling a second time, he came up behind the giant and placed the stone in his sling. Goliath turned and followed his fleeing opponent. But now he found himself on new ground and he looked down to avoid stumbling.

David saw that, stopped, swung his sling, balanced it, and let fly. The stone struck the giant's forehead with such force that it pierced the bone. His eyes streaming with blood, Goliath stamped a few feet farther, then reeled and fell forward so heavily that the ground rumbled.

Like a flash David ran to him, wrenched his powerful sword out of the sheath, and holding it in both hands, whirled it over his head and brought it swiftly down. The blow cut off the giant's head cleanly from his body. Then David pulled away Goliath's helmet, grabbed the head by the hair, and held it high, with the stone still in the bone of the forehead. From before and behind came a roar from ten thousand throats.

The Philistines' front swayed back and forth, then broke. They ran, those heavily armored warriors, heedless of the angry shouts of their officers, who were themselves carried along by the surge of the fleeing mobs.

Then the Israelite front broke too—but in a wild forward rush. Long pent up rage at the shame of the past weeks found release, and the men stormed straight through the valley, swinging their spears and clubs and bellowing like wild beasts.

"They've broken ranks!" shouted Jacob on the king's hill. "If the enemy turns, they'll be slaughtered."

"The enemy will not turn," said Saul, and he drew a deep breath. "He's had the fear of God put into him."

Abner stared in astonishment as tears rolled down the king's cheeks. "What is the matter, lord?" he asked. "Israel is victorious —and you weep?"

Saul passed his hand over his eyes. "This boy has done what I should have done and could not do. And I am the king." He stared at Abner, his face a tragic mask. "Or—am I not king any more?"

Abner knew his master. "As long as I live, you are the king," he said simply.

The Philistines never stopped running. They fled steadily to the west, back to their cities, some to Gath, others to Ekron. On the other hand, the victorious Israelites plundered the enemy's camps on the homeward march, and whole sections of the army could now be outfitted with good weapons which the Philistines had left behind.

Shortly before dark Abner reported to the king. Saul sat in his tent in the midst of the wagon barricade with several of his officers, who were studying reports as they came in. "At last I have been able to find our young hero, lord," Abner smiled. "Our men had trouble bringing him back. I think he would rather have pursued the Philistines to the coast."

"I will see him," Saul commanded and Abner flung back the tent flap and motioned.

David entered and bowed low.

"You have kept your word," said Saul slowly. "Where do you come from?"

"I am the son of your servant Jesse, lord, from Bethlehem."

"But I've seen you before," murmured Saul thoughtfully, "and not just today." He rubbed his forehead. "Where—"

"I am your harp player, my king."

Saul nodded. "Quite right. How does it happen that I did not recognize you at once?"

"The king sees so many faces," said David modestly, "I was an instrument and a voice, nothing more."

"You did me good," Saul admitted, "and today you have served the entire people well. We owe the victory to you."

"The Lord was victorious, not I," David said simply.

The king bit his lip. "I shall send a messenger to your father. He and your entire family are freed of the king's tax for life. But you will come back with me to Gibeah. Young as you are, you shall be given command of a thousand."

Then something unexpected happened. From the group of army commanders a young officer in rich armor stepped forward, went up to David, and laid both hands on his shoulders. "My father has given you rank and position," he said. "I offer you friendship."

David saw the boundless admiration on the handsome, open countenance of a young man only a few years older than himself. He smiled happily. "It is a great honor, my prince."

"Yes, for me," replied Prince Jonathan. He took off the *me'il*, the overgarment worn by princes, and the buckler and the sword, together with the girdle and the marvelously wrought bow. "Wear these from today on. And the Lord bless our covenant." As David started to kneel before him, the prince quickly drew him to his feet and embraced him.

"That, too, is a victory," said Saul, and those who knew him well could hear the dryness in his tone. "My son Jonathan is not in the habit of making friends so quickly."

The two young men scarcely heard him. "How does it happen we haven't known each other before?" David exclaimed.

Prince Jonathan laughed. "That's easily answered. I command the king's troops in the north and only came back here two weeks ago. But in the future we shall never lose sight of each other."

*   *   *

41

The king's spies reported that only a few small detached groups of the enemy were still left on the soil of Judah. Saul, therefore, gave the order to send the reserves home, and he himself set out on the return to Gibeah. The route led through a number of small towns, among others Bethlehem. But everywhere they went, news of the overwhelming victory had preceded them. Women and young girls in gala attire came out to meet them and bedeck them with flowers; they beat the tabret, the little hand drum, and cymbals made of little copper plates; and they danced and sang in honor of the victor.

Saul sat up and listened. What were the women singing?

hikkah sa-úl ba' alaphàw
wedawíd beribebôtâw

"Saul slew his thousands and David his ten thousands . . ."

The king's face darkened. He ordered the army to march on without stopping.

David's brothers marched with the army as far as their home. Their farewell from the "boy" who had so suddenly become the hero was awkward and embarrassed, and David asked impulsively what they were going to tell their father, but then he realized that it did not matter. Ezra and his men were going back to Bethlehem too and they would tell the whole story. Probably in the end his brothers would bask in his fame, a little of which was reflected on the whole family. Now *they* were the "little ones" —but the thought aroused neither satisfaction nor pity. Eliab, Abinadab, and Shammah were what they were. He had never had much in common with them. However, he wished he could go back to Bethlehem with them to embrace his parents. It would have been a pleasure, too, to be able to tell his father that from now on he need never worry about collecting money for the king's tribute. But the king was in a hurry and he did not stop in Bethlehem.

Delegations from all the cities of Israel took part in the victorious entrance into Gibeah. The shouting and rejoicing never ended, and here too they sang the new song: "Saul slew his thousands and David his ten thousands."

Saul looked at Abner. "Now all the young hero lacks is to be king," he said, and he smiled a crooked smile.

Abner shrugged his shoulders. His answer was an old proverb: "He who listens to women hears much, but nothing true."

Saul slapped him on the shoulder and laughed. But that night, to the astonishment of all, the king did not appear at the great banquet. Prince Jonathan took his place.

The banquet lasted far into the night and the men drank heavily. Prince Jonathan toasted the conqueror of Goliath, and after him, Abner and the other commanders followed suit. Later, in the early morning hours, someone began to sing the song—who it was no one ever discovered—and most of the guests joined in.

> Saul slew his thousands
> And David his ten thousands!

In the midst of the song there was a wild shriek, and then another, and another. The singing stopped abruptly. A palace servant ran into the hall, his face streaming with blood; glaring wildly around, he fled through the nearest exit.

The guests sat as if turned to stone. Suddenly the king appeared and they rose, many of them unsteady and staggering, few of them without fear.

Saul strode slowly forward, the royal spear in his hand—and the tip was bloody. His eyes flickered unsteadily.

"The evil spirit is upon him again," someone whispered.

Prince Jonathan silently gave up the seat of honor.

"Traitors," Saul said in a heavy voice. "How many of you are traitors?"

No one spoke.

The king seated himself and looked around. "You thought perhaps I was already dead?" he sneered. "You have already laid me in my grave in spirit and rolled the black stone before it. But I am alive. I am alive! And as long as I live, I am the king, the anointed of the Lord, I, I!" He roared out the words. Then his eyes fell on David. "So you are here too, harp player," he said, and suddenly his voice was calm, almost gentle. "Then play something—and sing us a song. A new song, harp player—a song in

43

which there is nothing about the vanquished, nothing about thousands and nothing about ten thousands."

"My harp," David said, and a servant ran to fetch it. In the great hall there was total silence. Saul stared in front of him. It seemed an eternity before the servant returned with the harp.

David picked it up. "A new song, lord," he said firmly. The harp twanged and David sang:

> Hear, O Lord, my justice:
> Attend to my supplication.
> Give ear unto my prayer,
> Which proceedeth not from deceitful lips.

Saul's upper lip was drawn back. His strong teeth were clenched.

"Let my judgment come forth from they countenance," sang David.

> Let thy eyes behold the things that are equitable.
> Thou hast proved my heart, and visited it by night,
> Thou has tried me by fire:
> And iniquity hath not been found in me.

"You lie, you dog!" shouted Saul. "Here, take that!" and raising his spear, he hurled it. David leaped aside and the spear pierced the top of a wooden table. With uncanny speed the king sprang forward and pulled it out again.

"Father, Father, what are you doing!" shouted Jonathan. Abner tried to grasp the king's arm, but with the strength of a giant Saul pushed him aside, aimed and threw the spear again. The throw was well aimed; David just managed to get out of the way. The spear whizzed past his head and stuck in the wall.

"Father, Father," shouted Jonathan, "come to your senses!"

Saul looked at him with empty eyes. He ran his hand over his forehead. "Cobwebs," he moaned. "Cobwebs everywhere. I cannot see. Is that you, Jonathan?"

"Yes, Father, yes. Come, lean on me. I'll take you to your bedroom."

But Saul shook his head. "I dare not sleep," he said darkly. "The Lord does not want me to sleep." A quiver ran through his

44

powerful body. Suddenly his eyes cleared. It was as though he had wakened. "What has happened?" he asked shortly.

"Nothing, lord, nothing," Abner soothed him. But Saul saw the spear in the wall. He pressed his lips together, crossed the room, drew it out, and looked at it attentively. Then he went to his seat. "Who sits beside me?" he asked pointing to the empty place.

"Your harp player, lord," said Abner.

"My harp player? Do you mean David? No one must call him that again. He conquered Goliath and I have appointed him captain of a thousand. Where is he?"

"Here I am, lord," said David, and his heart was heavy.

Saul nodded to him. "I offered a reward to the man who conquered Goliath," he said. "But you have received only half. The best is yet to come. You shall receive the hand of my daughter."

Prince Jonathan rushed to David and clasped both his hands. The guests broke into cheers.

For the first time in his life David felt dizzy. The change was too quick, too unexpected. Only a few moments before he had been at death's door, and now—it was inconceivable. Princess Michol was something unattainable, as distant as a wondrously beautiful star. No, Chusai was right, as distant and as ardent as the sun. "Lord," he stammered, overcome, "who am I and what is my race that I am worthy—"

"I am the one to decide that," Saul interrupted him calmly. He stood up. "In three months you shall take my oldest daughter, Merob, to wife." All rose as the king walked slowly from the hall.

David stood like a statue. "Merob," he whispered, "Merob?" But already the courtiers were crowding around him, wishing him happiness.

Princess Michol was watching her older sister dress. "Poor Hadriel will be deeply disappointed," she said. "You had been definitely promised to him."

Princess Merob looked at herself in her silver mirror. She had her father's sharp hooked nose, but her eyes were large and expressive and her long silken hair hung far down her back. "How can I help it?" she replied indifferently. "Father has just changed his mind, that's all."

"Hadriel is very rich," Michol reminded her. "He is the richest man in Israel after the king."

"Yes, yes, I know. But Father will see to it that I do not lack for anything." Satisfied with herself, Merob laid the mirror aside. "As I have never seen either Hadriel or this David, it is all the same to me," she added with a cool smile. "But I want to have children, many, many sons."

"I really don't know what Father was thinking of," declared Michol, annoyed. "This David is nothing but a shepherd, who accidentally happens to be able to play the harp. How dare he raise his eyes to the king's daughter?"

Merob began to comb her shining hair.

"But he conquered a great enemy of Israel's, a giant—I forget his name. Esther told me a lot about it, but I was only half listening as usual. They have even made a song about him because he killed so many of the enemy." She began to hum it: " 'Saul slew his thousands and David his ten thousands.' Ten thousand! That's something you can't even imagine!"

"Perhaps he has a brutal temper and then he'll beat you," Michol warned.

"Oh, that doesn't matter, it's quite good when a husband is strict," replied Merob.

"Perhaps we can still convince Father that Hadriel is a much better husband for you," said Michol. "My sister and a shepherd! One would think we were the daughters of a peasant."

"And so we are," retorted Merob unmoved, and she shrugged her shoulders. "Father did not begin as a king. I really don't know why you get so excited. After all we're just stupid women and have to do what we are ordered to."

"That's the way to talk!" Michol burst out. "That's the way to think if you want to be a slave all your life long! I want more from life than that." Her eyes flashed, but in a moment she had herself under control. "Let me speak to Father," she begged. "Let me tell him that you don't want to hurt Hadriel, that you love him and—"

Merob's laughter cut her short. "How can he believe you? He knows perfectly well I've never seen him. Nor have I seen the slayer of ten thousands." She began to paint her lips. "And why are you so concerned about my happiness?" she asked, examining her work critically in the hand mirror. "If it doesn't matter to me, why should you care whether I marry Hadriel or the harp-playing, giant-killing shepherd? Oh! Oh! Michol, have you seen the shepherd? What does he look like? Are you perhaps . . . Michol! Michol!"

But Michol had left the room. In her own apartments she had a long interview with Nossu, her favorite slave. Nossu was a Negress of almost grotesque ugliness, with a shining black skin, thick lips, and a flat nose that spread over almost half of her face. But she was young and merry, and to her Michol was a goddess.

"I understand, mistress," said Nossu. "It's as good as done. You know you can rely on me."

"Yes, and that's a pity," said Michol slowly.

Nossu opened her eyes wide. "A pity, mistress?"

"Yes, you black cat. For this time it would be a good idea if someone were to learn my secret . . . Jacob, for instance."

"Didn't you say that he hates David, mistress?"

"Of course. That's just why. So what will he do if he hears of it?"

"He will betray it to the king."

"Clever Nossu," praised Michol, stroking the slave's black cheeks.

"And the king will be very angry."

"Perhaps he won't," said Michol, smiling. "In any case, see to it that Jacob gets the whole story."

"Perhaps he won't believe me."

"Of course he won't believe you. But he'll send out one of his agents. A spy. And that man he will believe. And don't forget Jacob is to pay you for your message. Just let him think you have sold him my secret, that you are betraying me."

"If he can think that, then he must be very stupid," said Nossu, rubbing her flat, black nose.

"Most men are stupid—in their way," remarked Michol. "Even

47

my father. If I go to him and tell him frankly: 'Give David to me and not to Merob,' he would refuse me. Oh, he would thunder at me, and for months I would be in disgrace. But if I can bring him to that thought himself— Go, Nossu. You know what you have to do!"

David was on his way to the castle gate when the veiled woman glided up to him. "David, son of Jesse," she murmured. "No, do not stop, keep on walking; act as if you did not notice me at all."

"What is this? Who are you?"

"The maid of my mistress. And my mistress sends word to you: Be at the merchants' gate at sunset."

"Who is your mistress?"

"When you first came here, she showed you the way to the king." The woman glided quickly away and disappeared in the crowd.

At sunset David stood at the Gate of the Merchants and peered cautiously around. At this time of day the place was crowded. All the people who did not live in the fortress now had to leave, and all fortress dwellers came home. In half an hour the heavy gate would be closed and it would not be opened again until sunrise. David tried to appear unconcerned, but his heart was pounding like a trip hammer. It was hard, it was almost impossible, to believe that she was the one who had made a rendezvous with him here. It might be a trap, some sort of intrigue, though he could not understand why anyone would be interested in trapping him. Oh, there was no use going over all that for the hundredth time! But even if it was foolish of him—he had had to come.

On all sides the traders were hastily winding up their business for the day, the air was full of bargaining, shouted offers, and protestations.

"Harp player!"

He looked quickly around. Behind a projecting wall stood a heavily veiled woman. It was not the same one, not the maid;

this one was taller and slimmer, the hand that held the veil over her face was ivory-colored and wore costly rings; it was the hand of an aristocrat, *her* hand.

"Princess!"

"Hush. Not that word. Listen. Do you want to marry my sister?"

"It is the king's desire."

"Is it also yours?"

"No."

There was a slight pause. From the gate came a quavering voice: "Seven shekels for this shipment of fruit? They are already rotting, you thief and son of a thief!" And the trader answered something indistinguishable in a rumbling voice.

"Why don't you want to marry Merob?" asked Michol.

"He who loves the sun cannot be satisfied with the moon," said David, and a soft laugh rewarded him. "But what hope has a poor mortal of possessing the sun?" he went on. "Isn't that impossible?"

"It was also impossible to conquer Goliath, and yet you conquered him. He who would conquer must fight. Farewell."

"Stay," called David, beside himself. "Stay! Let me see the sun just once again—" But she was gone. Slowly he went back to the palace, bewitched, his mind in a whirl, incapable of thinking.

A short, thickset man in nondescript clothing stepped out from a nearby corner, waited until David was out of sight, then strolled slowly away. Half an hour later he stood before the captain of the bodyguards and made his report.

"David and the Princess Michol," murmured Jacob. "So the black girl wasn't lying. But are you sure it was the princess?"

"Quite sure, my lord."

"She was veiled. You could have been mistaken."

"It was the princess's voice. She wore the ring with the red stones, the one the king gave her last year. And she called Princess Merob her sister."

That same day Jacob informed the king. To his bewilderment Saul took it very calmly, he even smiled a little. "You are a vigilant servant. I thank you. You may go." Jacob went and the king smiled to himself again. David would never have dared to approach Michol. This rendezvous was her doing. She loved the young hero and he—he loved her. It was good and important to know what bait to dangle before him. What had Michol said? "He who would conquer must fight." He laughed soundlessly.

"Chusai!" and the secretary entered. "Chusai, you are a friend of David's, aren't you?"

"I am the king's servant and David's friend, lord."

"Yes, yes, I know. Tell him—I don't want to do it myself—tell him Princess Merob has been promised to another for a long time. But I will give him my second daughter, Princess Michol—when he has paid the price for the bride."

Chusai's long hands opened and closed. His face remained expressionless. "As you command, lord."

"If he asks about the price," Saul continued, "tell him, I know he is not rich enough. The king is just—he wants neither gold nor silver from him, only what he can give. One hundred slain Philistines, that is the price."

When Chusai had left the room, Saul leaned back in his chair, well satisfied with himself. There were no more enemies in the land. If David wanted to earn the bride's price, he must invade the enemy's country. At the most he had only a thousand men at his command. As soon as the Philistines learned of his presence, the great hero with his thousand men was as good as lost, and with his death the danger was averted, the terrible danger of which only a few were aware, perhaps only Saul. Saul thought of the song that was being sung so triumphantly: "Saul slew his thousands and David his ten thousands." He smiled grimly. The song began with the thousands Saul slew—but they did not dream it could be David and his thousand that Saul would slay by the hands of the Philistines.

After a while Chusai came back.

"Well? Did you speak to him? What did he say?" asked the king quickly.

"He sends his thanks to the king," said Chusai stiffly.

"Why doesn't he come himself?"

"He has already left, lord."

"Left?"

"Yes, lord. He said he was in haste to fetch the bride's price."

"How many men did he take with him?"

"One hundred, my king."

Saul glanced down to hide the sudden light in his eyes. "It is good," he said. "You may go."

Chusai withdrew in silence.

"One hundred," said Saul to himself. "One hundred he has taken with him!" And he laughed long and loud.

David was lost. The throne was safe.

4

NOSSU CAME RUNNING into her mistress's bedchamber. "He is back," she cried. "He is back! And *how* he has come back! Oh, mistress, that is a great man, that is the right one, the only one!"

"Control yourself, you black beast," Michol commanded. "Who has come back? Why all the excitement?" But she smiled and her cheeks glowed.

"David, of course," announced Nossu with a grin that seemed to split her face in two. "And he has brought the price with him."

"I knew it," cried Michol, triumphantly. "Father did not expect that. I could see it when he talked with Abner last week."

"Look down in the courtyard, mistress. There you can see it for yourself."

Michol ran to the window. Far below, soldiers were building pyramids out of human heads. She wrinkled her aristocratic nose. "Ugh! how ugly!"

"Ugly?" Nossu was shocked. "It is wonderful." She rolled her eyes.

"How they handle them!" said Michol. "As if they were loaves of bread. And there are more than the king asked for—many more." She took a deep breath. "Now Father must keep his word. David is mine, mine, not Merob's. And at my side—" She broke off. There were things that not even Nossu needed to know.

*　　*　　*

The king slept late. No one dare to wake him; that was almost always dangerous. But when finally he awoke he knew immediately that something unusual had happened. The antechamber hummed like a swarm of bees, and from the outdoors came the sound of many people. He rose, quickly rubbed the sleep out of his eyes, and went to the window. It was a small window, so small that even an expert archer would have had difficulty shooting an arrow through it, to say nothing of hitting anyone.

The pyramid of heads in the courtyard had already been built, and beside it a band of soldiers, barely a hundred men, were drawn up behind a young captain whose reddish-gold hair curled out from under his helmet. He waited. His men waited. The pyramid of heads waited.

Saul stepped back and suppressed an oath. It was bad to begin the day with a curse. And what good did it do to curse a man who had the Lord on his side? Saul turned away and prayed to God, who was on the side of his adversary and let him win where any other man would have lost his life. But what was the use of praying? "Everything goes right for him," he thought in despair. "And everything goes wrong for me." Faintly the thought occurred to him that he should win this young conqueror over to his side. And a second thought, dark and ugly, approved maliciously. Yes, he must let the young hero work for him—for the time being. Later, when the time came, he would see . . .

He called for his servants. Half an hour later, girdled and armed, the king walked slowly down the steps to the courtyard.

"Hail to the king!" shouted David. His men took up the shout and after them, Abner, Jacob, and a throng of dignitaries who were also waiting in the courtyard. "The king's servant brings the bride's price doubled," David said with quiet pride.

Saul looked at the heads of the Philistines. They paid him no tribute—they *were* tribute. And there were many more heads than he had demanded.

"Two hundred Philistines are missing on the list of the enemy army," added David calmly.

Saul nodded. "Again you have fulfilled, and more than fulfilled, what I asked of you." His own voice sounded strange to him.

"Hear ye all," he went on raising his voice. "David, son of Jesse, shall receive my daughter Michol as his wife. The marriage will take place on the first of the Month of Summer Fruits."

The months to the beginning of the Month of Summer Fruits were long, and had it not been for Prince Jonathan they would have been intolerable. David and Jonathan were together every day. They rode on the famous, swift asses from the royal stables; in the heat of the day they lay on the flat roof of the palace under cool awnings. The young prince taught the conqueror of Goliath the art of swordplay. "I'll never learn," sighed David. "I could see both of the first feints, but not the quick double feint."

"You are almost as good now as I am," Jonathan declared. "And I have five years' practice behind me."

"Which were very useful to you in the Battle of Machmas," said David. "I wish I had been there, but at the time I was not allowed to guard even the goats. Without you and your courage the battle would not have been won."

"Don't remind me of it," Jonathan raised his eyebrows. "I disobeyed an order of my father's. He wanted to have me killed for it—seriously." He sighed. "He can be—very impulsive in thought as well as in action. And when the evil spirit comes over him . . ."

David would have liked to ask what this evil spirit was, but he was afraid to hurt his friend. And then Jonathan was already saying: "You have never told me how you mananged to carry out the king's last order—to double it—and with only a hundred men."

David laughed. "Should I take a thousand men to capture one hundred Philistines? It would have been a disgrace to us. A thousand men are a goodly number. They cannot pass unnoticed. The Philistines would soon have known we were on the way. Either I should have had to withdraw at once, or they would have cut off my retreat. I did not keep even my hundred together, but separated them into five groups. Twenty men are not noticed. And twice we attacked by night."

"By night?" Prince Jonathan was horrified. "But that is—you can't do that! It brings bad luck!"

"Yes, to those who are attacked—especially when they also believe in that old myth. The lion doesn't believe in it and he is often successful in his night raids."

"Except when he runs into you." Prince Jonathan smiled.

"The two night attacks alone brought in seventy heads," David continued. "And then we had the luck to run into a troop of two hundred men who had been sent out to avenge our attack. It seems they thought we were bandits from Edom or Moab. We saw them in time and I was able to bring my men together and place them on both sides of a long valley through which our pursuers had to pass. Only a third of them escaped. You see, it was all quite simple. Your double feint is much more difficult."

Prince Jonathan shook his head. "Those are brand-new methods of warfare. What would Abner say to it, I wonder?"

"I ordered not only the heads of the slain to be cut off, but also their weapons taken from them," David went on. "Good swords— spears with iron tips. Weapons, that is our greatest problem. We must have smiths."

"The Philistines will never permit it."

"Do you talk that way too, Jonathan? I know how things are; clever Chusai has told me about it. The Philistines claim that we must still pay them tribute, in spite of our victory in the Valley of Elah. We have to shake off that yoke, and for that we need weapons that are as good as our enemies'."

"In the Valley of Elah we had only a few Philistines to fight," warned Jonathan. "Not the whole people."

David nodded. "We lack not only weapons," he said softly. "We also lack the will—and a farsighted, comprehensive plan."

"That is not my father's method," Jonathan admitted. "He is a man of the moment, always for the sudden decision. That's the way he always was."

"One day you will be king," said David earnestly. "And I shall stand by your side as *your* Abner. Then—"

"The king and his commander-in-chief," said Jonathan with a goodnatured smile. "Who knows whether it will ever come to that? Perhaps it is only a beautiful dream. But one thing is certain: You and I are friends as long as we live."

*　　*　　*

As custom demanded, the bridegroom wore a coronet when, accompanied by his friends, he went to the palace to receive his bride. Musicians walked before him with tabret and cymbal. In the great hall, richly decorated with flowers and costly rugs, dignitaries and notables stood in front of a cordon of officers. The king himself in full regalia, the *nezer* or crown on his head, held the bride by the hand. She was heavily veiled; only in the bridal chamber would the veils fall. On her arms sparkled gold bracelets set with precious stones, and a triple chain of rubies shimmered against the bright yellow of her gown. Behind her stood her waiting women.

Saul stared at the coronet David was wearing. It was small and unassuming, and it was the custom—every bridegroom wore a coronet on his wedding day. And yet . . .

Prince Jonathan, who stood close beside the king, beamed for joy.

Jacob, in the midst of Saul's retinue, pressed his lips together. The king's new son-in-law had been given command of the bodyguards. Not that Jacob had fallen from grace; on the contrary, he had been made a member of the Crown Council. And yet . . .

Chusai, far in the background, looked pale and resigned. Ever since David's victory over Goliath he had realized how far his young friend from Bethlehem had risen above him. It was logical and therefore right that he and none other should wed the Princess Michol. And yet . . . Chusai smiled sadly. One had to be a David to find the way to the stars, to the sun. David and Michol, they were a royal pair.

The trumpets blared and fell silent. Slowly Saul placed his daughter's hand in David's. "The alliance is sealed," he proclaimed in a loud voice, and the hall rang with shouts and cheers.

The wedding feast lasted all night long. But after an hour the bridal couple left the palace, and accompanied by a crowd of their friends, went to the house the king had placed at their disposal, a new, two-storied house at the other end of the fortress. Not until they came to the threshold of the bridal chamber did David's friends and the friends of the bride leave them. And not until she entered the room did the princess remove her veil.

"The Lord bear me witness," said David, "before I saw you I did not know what beauty was."

Michol smiled. "You remind me that I have married a poet."

"Two hundred Philistines had to die for this honor," said David. "Far too few. The price should have been ten times higher."

"Poet and warrior," said Michol. "Shepherd and giant-killer. You are many men in one. No, don't kiss me yet . . ." She went to the window. "The palace is still lighted. They are celebrating in our honor. For fifteen days they will celebrate in our honor, just as they did for Merob and Hadriel." She laughed softly. "Good old Merob! All she wants is to have children, many, many sons. But I—"

"My whole life has become a blazing flame—"

"You say beautiful things," Michol smiled, "and you are brave and strong. But those are not the reasons why I wanted you to be my husband—yes, I wanted to marry you, David, and I did everything in my power to bring it about."

"And what is the real reason?" he asked. "What can it be—save that you love me?"

She turned to him. "Yes, I love you, David," she acknowledged earnestly. "But not as ordinary women love. I love you because you are of royal caliber, like me. Therefore we belong together."

Involuntarily David ran his hand over his hair as though it were still smooth from the balsam the prophet of Ramatha had once poured over it. Could women sense things when they loved —as his mother had always known when he was in danger? But he had not time for further thought.

"You and I together," Michol went on insistently, "can accomplish a great deal. Everything, even the highest and the greatest. I have thought much about you and me."

He flung back his head and laughed. "I have everything I could wish for," he said passionately. "And now I will not wait any longer!" he cried and drew her to him. Yielding and cool she lay in his arms, let him kiss her, and listened smiling as he stammered words of love. Then she, too, glowed with passion.

* * *

57

"You sent for me, lord," said the scrawny man with the deep set, piercing eyes. Jacob nodded. "Sit down, Doeg. Have some wine." He poured out a glass for the man.

Doeg merely took a sip from the beaker. "You are kind to a man from Edom," he said. "Not many Israelites offer me anything to drink."

Jacob smiled thinly. "You are the king's head shepherd," he replied. "That is no mean rank—especially if one considers what a shepherd can become nowadays."

Doeg grinned and showed four or five blackened stumps of teeth. "That's true," he said. "But I'll never get to be the king's son-in-law."

"However, you have managed to be other things," replied Jacob dryly. "You are the king's eye."

"I don't know what you mean, lord," said Doeg coldly.

Jacob laughed. "You have forgotten that I'm a member of the Crown Council. There one hears all sorts of things that otherwise no one knows."

Doeg was silent.

"That's why I have sent for you," Jacob went on. "But you're not drinking?"

"It could be you have something important to say to me. So it is better to stay sober."

Jacob nodded in relief. "You are right, we are living in strange times. A man who one or two years ago was nothing but a shepherd boy becomes the king's son-in-law, the people's hero, the idol of women and girls, the most popular man in the whole court, captain of the bodyguards, leader of great army divisions, victor over the Philistines—"

"—but does not enjoy the favor of all the members of the Crown Council," added Doeg dryly.

"That would not be so important perhaps," said Jacob with a shrug. "What is important, however, is that the king has decided he must die."

Doeg opened his eyes wide. He had no eyelashes. "Are you serious?"

"One hour ago he so informed the Council," replied Jacob shortly.

"But why? What has David done?"

"What is that to you? It's the king's will that he die. And you are to carry out that will."

Doeg took a deep draft of wine. "I am the king's dog," he said. "When he commands: 'Lick my hand,' I lick his hand, and when he says 'Bite!'—then I bite."

"Good. That's what I expected of you."

"But it's no light task, lord. The man who conquered Goliath can't be spitted like a desert fox. I need men for that, men on whom I can rely."

"The guards are now under his command, and they can't be called on," Jacob explained. "And the men of Israel seem to be bewitched by this man. Haven't you enough Edomites among your people for that?"

Doeg hitched around uncomfortably on his chair. "Sure, but we have to go to work carefully. Otherwise people will say that men from Edom have killed the husband of the king's daughter, the great conqueror of Goliath and the Philistines; and if we tell them it was the king's orders—who will believe us?"

"Everyone," replied Jacob calmly. "For you will wear the king's own ring. Here it is."

Doeg took the ring and examined it carefully. "Yes. It is the king's ring." He nodded in satisfaction. "When shall it be?"

"Tomorrow morning early, two hours after sunrise, when he leaves his house to go to the palace."

Even before sunrise, Doeg with fifteen Edomite shepherds was at his post. They waited impatiently. Hour after hour went by, but David did not appear. Doeg waited until midday. Then he dismissed his men and went back to the man who had sent him. Jacob was not at home. Again he waited patiently.

Around the ninth hour Jacob finally came. "I know about it," he said wearily. "You didn't get a chance to see him. He was warned."

"A traitor in the Council?"

"Yes. The king's eldest son, Prince Jonathan. And what is more, he has succeeded in making the king change his mind. It was all in vain. Give me back the ring, Doeg."

"Here it is." The chief shepherd obeyed good-naturedly.

"Forget what we have talked about. And see to it that your men don't talk. Here is silver."

Doeg weighed the pouch. It was heavy. "They won't talk," he promised, and he showed his tooth stumps again.

Michol leaped up from her pillows. "Who is there?"

"It's David."

"David! What has happened?"

"The king tried again to kill me."

She groaned. "So that's it! And this time Jonathan did not warn you?"

"He couldn't. It came over your father suddenly—like that time at the banquet after the victory over Goliath and the Philistines. He threw his spear at me. I just managed to get out of its way."

"They say Father has an evil spirit," said Michol in a muffled voice. "Perhaps it is really so. Quick to anger he always was. Even as children we never knew whether at the next moment he would give us beautiful presents or strike us. And since—since the curse of the old prophet, it has been much worse."

"What is this, actually, about the curse? I have never been able to find out."

"I myself don't know exactly. He never talks about it." She got up and began to pace up and down the room. "It is too soon," she murmured. "He is still too powerful. And there is no stopping him. Day before yesterday that scum of a Doeg with his men! Jonathan warns you in time, he talks with Father, everything is all right again—and now he is beginning all over. It goes too fast. And we need another year, at least a year—"

"I don't understand you, Michol."

"Jacob is your enemy and always will be. But Abner must be won over; he is Father's best general and the men swear by him. And Hadriel must be won, he has the money we need. That will not be so difficult. He worships Merob."

"What are you talking about, Michol?"

Suddenly she stood still. "About the new king of Israel!" she cried violently. "Who else? How much longer shall the land be ruled by a man who cannot even rule himself, who today swears love and devotion to you and tomorrow tries to murder you?"

"You must not even think such things," warned David. "Certainly you must not speak them. Saul is the anointed of the Lord. And Jonathan would never rise up against his father."

"Jonathan? Who is talking about *him*? There is only one man who dares wear the crown and that is you! You are the new king! And my brother Jonathan will swear fealty to you or he falls with our father!"

"Michol! You have lost your mind!"

"You are the king and no other! I have known it, I felt it—oh, I don't know for how long now. But the pity is that Father also feels it. That is why he hates you. That is why you must be killed."

"But I have never thought of such a thing—"

"No? Really not? Not in your innermost heart, not in your dreams? Then you would be a fool, and that you are not. The bad thing is not that Father realizes it, only that he has recognized it too soon."

"Michol, by the holy name of the Lord I never wanted—"

"Then want it now! Father is forcing us to act before we are ready. There will be a hard struggle. What would I not give if Abner were already on our side! But you are the captain of the guards. You can—"

"Hush, Michol! I will not be a traitor to the king. And even if I wanted to, I could not. The king has taken the guards from me. They are under Jacob again."

Michol was startled. "Then it was no mere fit of anger! It was a plan." Swiftly she rushed to the window and peered down into the street. When she turned back to David, her face was pale. "They are already outside," she said. "A whole troop."

"Doeg and his men?"

"No, David. The king's bodyguards. No one in Israel and Judah disturbs the peace of a house at night. But as soon as morning comes, they will force their way in and kill you. You must flee."

"Flee? Like a thief, a criminal?"

61

"Like a healthy man before illness—like a wise man before a desert storm."

"And you? What about you?"

"I must stay here," she answered quickly. "Father will not harm me. I am only a woman; that is as good as nothing in his eyes."

"Without you—"

"It must be, David. On your flight I would only be a hindrance. And here I can keep watch, see what happens, and send you word as soon as I know where you are."

"Flee," he repeated mechanically. "But where to?"

"To Moab—to Edom—somewhere where you will not be murdered. I implore you, do not waste time! It is only a few hours to sunrise. The farther away you are by then, the better it will be."

"You are right," he said heavily.

Now that the decision was made, he acted immediately. For a moment he stood at the window at the back of the house and looked down at the little garden and the empty street below. Not a man in sight. "A rope, Michol. I must let myself down here."

"Nossu will know where I can find one. Don't worry, she is loyal. I'll go and wake her."

A few minutes later she came back with the black girl. They had found ropes, but they were not long enough. David tied them together and knotted one end around the foot of the bed nearest the window. Then he seized the other end and let it down outside. It was still not long enough, but it would have to do.

Once more he turned to Michol. "I forgive you for thinking me capable of being a traitor," he said softly. "For you did it only because you love me. What lies before me I do not know. But if I live, I shall come and get you; this I swear to us both by the holy name of the Lord. Farewell." And he kissed her.

"Go," she gasped and tore herself from his arms.

"Hold the rope tight," he commanded in a hard voice. "The bed alone isn't strong enough."

The two women obeyed. The next moment he was over the window sill. The rope went taut, then slackened again. Michol ran to the window. She saw David wave to her once more; then he disappeared down the dark street.

5

Nossu began to sob. "Be quiet!" Michol commanded, and the sobbing ceased. She thought hard. How long would it be to sunrise? Two hours perhaps, not much more and then they would come. Two hours' start, then the pursuers would gallop after him. The king's white asses were swift, and it was doubtful whether David could outdistance them. Michol gnawed her lower lip. "Nossu!"

"Y-yes, mistress," and Nossu lifted her tear-stained face.

"Bring me the teraphim from your room."

"The . . . ?"

"The wooden statue, the one you pray to, idiot."

"Yes, yes of course, mistress." It was a hideous thing in light brown wood, a head with no nose and with holes in place of eyes and mouth, a short, thick body, and even shorter, shapeless legs. "Lay it in the bed," Michol ordered. "That's it. And now bring me a couple of towels and the little goat's-hair rug from the entrance hall. The reddish one." Eyes bulging with surprise, the slave obeyed.

As dawn broke Jacob hurried to the waiting bodyguards and gave the order to force an entrance. Michol received them on the steps leading to the upper story, her finger on her lips. "Hush," she said. "My husband is sick. What do you want?"

"The king's orders," said Jacob. "I'm sorry, Princess, but we have orders to take your husband to him at once."

"Impossible," she replied coldly. "He is very ill." Jacob hesitated. "Come with me if you don't believe me," she added icily. "But don't make a noise; he has just fallen asleep." Jacob followed her up the stairs. At the entrance to the bedroom she stopped. "You will do well not to go too near him," she suggested. "He has spots all over him. It might be leprosy."

Jacob looked at the covered figure on the bed. He saw the red hair, not curled now, but straight and wet from fever. "I'll report it to the king," he said and withdrew as hastily as his dignity permitted. "Wait outside," he ordered his men. In the house quiet reigned. Nossu wanted to rejoice over their successful trick, but Michol silenced her. "They will come back," she said. "Pray that they don't come at least for a few days. Pray that our lord may meantime get to a safe place. Pray that he comes back with a great army to fetch me." But then she remembered that Nossu's god was now lying in her bed, with the little goat's-hair rug on his skull. "Leave me alone," she ordered sternly, and Nossu glided from the room.

Where would he flee? How long would it be before he came back? It was well that she did not know which direction he would take. In that way she could not betray him if they tried to force her. Silent and dry-eyed she sat on the edge of the bed in which lay the grotesque figure of the teraphim.

But before an hour had passed, heavy fists pounded on the house door. The myrmidons of the law had returned. Again she met them at the head of the stairs. "What do you want this time?" she asked with wildly beating heart. "Have you no pity for a sick man?" Jacob had brought more than twenty men with him.

"I'm sorry, Princess," he said, "but the king has ordered us to bring the sick man on his bed to the palace."

She bit her lips, and in silence she moved aside as six armed men mounted the stairs and stalked past her. Then came an angry shout: "It's a trick! She's let him escape!" Jacob rushed up after his men. When he came out of the room again, he shouted to the men below, "Search the house!"

64

"It's no use," said Michol, her voice trembling with hatred. "He has gone."

"The king himself will have something to say to you about this," growled Jacob. "You will do well to come with me to him."

"Do you intend to lead me through the streets under armed escort?" she asked scornfully.

He made a short bow. "The princess will be accompanied by her women as usual. I shall follow with my men."

At the palace Jacob went in alone to the king and made his report. Saul immediately gave orders to pursue the fugitive. "One hundred silver shekels to the man who brings him back, dead or alive. Be off now and send my daughter to me." Jacob disappeared swiftly.

Michol entered the king's room.

"You helped him escape," growled Saul. "What is to prevent me from cutting off your head?"

"I am a poor woman," said Michol meekly. "First my husband threatened to kill me if I betrayed him. And now my father threatens to kill me because I did not betray him."

Saul gave her a long look. "All women are liars," he said finally. "Where has he gone?"

"He wasn't so foolish as to tell me, Father."

The king nodded. "You were his wife. Now you are his widow," he said. She gave a start and her eyes widened. "His widow," he repeated coldly. "For he is as good as dead. But don't mourn him too deeply. I'll soon give you to another man. Go." Michol bowed and withdrew. In the antechamber she collapsed in a faint.

The eyes of the ancient man were closed, and he sat on the boulder as still as if he were part of the wild countryside. A light breeze played with his white beard. He wore only a wide, loose garment that came to his thighs and a long, flowing cloak. His feet were bare and his body so emaciated that one could see his ribs, as yellowish brown as the desert sand around him.

Far away on the horizon rose a tiny cloud of sand and high above it a vulture wheeled in circles. The little cloud grew bigger —a man on an ass was riding toward the maze of rocks. The ancient man could not possibly hear the animal's hoofbeats in the soft sand and yet he turned his head in their direction, nodded to himself, and opened his eyes.

"Welcome to this refuge," said Samuel to the rider.

David dismounted. The long journey had exhausted him and he staggered as he stammered a greeting.

"Neither your animal nor you are thirsty," said the prophet from Ramatha. "You found enough water two hours ago, at the great well of Shochoh. Sit here beside me and wait till you have strength enough to tell me what I already know."

Without a word David obeyed. The eyes of the old prophet were upon him, the only eyes that had ever filled him with fear. And they had lost none of their power. After a while he began: "I am being followed."

Samuel nodded. "I have already told you that you are safe here."

"The king seeks my life. He has tried to kill me . . ."

"Three times he flung his spear at you and three times he missed. And yet he is the best spear thrower in Israel. How do you think that came about?"

"I do not know. I have never harmed the king."

"Every day he has killed you seven times—in spirit."

"I have done him no harm," repeated David. "Why does he pursue me? People say there is a curse on him. Your curse. But no one has told me the cause."

"Disobedience," said Samuel hoarsely. "The Lord demands obedience. He who disobeys the Lord brings down His curse on himself. So it was in the beginning in Paradise and so it is now. And when a man is anointed king, he becomes doubly responsible to the Lord, for himself and for his people. I carried a command to Saul from the Lord. He disregarded it. Then he wanted to sacrifice. 'Obedience is the best sacrifice,' I told him. 'You have spurned the word of Jehovah, therefore Jehovah spurns you as king.'" The ancient voice trembled. "It hurt greatly—and not only Saul. I loved Saul, the strong man who always wanted to act promptly. But the Lord comes first, always. A king can seldom relent; a prophet never." He sighed, and the sigh seemed to come

66

from the center of the earth. "Since then Saul suffers from what men call his evil spirit."

"You anointed me too," said David with burning eyes. "I did not understand it—then. Even today I still do not know what the Lord wants of me. I cannot betray the king, not even though he considers me a traitor. His son is my best friend. His daughter is my wife."

"But she doesn't think as you do."

"You know that too? No, she doesn't think as I do. Still that does not disturb me. I must go my way. And the Lord cannot wish me to be disloyal."

Samuel nodded. "Even if I had not long known that the Lord was pleased with you, I would know it now. Come! Your pursuers will soon be here."

Now for the first time David saw the huge dust cloud on the horizon which was drawing swiftly nearer. "That is Doeg with his crew," he murmured, "or a section of the royal bodyguards. Only a few days ago I was their commander. In five minutes they will be here."

Samuel stood up calmly. "Come!" he commanded and began to clamber up the rocks above him. The old man climbed with astonishing agility. David had trouble following him as they mounted higher and higher in the pile of fissured rocks. "Where are you taking me?" he asked. "And what about my animal?"

"Come," Samuel repeated, and they went on climbing.

Suddenly David stopped. The stone on which he was about to set his foot had moved; it was no stone, it was a hairless human head, a man, an old man caught there in a cleft in the rock, and holding something in his hand, a horn. And scarcely ten steps farther on stood another man leaning against a rock wall and gazing up—no, he was not looking at anything, for only the whites of his eyes were visible.

"Come on, come on," warned Samuel's voice.

Mechanically David climbed on. Two old men, clad only in short shifts, squatted back to back; he passed so close he could have touched them, but they did not stir and kept staring straight ahead. One of them had an instrument that looked like a flute. A little higher up three other men lay on their backs and looked into the sun. And now at last they came to the summit, a broad plateau without a sign of vegetation, and Samuel stood there and looked down at the plain below. It was as still as if the whole world were holding its breath.

"Where are we?" asked David in a whisper.

"Najoth," said Samuel simply.

David shuddered. Najoth—that was the sacrificial mound of Ramatha, the holiest sacrificial mound in Israel. None but men who had given up all personal desires and instincts, who lived only for God, holy men, prophets dwelt here. Pilgrims came from afar and laid sacrificial gifts, bread and parched corn, dates and figs, at the foot of the heights, and it was said that one single date was enough to keep a holy man alive for a whole week. Perhaps here he was really safe. It was difficult to imagine that the king's men would dare to climb the sacrificial mound. To be sure, Doeg and his men were Edomites; they did not believe in Jehovah. David looked back. The troop of pursuers—there were at least forty or fifty of them—had just reached the foot of the mountain. They swung themselves off their animals; one of them, a tall, lean man—that was Doeg—pointed to the top and they began to climb.

Then Samuel raised both arms. In his high, throaty voice he sang something David did not understand—ancient words, older than the speech of Moses. Perhaps Abraham would have understood, Abraham from the land of Ur.

The climbers stopped and looked up.

Then the long-drawn-out note of a horn rang out. A second horn joined in, a third, and a fourth. From all sides of the sacrificial mound at the same time came the muffled roll of drums. Flutes wailed loudly. The holy men were all standing now; many of them held instruments in their hands, others began to sing, and it seemed that the whole mountain sang and rang, and the very stones came to life.

The pursuers stood as though turned to stone. Then, as if at a command, they flung up their arms, dropped their weapons, and began to dance—at first slowly, then faster and faster. They fell and stood up again and went on dancing. They rent their clothes from their bodies as if they were fetters that hindered them, and they danced and danced. . . . They could not stop dancing. They sang, too, or shouted, but their voices could scarcely be heard above the wild roll of the drums and the shrilling of horns. Doeg danced, the long, lean Doeg, and all his men.

"Why doesn't it seize me too?" thought David, and at the same moment he felt the light pressure of cool fingers on his head, Samuel's fingers; the ancient one stood behind him, nothing could harm him. There—another of the dancing men fell, but this time he did not get up again. Three, four—no, more, many more. . . . The pressure of the cool finger on David's head grew stronger. Looking around, he saw that Samuel was smiling, a wintry, weatherbeaten smile, the smile of the mountain more than of a man. "Look there," said the old prophet. "Where are your pursuers?" And David saw the last of the dancers fall and lie without moving. He was seized with horror. "Are they dead?"

"No," said Samuel. "But for some of them it would be better if they were. Come, now. You are very tired and need a long rest. It isn't far." He led David to a little cave just below the plateau. It contained a couch of goat skins, beside which stood a pitcher and a little basket of dates. David sank down on the couch. "Sleep," said Samuel's high voice. "Sleep long and the Lord give you fresh strength."

But David was already asleep.

Confused dreams drifted through his mind. The prophets were singing a solemn song; some of the lines David could hear quite clearly. "Who is like unto the Lord, our God, enthroned in heaven? Who has raised up the lowly from the dust and placed him among the highest . . ." Strange, it almost sounded as though they were singing of his destiny. Then riders came dashing up, leaped from their animals, and began to climb the holy mountain. But the drums rolled and the horns blew and these pursuers, too, began to tear off their clothes, and they danced until they fell down and did not move. Again the prophets sang. This time David could not hear any words, but he knew, with the strange certainty of dreams, that he dared not hear them because they

69

concerned the future. Why not? Was that future so bitter, so full of pain and disappoinment? But for that question, too, the dream had no answer. Instead his pursuers came a third time. It was the bodyguards this time, and Jacob was with them. Jacob and his men danced, too, and fell down. The dream seemed to go on and on. Shoulder to shoulder stood the prophets as for the fourth time pursuers came, their number greater than ever, and the man who led them wore a crown, for it was the king himself. But the drums thundered and the horns blew as if they would throw down the walls of Jericho, and the king tore all his clothes from his body and danced the dance of ecstasy, as did all those with him. His men soon fell, but he danced on, his eyes wide, his hair wet with perspiration and hanging down on his forehead, his mouth open. Then at last, he too fell—and David awoke.

Samuel stood beside his couch. "Eat," he commanded. "Then you must go."

Suddenly David felt a wild, gnawing hunger. He remembered the little basket of dates. It was still there, and beside it lay a small loaf of bread. He ate all of it and drank water from the pitcher. With the rest of the water he washed himself. Then he went out of the cave. Above, on the plateau, Samuel was waiting for him. "Come," he commanded, and they began to descend. There was no sign of the prophets, but halfway down the hill lay a tall, strongly-built man, no longer young and almost naked. With difficulty David repressed a cry. For the man was Saul, and he was sound asleep.

David stood still. Was he still dreaming? Or had everything he had dreamed perhaps been true?

Samuel answered his mute question.

"On Najoth realities flow into each other," he said calmly. "Three times the king sent police spies after you and you know what happened to them. Then he came himself. He will sleep a long time—for a day and a night. You have time to escape."

"And his men?"

Samuel pointed to the foot of the hill. There they lay, all in a heap, fifty or sixty men.

"How long did I sleep?" asked David.

"Four days. But time means little on Najoth. There stands the ass. He has been fed and watered. He is fresh. No, don't thank me. I do what I should, no less and no more. Go with God. He alone is your helper."

David was approaching Nobe, the priests' city south of Jerusalem. In a little village he had exchanged the white ass for a donkey so as not to arouse attention, and he wore a headcloth that covered his reddish-blond hair. To recognize him one would have to come close to him, and he avoided all meetings as far as possible. To be sure it was not always easy. He had to eat and drink, and where there was a well there were always people who asked questions. Never in his life had he felt so alone. Day after day he had ridden straight across the land. He had even passed by Gibeah—yes, he had managed to get in touch with Jonathan and the prince had come to his hiding place, the ruins of a farmhouse in a deserted field. Weeping, the friends had embraced. Jonathan told him that the king had returned from Ramatha, pale and angry, and that he had sent out spies in all directions. The king had cursed him, Jonathan, even threatened him with his spear, because he had intervened on behalf of David. It was plain to David that Jonathan suffered much more because his father hated his beloved friend than because of the countless curses which had been called down upon his own head, and he was deeply moved. It hurt him to be separated from Michol, hurt so much that sometimes he lay awake half the night thinking only of her. And yet, the separation from his noble, selfless friend was an even greater sorrow. "God alone is thy help," the prophet had said. Perhaps it was God's will that he should renounce all human help, even human love and friendship, and depend on Him alone.

Now, therefore, David rode to Nobe, the priests' city, for there he would find Achimelech, the high priest. There, too, was the holy ephod, the wide garment of wool and linen, richly embroidered with gold, to which also belonged the breastplate with the Urim and Thummim stones with which the priest could ascertain the will of the Lord. No less than fifty-eight priests with their wives and children lived in Nobe.

The first to receive David was Abiathar, the son of the high priest, a husky young man with a black spade-shaped beard. He, too, wore the priestly garment. Abiathar's eyes widened in surprise, but he bowed courteously.

"I shall inform my father immediately," he said, and he disappeared quickly into the house.

A moment later the high priest stepped out of the door, a dignified, gentle old man, with beautiful, almost womanly hands. "Peace be to thee," he greeted David. "How does it happen that the son-in-law of the king, the commander of the bodyguards, travels without an escort?"

David took a deep breath. Here, at least, no one knew his situation. It was not pleasant to lie to the good old man, but there was nothing else he could do. "The king has given me a secret mission," he explained. "I am to meet my men at the Sichar oasis. They will be hungry. Can you give me five loaves of bread?"

"We are fasting now," replied the High Priest. "I have only holy shewbread. The loaves must now be changed for fresh ones and I can give them to you—but only if you are clean and your men likewise. Have you been with women since yesterday?"

"We are clean," replied David curtly and put the thought of Michol out of his mind. "I also need a weapon," he added. "I had to leave in such haste that I did not even have time to go home and fetch my arms. Have you a spear or a sword for me?"

Smiling, the old man shook his head. "We are peaceful folk here in Nobe. But wait—there is a weapon here, one you know better than anyone else. It is Goliath's sword. The king gave it to us to put in safekeeping. It lies behind the ephod."

David's eyes gleamed. "Give it to me," he said. "There is none to equal it. One thing more: I beg you earnestly, ask the Lord's will for me."

"Gladly," replied the High Priest. They entered the Holy of Holies together. "Which comes first?" asked Achimelech with his gentle smile. "The sword or the will of God?"

"Always the will of God," said David earnestly.

Achimelech nodded. Abiathar helped him to put on the ephod

and fastened the breastplate around him. Both priests prayed. Then Achimelech said simply: "Ask."

David also prayed. It took him some time to formulate his questions so that they would not betray him to the priests. "In which direction shall I go, Lord, to find what I seek?" he asked finally. Now they could think what they pleased; that he was after some secret of the enemy, that he had been sent after spies, hidden treasures, or the like. They could not guess that he was seeking a place where he could sleep without fear of being awakened by the spears of Saul's bodyguards.

The high priest shook the breastplate with both hands, so that the Urim and Thummim stones clattered. Then he reached in. The stone he pulled out was white—"Yes."

"In which direction must I go to find it?" asked David again. "To the east?"

This time the stone was black—"No."

"South?" asked David.

The answer was again a black stone, but it fell out of the high priest's hand. No, but not entirely no.

"To the southwest?"

The stone was white. So, then, to the southwest. Not to the people of Moab or Edom, not to the Amalecites or Aramaeans. To —the Philistines! It was the most dangerous answer he could have received. But it was the answer. He would gladly have asked more, but he could not ask his question without letting the priests know that he was a fugitive. He bowed his head. "It is enough," he said. All three said a prayer of thanks. Then David took the sword. It was a wonderful weapon, but very heavy. Would he be able to parry or use it in the double feint, as Jonathan had taught him? Jonathan—Michol—home!

Abiathar brought the five promised loaves. "It must be a very dangerous undertaking the king has entrusted you with," he said.

David could not trust his voice. He merely nodded.

They went out of doors again. Abiathar put the bread in the pockets of the cover David had spread over the donkey's back. "Don't forget to tell your men that these loaves have lain on the altar of the Lord, that they must handle them with respect and not fling the crumbs to the birds," said Achimelech anxiously. "And the Lord bless your enterprise."

"I thank you," David replied in a choked voice. Then he mounted and rode toward the gate. The forecourt was filled with a great number of people, petitioners and those who wanted to make sacrifices. They all turned and stared at him. But one of them, a long, lean man, turned his back, and David suddenly knew that he had done it on purpose. He knew that man. As he rode past him he saw his profile, the short, stubby beard, the deep-set eyes. It was Doeg, the Edomite.

6

DAVID RODE QUICKLY out of the gate. He hadn't the slightest
doubt that Doeg had seen and recognized him. Perhaps some of
his men were among the petitioners, but possibly he was here
only as a spy for the king. In any case he would report to Saul.
David must get away as fast as he could. The thought occurred
to him that it was now impossible to ride southwest. Doeg would
be sure to learn that this advice had been given him. Then he
thought of Samuel: "The Lord demands obedience." He had
asked the Lord where he should go and the Lord had answered
him. There was only one direction for him—to the southwest.

He rode until late evening. Shortly before he approached the
oasis of Maruth, he halted. Thirsty though he was, he would have
to wait till it was dark before he could venture to the well.

One hour after sundown he rode into the oasis. There was no
moon, but he found the well, carefully let down the bucket, drew
it up again, drank until he could not hold any more, and gave the
donkey a bucketful. Then he rode on into the night, always toward the southwest.

The city that appeared before him was larger than Gibeah and
Jerusalem put together. The guards on the strong walls carried
shields with metal fittings—therefore they were Philistines. This
must be Gath and here Achis reigned. In spite of his kingly title

he was by no means the most powerful of the five Philistine rulers, but, so it was said, a rather mild man—for a Philistine. He was also said to be a just man. How much of this was true David would soon find out.

And yet he hesitated. Ever since he could remember, the word Philistine had always meant "enemy." Again and again the Philistines had attacked Judah and Israel and had relentlessly exacted their tribute. They were wild and brutal like the abominable gods they worshipped—Dagon above all, Beelzebub, and Astarte. Could the Lord really wish to send him to those people? Was it really possible that the Lord wanted him to serve Achis instead of Saul?

He pressed his lips together. Gath lay to the southwest. And there was no choice. Urging his donkey on, he rode into the city. The guards at the gate, wearing the hated high helmets and metal shields, let him pass unchallenged, but almost immediately he was surrounded by a throng of curious folk.

"Where do you want to go, stranger?" asked a well-dressed man.

"To King Achis to enter his service."

"And who says the king can use you, little man?" scoffed a workingman. "What's he got there in that cloth? Looks like a sword. Oh! Oh! Such a big sword and such a little man!"

"D'you want to sell it or did you steal it?"

"Let's have a look at it," demanded a soldier as he reached for the sword. David shoved his arm aside. And as he did so, his headcloth fell off.

"He's got red hair," cried a fat woman, laughing uproariously. But the soldier turned pale. "I know that man," he burst out. "By the wrath of Dagon, that's the man who killed Goliath."

"Impossible," laughed the well-dressed citizen. "Do you think this little shrimp could have killed a giant? What's the matter with you? Our Goliath would have had to stoop down to get so much as a look at him!"

The crowd laughed, but David suddenly burst into perspiration. Gath—the home of Goliath! How was it possible he had not thought of that! At the time he had fought Goliath it had made no difference to him which of the Philistine cities the giant came from. He must die—that was all that mattered then. But these people had not forgotten their greatest hero, the unconquered, the pride of the army. The soldier had already began to shout: "Hold him, hold the red devil! He's the man! I was there—I saw it all! He's the one!"

David kicked the donkey forward, but the crowd ran along beside him to right and to left. "Kill him!" screamed the fat woman. "Tear him to pieces!"

"What's all this shouting about?" roared an authoritative voice as a high-ranking dignitary forced his way through the excited crowd. "Don't you know the king wants quiet when he sits in judgment on quarrels? Scarcely fifty paces from here he sits on the judge's bench and you howl like jackals!"

"Lord, this stranger here—"

"An enemy has entered our gates, an enemy from Israel!"

"It's David," shouted the soldier. "The red devil!"

The dignitary smiled. "David married the daughter of King Saul; he sits in Gibeah and has no intention of coming here. Devil or not, he's not that crazy. Haven't you asked the fellow what he wants?"

"Yes, lord," answered the well-dressed citizen. "He says he wants to take service under the king."

"Indeed?" The dignitary glanced at the man on the donkey. "Well, I'll tell the king," he said leniently. "Then we'll find out what it's all about." And off he went.

Meantime the crowd around David had trebled in size. "You can believe me," shouted the soldier. "I was there when he killed Goliath! That fellow wasn't there, of course!" And he jerked his thumb in the direction in which the dignitary had disappeared. "That one was sitting home, eating four meals a day. Hey! Kamar! Kamar! Come here—you were there too! Tell us whether you recognize this man here?"

"Someone go and get Hameth!" shrilled a woman's voice. "Widows don't have much fun. Let her see how we deal with her husband's murderer!"

"Pull him off his donkey!"

Half a dozen eager hands pulled David from the animal.

"Murderer of our husbands!" the woman shrieked again. "Didn't they sing about you: 'Saul slew his thousands but David his ten thousands?' We'll tear you in ten thousand pieces, you red dog!"

At that David began to laugh. What else could he do? The dignitary was right, he would have to be crazy to go to Gath, stark, raving mad. He laughed and laughed and could not stop laughing.

Amazed, the crowd let him go; they even stepped back as if they were suddenly afraid of him. He noticed it and as swiftly as it had begun, his laughter broke off. So they were afraid of him! He remembered that the Philistines, like the Edomites and Moabites too, had a superstitious respect of madmen; they thought they were possessed of some sort of godhood and must be respected. To attack them was the same as attacking the godhood. And David's laughter had made them think he was mad. He began to laugh again as loudly and shrilly as he could. He showed his teeth, flung his arms around, and let spittle run over his chin.

The people moved farther back and stared shyly at him.

Then the dignitary returned, bringing six soldiers with him.

"That is the man," he said pointing to David. "Bring him to the king."

David laughed wildly, tapped one of the soldiers playfully on the helmet, and followed them dancing, even turning around and walking backward, much to the amazement of the dignitary who had not witnessed the beginning of the mad scene and did not know what to make of it.

King Achis sat in the judge's chair with the heavy gilded armrests and the Phoenician purple cushions. He liked to hold court in the open marketplace where more people could be convinced of the ruler's justice than in one of the palace rooms. The quarrel he was trying to settle was complicated and he was not displeased to stop for a few moments and give his attention to the stranger who wanted to enter his service.

Still dancing, David approached the king, stood still, rolled his eyes, laughed, and ran to the nearest house wall, on which he began to drum as if it were a musical instrument. As a soldier drew near him to bring him back, he kicked both legs behind him like a mule.

The king raised his eyebrows. "Why do you bring this man to me? If it's supposed to be a joke, it's a very unseemly one."

The dignitary's face flushed scarlet. "Lord, I don't know what has come over the man—"

"A demon probably," declared the king dryly. "Can't you see he is not in his right mind? Why do you bring him to me? Don't we have enough crazy people in Gath? And is that the sort of creature I'm supposed to take into my service? Away with him— and see that he is left in peace. You there, lead him out of the gate. And now back to our lawsuit. Kargath, you maintain therefore that your neighbor has purposely damaged your fields in order to buy them cheaply from you. But in your statements—"

David heard no more. The soldiers had set him on his donkey again and were already leading him back to the gate and out of it. After raising their hands with fingers spread in order to ward off the demon that had taken possession of him, they returned in haste to the city.

David was in just as much of a hurry. It was a tremendous relief to leave Gath and the Philistines behind, and he had no desire to wait until King Achis became convinced that the conqueror of Goliath had been in his city—no doubt to spy—and until he sent a hundred riders after him. To the southwest the Lord had said, but He could not have meant Gath. Perhaps He had not meant that David should leave the land of Judah at all. In the stone desert through which he had passed yesterday, in the ruins of the old castle fortress of Odollam, there were plenty of caves in which a man could be safe from discovery. It would take him only a few hours to reach the place. He decided to look the region over carefully, and it was fortunate that he did so, for just in time he saw a man step out from behind a group of rocks and fling an enormous stone at him. David jerked the donkey aside and the stone whizzed sharply past his head.

Immediately David galloped at the attacker, who waited for

him, grinning, a sword in his hand. Six paces away David halted the donkey, sprang down, and pulled Goliath's sword out of its cloth cover. "You have a friendly way of greeting travelers!" he said ironically.

The man was a head taller than David and strongly built. He was still grinning. "Where is your sword going with you, little man?" he scoffed. "Better throw it away or you'll hurt yourself with it."

David had never liked the term "little man." Instead of answering, he knocked the man's sword out of his hand and thrust the hilt of his own sword so hard under the man's chin that he fell forward and writhed on the ground.

"What's the matter with you, big fellow?" cried David. "Come, stand up and fight!"

There was a sudden roar of laughter from many throats. David swung around. Behind him stood at least one hundred men, and more and more men came running up. It was as though the whole stone desert had come alive. David looked at the men. They were all armed; they had spears with sharp stone points, pointed sticks, clubs, even a couple of swords, but the majority were in rags. Robbers! Caravan robbers! They had sought the same hiding place as he—and for the same reasons.

"Pretty neat, the way you made short work of big Ruben," laughed a thickset man with a face burnt almost black from the sun, as he wiped the tears from his eyes. "It's almost a pity you have to die."

"Kill him!" gurgled Ruben. He was sitting on some loose boulders and spitting out teeth. "What are you all waiting for?"

"Yes, truly, what are you waiting for?" asked David scornfully. "A hundred men certainly aren't afraid to attack one lone man!" Grabbing the sword with both hands, he swung it in a circle so swiftly that they all involuntarily stepped back.

"Wait!" croaked a voice, and an older man with a dirty yellow headcloth pushed his way through the crowd. "I know who he is," he went on in great excitement. "That's David, son of Jesse!"

"No matter who the fellow is," howled Ruben, "he knocked out all my teeth. Kill him!"

"It's David, you fools," repeated the man with the yellow head-cloth. "The man who conquered Goliath—no wonder he could handle big Ruben too."

Silence. The eyes of the ragged men were filled with respectful curiosity. A bearded man stepped forward. "It is truly David from Bethlehem," he declared. "I knew him when he was still a boy."

"And I know you," said David. "You are neighbor Simon, who could not pay the king's tribute and whom they drove from house and home."

"If you are David," said the thickset man gloomily, "then you are the son-in-law of the king. Give yourself up. And when Saul's troops come to take us, you will be the first to die."

"That's true," David nodded. "I certainly will. They've been after me for some time." He laughed bitterly at sight of their astonished faces. "No matter why you are here in the desert," he went on, "whether because of debts, like Simon here, or whether you have stolen or killed—the king would let you all go free before he would let me escape."

"Don't you believe him!" shouted Ruben as he staggered forward. "It's a trick, a barefaced trick! He wants to hand us all over to the king!"

"If that's what I wanted, would I have come here alone?" asked David calmly. "Go and ask anyone you see. You will soon find out how much the king loves me. Bethlehem is not twelve miles from here. The people there know."

The thickset man grinned. "Out of favor, eh? And why? Don't tell us, I can guess what it is." In a hoarse voice completely out of tune he sang: "'Saul slew his thousands, and David his ten thousands.' That's something a king doesn't like to hear." He turned to the men. "This is the best catch we've ever made!" he cried. "Now at last we have what we badly needed, a man to lead us. Am I right?"

"Aye, aye!" they shouted.

The thickset man turned to David again. "You see, they want you, lord," he said. "Will you join us? You are a better leader than Ruben here."

81

"Will you really dare to brave the king's sevenfold scorn?" asked David. "Without me it might well be that he would not do anything to you, or at least not much. But if I am your leader and he hears of it, he will certainly come. Knowing that, do you still want to risk it?"

There was a short pause. Then the thickset man cried: "He'll come even so! And you will know what we must do to keep alive. Saul slays his thousands and David his ten thousands." Now all the men were shouting enthusiastically.

"Good," said David very earnestly, "I accept." Taking no notice of their cheers, he walked over to Ruben. "I treated you badly," he said with a smile few men could resist. "But even so, better than I did Goliath! Be my friend."

Ruben stared at him. Slowly his face lighted up. "To lose to you is no shame," he grumbled. "I'm only sorry about my best teeth."

The group numbered not merely a hundred men, but almost double that, and they were no more poorly armed than Saul's men. David caught himself thinking that the Lord had given him a little army, but he immediately put that thought aside with a grim smile. An army of ne'er-do-wells, good-for-nothings, evil-doers of all kinds, and a few poor fellows who had suffered cruel injustice and for whom there was no other refuge. From now on he was responsible for the acts of all these men, and also for their well-being.

He began by acquainting himself with the general situation. There was no lack of water; two brooks gave them all they needed. A decent flock of sheep and goats—doubtless gathered together piece by piece—provided them with meat, milk, and cheese, and there were plenty of roomy caves in which the provisions were stored. He decided to forbid thievery on the territory of Judah, and instead to allow the men to prey on the not-too-distant border villages of the Philistines—an idea that at first met with little enthusiasm. The Philistines were dangerous and better armed. "Then we'll get ourselves arms from them," David retorted. "It wouldn't be the first time." He appointed Ruben and the thickset man, Tufiah, as his seconds in command. He had no great confidence in Ruben but neither did he wish to make an enemy of him unnecessarily. "Harmless travelers must not be molested," he ordered. "Nor soldiers of the king either."

"But what if they attack us?" asked Ruben.

"To do that they must first find us," replied David. "Just leave that to me."

A few days after he had taken over the command, additional forces arrived, over sixty men from the neighborhood of Hebron. "We want David to be our leader too," they declared. How had the news spread so quickly to the south? Almost every day small groups joined the band. A week later forty more well-armed men from Tekoa arrived. And in less than three weeks their number had increased to almost four hundred men, among them many who were not criminals but political dissidents, men who had been driven out as a result of the king's personal enmity.

The little caravan moving through the gullies of Odollam was watched by sharp eyes. "There are two or three women among them," Ruben reported to his commander. "And perhaps a dozen men."

David looked toward the caravan. "By the holy name of the Lord," he cried, "anyone who makes a move against them dies by my hand." Then in long strides he descended the hill.

"Father?" he called. "Mother!"

His parents embraced him, his mother wept. "We have all come," said Father Jesse. "Neighbor Ezra warned us. The king intends to send troops against us, on your account."

David nodded sadly. Saul wanted them as hostages.

"At my age to have to flee like a criminal!" moaned Jesse plaintively. "How could you have made an enemy of the king, your own father-in-law? What have you done to him? He is said to be absolutely implacable. I can only think that your new position at court has gone to your head. What good is it to me not to have to pay the king's tribute if at the same time all my possessions are taken from me—and that is what will happen now."

"It comes from trying to climb too high," said Eliab. Abinadab,

Shammah, and the other brothers were there, too, and David's two sisters. Sarvia, the elder sister, had brought her sons with her; Asael, the youngest, was still a child, but Joab and Abisai were young men, and what men they were! The last time David had seen them—how many years ago was it?—they had been wild lads terrifying the whole neighborhood, catching animals in traps and winning fights against six or seven boys their age. And now the two young men were the only ones who seemed gay and happy; to them it was a great adventure to come to their uncle David, who was now the leader of a band of armed men.

"You boys have grown so big and strong," said David in astonishment. "I would hardly recognize you." Joab, who was a year older than his brother, had black hair, and Abisai brown, but otherwise they looked so much alike one could not tell them apart—the same sharp, hawklike faces, the same bushy eyebrows that met over the bridge of the nose.

"You'll let us come with you, won't you?" begged Abisai. "Is that Goliath's sword?"

"Easy, brother," warned Joab. "Just wait."

David slapped them on their muscular shoulders. "We'll see," he said warmly. "If your mother is willing . . ."

Eliab, Shammah, and the other brothers stood silently by, casting anxious glances at David's men, who were streaming together from all sides. His mother and sister were also looking anxiously around, and it was clear to David that his family could not stay here. The rough life of the army camp at Odollam was not for them. And it would not be long now before Saul's troops came. The parents and brothers and sisters must get away. But where? Feverishly he thought it over as he led them to his cave, where he ordered a good meal set before them. Before the meal was over, he had found the right solution. He would see that they all had a comfortable bed—there were plenty of goatskins—and a peaceful night. In the morning he told his father that he would take the whole family to Moab. "I will have fifty of my best men escort you so that nothing can happen to you on the way. The king of Moab will give you a friendly welcome. Was not the mother of your mother a Moabite?" So often he had heard the story of Ruth and Boaz, but never had he thought that his great-grandmother Ruth would play an important part in his life. After the death of her first husband, Ruth had faithfully followed her mother-in-law Naomi to Bethlehem, where she met Boaz, who became her second husband—and now their grandson was obliged to return to Moab, because their great-grandson was at odds with his father-in-law. Ancestors and descendants were forming a strange, mysterious chain . . .

After talking it over, the parents consented, and to David's great relief his brothers also decided to go with them to Moab. Not so Joab and Abisai. They insisted upon staying with David, and pestered their mother so long that, sighing, she finally gave her consent. "It is the fate of widows to be weak and yielding with their sons," smiled Sarvia amid her tears. Her husband, who had been an Aramaean, had died four years before.

And so David set out with his family. During his absence he left Tufiah, the thickset man, in command, urging him to avoid any conflict with the king's troops. "Do as I tell you and you will have no trouble," he warned him insistently. "They don't know the terrain here so well as you and I. The moment they come, draw back into the southern caves. If the enemy discovers even one of you, then you must all flee, but in small groups of not more than twenty men. Scatter in all directions, then come back as soon as possible to the caves. Saul's troops will not follow you, because they do not dare split up. They have to stay together."

Tufiah promised to do his best.

7

Two weeks later David returned. Everything had gone well. The king of Moab had been proud to give asylum to the descendants of Ruth the Moabite and had sworn to treat them as if they were his own relatives. To be sure, that was a pledge of rather dubious value—the king had had two of his brothers executed because they were suspected of having aspired to the throne—but in general he was not a hard man and he seemed to mean well.

Tufiah, beaming with pride, reported that there had been no sign of Saul's troops in Odollam. "Perhaps that is because the king and all the notables of Israel have gone to Ramatha."

David looked up. "To Ramatha? Why?"

"Haven't you heard? For days people have talked of nothing else."

"I have heard nothing. We traveled by night, and by day we slept in some sort of hiding place. What has happened?"

"The old man from Ramatha, the prophet—"

"Samuel!" David nodded quickly and excitedly. "What has happened to him?"

"He died," Tufiah explained. "Even prophets are mortal."

David turned away: he was deeply moved. Samuel—his first, his greatest friend, the last of the judges over Israel and Judah, the man who had made Saul king, who had chosen and anointed David, son of Jesse. He had met him only twice, and yet no other man had had such influence on his life. Suddenly he felt completely deserted. What was he without the secret protection of the prophet? Leader of a band of thugs, commander of cutthroats, despised and pursued by the king of the land! People everywhere must look upon him as a guilty fugitive; even his own father could scarcely believe he was innocent. Samuel, as David now realized, had been a strong support for him. Not only had he saved his life that time on the sacrificial mound of Ramatha, but he had also given him spiritual support. With Samuel behind him, a man could not go wrong. And now the prophet was dead. As if from far, far away he heard the peculiarly high, throaty voice, "The Lord demands obedience—the Lord alone is thy helper." But the Lord had made known his will through Samuel . . .

"We have twenty-one new men." That was Tufiah who was waiting to continue his report. "There are some good fighters among them. And a priest has come. His name is Abiathar."

Abiathar? What was the son of the high priest doing in Odollam? "Where is he?"

"In your lodging."

David hastened to him. "Abiathar! In the name of the Lord, what has happened to you?" The young priest wore a thick bandage around his head and carried his right arm in a sling.

"That is nothing," he answered with a melancholy smile. "But I bring terrible news."

David turned white. "Sit down. You must spare yourself. I can guess what you have to tell me."

Abiathar sat down. "No matter what you may think, my news is worse," he said quietly. "No man can guess it. Two days after you left us, the king commanded my father and all the priests to come to Gibeah. Naturally we obeyed, my father, the other priests, and I, eighty-five of us in all. He overwhelmed us with reproaches—that we had stood by you, given you bread and weapons, although you were his enemy. My poor father tried to explain that he had known nothing of this. You were Saul's first servant, his son-in-law, the captain of the bodyguards! How could he have known that you were the king's enemy? The king did not believe him and ordered us all to be killed."

"Impossible! No faithful Israelite would lay his hand on the servants of God!" cried David.

"You are right," Abiathar said sadly. "Saul's bodyguards refused. Then he commanded Doeg, the Edomite. And Doeg obeyed."

"Doeg," groaned David. "I saw him that time in the courtyard. I knew he would report it to the king. It is my fault. It is all my fault!"

"It is Saul's fault," retorted Abiathar calmly. "And Doeg's. The Edomite killed my father first, then all the others. He struck me too. But his arm had doubtless grown tired and he gave me only a glancing blow. I pretended I was dead, and when they had gone and there were only corpses left in the palace courtyard, I escaped. The next day Saul sent his soldiers to Nobe and slaughtered everyone there, women and children, even the cattle. Nobe no longer exists."

David sank down on his couch and burst into loud sobs.

"I am the only one left alive," Abiathar ended his story. "And I come to you—with this."

David stared at the ephod as if he were bewitched. The gold-embroidered apron, the breastplate with the Urim and Thummim stones, the holy ephod was here, and legitimate, priestly hands had brought it. Saul had murdered all the priests. The sole survivor was here in his camp with him, the leader of the despised, the hunted. "God is my helper," he whispered. "The Lord has answered my questions." He took a deep breath. "Stay with me, Abiathar. Have no fear. Whoever tries to take your life must also try to take mine. And I think— I think that you are safe with me."

When the band had increased to six hundred men, David departed from Odollam. "Two hundred of us could easily hide here," he explained. "With four hundred it would be difficult; with six hundred it is impossible." He led his men to Jaar-Hareb where there were extensive woods. At first Ruben and even

Tufiah grumbled. They had become accustomed to Odollam. "One more reason for going elsewhere," declared David. "We can't let ourselves settle down and grow fat. And the forest offers us great advantages."

"I know what you mean," Abisai interrupted.

"I do, too," said Joab.

David took great pleasure in the two young men; they were alert and brimming over with ideas. "Well, what do I mean, Abisai?"

"That the king's troops can't maneuver here in the forest," was the prompt reply.

"Quite right," David commended. "Is that what you thought too, Joab?"

"Yes, but that's not all." The usually reticent Joab suddenly became talkative. "If the king sends an army against us, he has only two possibilities. Either he breaks into the forest, we make a sudden attack, and just as suddenly draw back—or he surrounds the forest. Then he has to spread his lines out so thin that we can break through them wherever we wish."

That was the time when David realized that in his two young nephews he had excellent material for future commanders, and from then on he included them in all the councils of war. He had them practice maneuvers, lightning attacks on a marching column, equally swift retreats, with a salvo of arrows from cover as a parting shot at the bewildered enemy. He taught them to dig deep pits lightly covered with brushwood as traps for the enemy. All archers had to practice climbing in order to get better aim at the enemy from the tops of trees.

David himself organized the spy service. Large numbers of his spies roamed the land and he chose them carefully for their particular tasks. Men from the north were sent only to the south and vice versa, so that they never ran the danger of being recognized. Men from Israel went to the cities of Judah, men from Judah to the cities of Israel. Soon his system was so well established that it was impossible for a strong force to attack them by surprise. Moreover, the daily training hardened the men and kept them in battle trim. Six weeks after they had moved camp, a spy reported that Saul's troops had been searching systematically in the neighborhood of Odollam. "There were at least fifteen hundred men. They had found the southern caves, your lodging, everything."

"But not us." David nodded in satisfaction. He knew, however, that the search would go on, and he was prepared for any eventuality. The next report he received, however, was of a very different nature.

"The Philistines are besieging Ceila," a scout reported. "They are laying waste all the country around the city and stealing the cattle."

Ceila was a city in Judah. "How many are they?" asked David.

"About a thousand, lord."

That meant only one tribe—a raid, not war. David lost himself in thought. A city of his native land was besieged by the enemy, the archenemy. Should he look on and do nothing? What did the Lord want of him? "Abiathar, I have a question to ask the Lord."

The priest put on the ephod, the apron, and the breastplate. They prayed. "Ask," said the son of the high priest calmly.

"Lord," said David, "shall I go and smite the Philistines who are besieging Ceila?"

Abiathar shook the breastplate, put his hand inside, and drew out a stone. It was white.

David sprang up, seized a ram's horn, and blew. When his men had gathered together, he told them of his decision. But the men were not enthusiastic. Big Ruben spoke out his misgivings frankly. "We are only too glad to have Saul leave us in peace. Why should we run into danger to do *his* work for him?"

Tufiah was against it, too. "We have learned to defend ourselves," he said. "But to attack experienced fighters like the Philistines?" He shook his head in disapproval.

David looked at Abiathar, but the priest was silent. So he must make the decision alone. "For you sake I will ask the Lord once more," he announced. "But you must all pray with me that He may make His will known to us." The jailbirds and the tramps, the tax evaders and the killers looked at each other in embarrassment, but they obeyed, and a strange silence fell over the camp.

"Ask," said Abiathar again.

"God of Israel," David prayed in a loud voice. "Wilt Thou deliver the Philistines who beleaguer Ceila into our hands?"

Abiathar drew out a stone and held it up so that all could see. It was white.

"We set out at once," David commanded.

Towards evening they came to Ceila. The besiegers had put up scaling ladders and the battle was in full swing. The Philistines had already driven together the farmers' cattle. David studied the position from the edge of the forest.

"Tufiah," he ordered, "take a hundred men and drive the thieves over there away from the cattle. When you have killed the sentries and the cattle thieves, leave twenty men with the animals and attack the besiegers on the farthest right wing—if they are still alive. I can't promise you they will be. Now off with you!" Tufiah grinned and disappeared.

David could clearly see that the Philistines had had considerable success against the defenders. Almost unharmed they had clambered up the ladders and crossed over the walls. A larger troop, standing in closed formation before the walls, were apparently waiting for their comrades who had entered the city to open the gates from within. There were about four hundred men in all. David drew Goliath's sword and pointed to them. "Down with them!" he commanded. "Forward!" Five hundred men broke out of the woods.

The attack on the flank was overpowering: The Philistines could not even put up an orderly resistance; they were overrun and cut down. "Leave the booty! We'll get that later," shouted David. He was about to order his men to climb the scaling ladders which the Philistines had left standing, when the city gates opened.

"Follow me," shouted David, and stormed the gates at the head of his men. It was exactly as he had thought—the invading Philistines who were already inside the gates had intended to open them to their comrades. Instead, they suddenly found themselves faced with hundreds of the enemy. David killed two and saw Abisai beside him stretch a third man on the ground. Then he was through the gate, and his men poured in after him in an apparently endless stream. The men of Ceila were no less surprised than their enemy when David's men fell upon the Philistines from behind. A quarter of an hour later the battle was over. Only a few Philistines escaped under cover of the oncoming night.

A tremendous victory celebration followed, when the elders of the city gave a great banquet in honor of their deliverer. In an inspired speech the commander-in-chief of the garrison lauded the best general in Israel, the conqueror of Goliath, the terror of the Philistines, and—the son-in-law of the king. "We beg you to convey our thanks to the king for sending us help so quickly," he ended amid thunderous cheers and applause.

Tufiah, Ruben, Joab, and Abisai were half amused, half embarrassed. They turned to David, who looked down and frowned. He had certainly not expected the people of Ceila to be ignorant of the real situation and to mistake his men for Saul's soldiers. Slowly he raised his head. "Between the king and me there has been an unfortunate misunderstanding," he began to the consternation of his junior officers. "It was not Saul who sent me to you, but the siege of Ceila has given me an opportunity to prove my loyalty to him. I and my men came to your aid on our own initiative."

A bewildered silence followed.

The commander-in-chief of the garrison cleared his throat. "In any case we shall inform the king that we have you to thank for saving our city," he said.

"Tell me another," murmured big Ruben, biting heartily into a juicy leg of mutton. David, who was sitting beside him, did not move a muscle. Later, when David was alone with his two young nephews, Abisai asked: "What will the king do if he hears about this?"

David sighed. "If he is in his right mind, perhaps he will come to his senses. If not, we are in greater danger than before."

"Do you think the people of Ceila are really grateful to us?" Abisai continued.

"I don't know," answered David, smiling. "Do you think so?"

"No," replied Abisai and Joab with one accord.

David shrugged. "Well, we'll manage somehow," he said lightly. But his heart was not light, and the two young men knew it, no matter how carefree he pretended to be.

The morning after the banquet, Tufiah came to David.

"A young girl wishes to speak to you, lord." He grinned gleefully.

"A young girl?"

"A two-legged gazelle, lord—lovely, with eyes like—like—I can't think of any comparison that would be good enough."

David laughed. "What does she want?"

"She won't tell anyone but you, lord."

"Stop grinning," David snapped, "and bring the girl in!" Since his mother and sisters had been with him in Odollam he had not seen any woman close at hand.

The girl came in. Her face with its regular features was beautiful, though the lips were perhaps a little too voluptuous. Tufiah was right, she had marvelous eyes, dark and full of fire. She wore a honey-colored gown and held a little coffer in both hands. "I am Achinoam, daughter of Salmon from Jezrahel, and I have come to thank you." Her voice was deep, but as soft as a Phoenician cushion.

"Thank me for what?" asked David.

She looked at him passionately. "You have saved my life and the lives of my people and everything we have."

"How is that?"

"We live near the city well, lord, and the Philistines had already forced their way into our house; they had tied us and stolen everything of value. They were going to set fire to the house and burn my relatives in it. Me they intended to take with them into their hated country. Then you broke into the city with your men, and the Philistines ran like jackals when the lion comes. Here, lord, I bring you a gift from my relatives; it is only a portion of the things you have saved for us." She opened the little coffer; it was full of gold and silver jewelry.

"You should keep these beautiful things for yourself, Achinoam," said David. "Wear them when your bridegroom comes to take you to his house."

Achinoam set the coffer down hastily on the nearest table. "I will have no bridegroom, lord," she murmured breathlessly, "for no man can be as you are!" Before he could say a word she had run out of the room.

"Achinoam!" he called after her. There was no answer. In three strides he was at the door.

There stood Tufiah, grinning as usual. "She's gone," he reported. "She runs like a gazelle, too."

"Find out what you can about her," David ordered. "Her name is Achinoam and she lives with relatives at the city well. Go." Tufiah grinned even more broadly and obeyed. David went back into the room and paced thoughtfully back and forth. He thought of Michol and of the spies he had sent out weeks ago to find out how she was. Achinoam was beautiful, even though hers was not an aristocratic beauty like Michol's. A man could have as many women as he desired so long as it was possible for him to support them. But there was only one Michol. And yet . . .

"Why are we still here?" asked Abisai impatiently.

David smiled. "Don't you like Ceila?"

"A forest suits me better."

"It's safer there, too," growled Joab.

"Indeed?" asked David. "But Ceila is a fortress."

"That's just why," explained Abisai. "Oh, of course, it would be a different matter if it were our own fortress! But I don't trust the people here. The mouse in the mousehole is safe from the cat—but not when a second cat is sitting with it in the hole."

David nodded. "You are not far wrong, Nephew. But we have been here only three days. The storm can't come so quickly—if it comes at all."

"You still think you can change Saul's mind!" cried Abisai. "But you can rescue ten cities for him and he will still be your enemy, the unthankful—"

"Hush," warned David. "He is the king."

"For me you are the king," cried Abisai and rushed out of the room.

"My brother is a hothead and he talks too much, but this time he is right," declared Joab dryly as he followed Abisai.

In the afternoon of the same day Huzal the spy arrived and David received him alone. "You were in Gibeah?"

"Yes, lord, I come from there. The king is assembling troops. I counted almost three thousand men and they expect more."

"He intends to come to the help of Ceila?"

"No, lord, he knows you have already done that."

"Then why the troops?" asked David, suddenly alert. "An expedition of revenge against the Philistines for their attack on Ceila?"

"I could not find that out," Huzal admitted. "The troops themselves know nothing, not even the officers. Abner knows and probably Jacob too, but I couldn't very well approach them."

David nodded absent-mindedly. "What do they say about me?" he asked softly.

"They love you, lord," said Huzal simply. "But they obey the king."

Again David nodded. "That is their duty." Then, as if casually, he added: "And how is the Princess Michol?"

Huzal looked embarrassed and his fingers played with the fringes on his sleeve. "She is not in Gibeah," he said.

David looked up. "Where is she?" he asked sharply. "Speak, man!"

Huzal avoided his eyes. "The king gave her to one of his dignitaries to be his wife," he managed to get out. "Phalti, the son of Lais from Gallium."

David stared into space. "Thank you, Huzal," he said soberly. "You have done good work and will receive a reward. Go now." Huzal crept out.

For two long hours David sat there motionless. Then Tufiah came. "The girl Achinoam, lord," he began in a businesslike tone. "She is an orphan and lives with her father's brother and his wife. They are well-to-do people and greatly respected in Ceila. The girl is fourteen years old and no one has anything to say against her."

"What are you talking about?" asked David.

Tufiah opened his eyes wide. "About the girl Achinoam, lord. You ordered me—"

"Yes. Quite right. I shall take the girl to wife, Tufiah. This very day. Now. Let her relatives decide at once on the price for the bride." He smiled grimly. "It will be easier to pay than the price for the Princess Michol. Attend to everything necessary, and send Abiathar to me with the ephod."

When he entered the room, the young priest was already wearing the apron and the breastplate. As always they prayed and Abiathar said: "Ask."

"Lord," began David. "God of Israel, will Saul come down to attack me?"

The stone was white. So then the assembling of troops in Gibeah was intended for him and not for the Philistines. "Lord," said David again, "God of Israel. Will the men of Ceila rise against me and deliver me into the hands of the king?"

Again the stone was white. David and the priest recited the prayer of thanks.

"They can be here tomorrow," said David. "We shall set out this very day." He called for Ruben, Joab, and Abisai. "The men are to make ready as unobtrusively as possible," he commanded. "We leave the city around midnight."

But before that, his marriage to Achinoam was celebrated. "You will not have an easy time with me, Achinoam," David warned. "We lead a very unsettled life. And if the king should succeed in capturing us, I don't know what would happen to you."

"Death with you is better than life with another man," replied Achinoam calmly.

"And I shall also have other wives."

"That shall be as my lord wishes," said Achinoam in a low voice, but she breathed a little faster.

At midnight they set out, quite suddenly. The Ceilans at the gate let them through—they were probably glad to be rid of their far too numerous rescuers, whose leader, moreover, was still in the king's bad books. But when they were near Jaar-Hareb, they saw the light of fires. The forest was burning in several places.

"That means he knows about our hiding place," thought David. He considered the matter briefly, then gave the order: "To the southeast."

"Southeast," repeated Tufiah incredulously. "That's where Hebron is—"

"We must bypass Hebron tonight."

"And then, lord?"

"Into the desert, friend. Now we must start moving. For from now on the king is not joking."

8

DAVID KNEW THE ZIPH DESERT WELL, for he had often hunted antelope there and occasionally even lions. Sometimes alone, sometimes with Prince Jonathan. He knew where to find water and where there were caves in which to take shelter. Moreover, the terrain offered many possibilities. If the king attacked, they could retreat farther into the desert. It was not easy to find enough water for six hundred men, but for three thousand it would be impossible unless Saul carried an enormous baggage column with him. In that case David's only recourse was to flee around the Dead Sea to the land of Ammon or Moab, with the danger of finding himself facing new enemies there. The king of Moab had already taken in a few refugees from Judah. Whether he would so graciously accept six hundred outlaws was another matter. And what if Saul or Abner should succeed in driving him away from the Dead Sea? But those were worries he could take up later. For the moment he had to make friends with the desert dwellers, or at least as well as he could, so that they would not betray him. He impressed on his men the necessity for the strictest discipline. As his headquarters he chose the mountain plateau of the desert, about five miles southeast of the city of Hebron.

Little Achinoam had shared all the marches uncomplainingly, and to David's great relief his men did not seem to take it ill of him that he alone had a woman with him. They treated her with a mixture of awkward respect and goodnatured liking, perhaps because they knew that she worshipped her husband. She was delighted with their quarters on the Ziph plateau, from where they looked out over a great part of the desert as far as Maon and Engaddi. "The view is magnificent," she declared, "and so is the prospect of not having to march every night!"

"Don't be too hopeful," David warned. "Any day we may be forced to move again."

His fears were soon realized. Only two weeks after their arrival Achinoam saw from a distance a long, glistening column, like a snake creeping through the desert. She called David to her side.

"That is the king," he said immediately. "And with at least three thousand men." Already the alarm was sounding from the outposts. And a few hours later David knew that the people of Ziph had betrayed him. The snake was heading straight toward the Ziph mountain. He ordered his men to set out for Maon, although even there his pursuers would quickly find them. "We'll see who holds out longest!" David called to his men, and laughed, though he felt far from cheerful. In no event must they join battle with the enemy. Six hundred men against three thousand—there could be no doubt as to the outcome. This was not war, it was a hunt, a manhunt, and he and his men were the prey.

In the gray dawn his sentries saw a solitary man hurrying toward them. They promptly took him prisoner and brought him before David. The richly dressed prisoner smiled.

"Jonathan!" shouted David and flung his arms around his friend. The sentries withdrew, astounded.

"I could not help it," Jonathan admitted. "I had to come and see you once more."

"Does your father know?" asked David. Then he thought of Michol and the sudden light in his eyes faded even before his friend could answer.

"If my father hears of it, I'm a dead man," replied Jonathan. "He hates you more than ever and his hatred is greater than his love for me—if he loves me at all, that is—"

"I reconquered Ceila for him," said David bitterly. "And what did he do? He gave Michol to another man. It seems that nothing I can do will convince him that I am loyal to him and will always be loyal. Nothing."

"I'm afraid you are right," said Jonathan calmly. "For the only thing he loves is his crown and he knows he will lose it to you."

"What are you saying?"

"He knows that the Lord has chosen you to be king over Israel," said Jonathan firmly. "But he cannot admit it. He suffers cruelly."

David ran his hand mechanically over his hair, on which many years ago Samuel had dripped balsam. "And what about you? What do you believe?"

"You will be king over Israel," said Jonathan gently, "and the best and greatest king I could ever imagine. We talked about it once before, you and I, a long time ago. At the time you said to me, 'One day you will be king, Jonathan, and I will stand by your side as your commander-in-chief!' Today I know that it will be just the reverse. You will be the king—and I, perhaps, the second man in the land."

"I still remember what you answered that time," said David in a low voice. "You said, 'Perhaps it will be only a beautiful dream. But one thing I know: You and I are friends as long as we live.' You have often proved it—and once again today. What would I give if you could stay with me! But you must go back to the king. Every moment you linger here puts your life in greater danger."

"Anyone else would have held me as a hostage," and Jonathan smiled. "Or he would at least have tried to sound me out as to the strength of my father's troops and his plans. It doesn't even occur to you. And yet they say you are the sliest fox in all Israel and Judah."

"Who says that?"

"Abner," replied Jonathan. "Although that is what he is himself."

"Is he with you?"

"No. He stayed behind in Gibeah in case the Philistines should show up. Goodbye, my friend. I do not need to say 'God guard you.' I know He is guarding you."

"Tufiah," shouted David. The officer stood in the doorway. "Prince Jonathan has safe conduct wherever he wishes to go."

The manhunt went on. Again and again David and his men had to change their positions. And again in the desert hills word came at dawn that Saul's army was on the direct line of march. This time David immediately broke camp, let his men take cover in the bushes of the secluded hillside, and sent Huzal the spy with six men to report to him the moment the enemy column came in sight.

The first report came a quarter of an hour later. "They are swerving toward the north, lord." That could only mean that they would march on the other side of the hill. David ordered his men to advance in the same direction, but in single file and as quietly as possible. "We are less than a hundred yards from the enemy and separated only by the chain of hills. If you so much as kick a stone loose they can hear it."

He knew that the road branched off before the end of the chain of hills. On his side there was a narrow pass ahead that led to the open desert. That was the only road to freedom. And so it came about that the troops of King Saul and the men of David marched for almost one hour parallel to one another. Only a short half hour and David's men would be at the narrow pass. At that moment Huzal, pale and excited, hurried up from the rear guard. "They have divided, lord! The troops on the other side of the hill are only a thousand men strong. Another thousand are fairly close behind us."

David bit his lip. "Where are the remaining thousand?"

"They must have gone on ahead. There is no sign of them."

Feverishly David pondered the problem. What would he do with the remaining thousand if he were in Saul's place? Use them in a flanking movement, of course. Then, with the pincers closed, the enemy would be encircled. That explained why the thousand had gone on ahead. They were now up forward somewhere. Abisai came from the vanguard, pushing his way past the column.

"I know what you have to report," said David. "The narrow pass is held."

Abisai opened his eyes wide. "Yes, we had to halt, otherwise they would have discovered us. But how could you know that?"

David waved him away. For the first time since his flight from the king began, his courage failed him. He was hemmed in on three sides; the fourth side led to open country where he would immediately be seen by the enemy ahead and behind. Then the marching column on the other side of the hill would descend the heights and swoop down upon him. "Saul is a good soldier," he thought bitterly. "God of Israel, have You let me come so far to ruin me now, me and all those You have entrusted to my care? Your prophet said You were my only help. Now help me—for I know no other way."

One of Huzal's men rushed toward him. "Lord, the pursuers in our rear have turned back."

David swung around. "Have you lost your mind? It can't be."

"I saw it myself," babbled the messenger. "They are retreating in great haste."

"Turn back," David promptly ordered. "Abisai, order the vanguard to turn immediately and march back."

"There is one of my men coming this way," cried Abisai in surprise. The man ran up, panting. "Lord, the narrow pass will soon be free. The enemy is withdrawing."

David clasped his forehead. It is Saul who has lost his mind, he thought. Or—or the Lord has saved us.

Tufiah and big Ruben sat side by side in the grass polishing their weapons. "Not much use doing this," grumbled Ruben. "It won't come to a decent raid anyway."

"Be glad we can have a few months' rest," Tufiah tested the point of his sword. It was a good bronze sword, part of the booty from Ceila. "Or do you have a hankering to be marching night after night again? Just don't think Saul has given us up."

"I'm not so set on marching," Ruben admitted. "But a little plunder now and then wouldn't be so bad."

"Since you married your Rachel you're out after silver jewelry,"

102

grinned Tufiah. "You know very well why David won't allow any raids. We'd have the whole population here in Negev down on us."

"They'd rather see us go than come, anyway," Ruben retorted. "And when Saul turns up they'll betray us just like the others in the Ziph desert."

"They've learned to respect us. That is, they respect David," said Tufiah thoughtfully. "Only yesterday women came to camp again with parched corn and fig cakes—of their own accord, too."

"Because we protect them," growled Ruben. "That's why. We're the king's border troops, you might say. Instead of cheerfully taking what we need, we see to it that no one takes anything from the people."

"I really believe you're bored," laughed Tufiah. "When have we ever been so well fixed?"

"In the old days we didn't have so much trouble getting provisions, you can't deny that."

"Yes, when we were only two hundred men strong; there was nothing so very clever about that. But have we ever had to go hungry? David has always seen to it that you had a bellyful, you old glutton. And half of our men have been able to take wives, the first batch of youngsters is already here, and more on the way."

"With us, too," Ruben admitted with a smirk. "Rachel told me only yesterday."

"May the Lord give you a strong and healthy son!" said Tufiah earnestly, as was proper.

"Me, the father of a family!" Ruben shook his head. "But what you said about respect for us, that's right. They all talk about David as if he were the king and not Saul."

Tufiah nodded to himself. "I almost believe it myself. He has a guardian angel. Nothing can harm him. Remember that time in the desert foothills? Why, that was a miracle!"

"Nonsense!" laughed Ruben. "We've known for a long time why Saul suddenly retreated instead of springing the trap. Because he had to! Because the Philistines were on the march again. That was more important to him than catching us. Miracle! Bah!"

Tufiah looked at him pityingly. "Thinking was never your strong point," he said. "Why shouldn't a miracle have a sensible basis? And why did the Philistines come at just that moment? Why didn't Saul get the news two hours later, after he had cut all our throats?"

"The real miracle is that Saul has left us in peace so long," said Ruben changing the subject. "And if David can work miracles, he'd better see to it that we get more to eat. The little bit of corn and the few fig cakes from yesterday won't go very far."

"David doesn't work miracles, you fool. But the Lord does and He won't forsake us."

"The lord on whom our food depends now is named Nabal," retorted Ruben grumpily. "He has three thousand sheep and a thousand goats, and he's a tremendously rich man, one of the richest here in the south, and why? Because we're keeping the desert thieves away from his possessions. And the ten messengers David sent to him should have been back long ago."

"It's not a bad sign that it takes so long," declared Tufiah calmly. "They're just waiting till Nabal has loaded all the good things and then they'll come right back with them."

The messengers came two hours later—with empty hands. "Nabal is very highhanded," reported Huzal, the leader of the ten. "His people eat and drink to their hearts' content. But for us he has not one tiny sheep's tail."

David frowned. "You gave him my greetings courteously, as I commanded?"

"Of course, lord, and we pointed out modestly that we have protected him and his people for many months and all that time he has never lost any of his cattle, and then we begged him to help us out now."

"And what did he answer?"

Huzal gulped. "He asked scornfully, 'Who is David? And what is the son of Jesse? Servants who flee from their masters are multiplied nowadays. Shall I then give my bread, my water, and the flesh of my cattle I have slaughtered to such rabble? I have no intention of doing so. Begone.'" David knew the language. Even in Bethlehem there had been rich, stingy landowners who had haughtily turned away anyone asking for help. But here the case was different. Not only was this a question of give and take, but he dared not accept this treatment of his messengers or it would set a precedent. He would lose respect of all the farmers and cattleowners in the neighborhood, to say nothing of his own men. He sounded the alarm signal on the ram's horn and the men gathered together.

"Tufiah," David ordered, "you stay here by the baggage with two hundred men. You others gird on your swords and follow me."

A quarter of an hour later he was on the way at the head of four hundred men. Nabal had perhaps all told a hundred servants and herdsmen. Before sunset, if David had his way, not one of them would be alive, nor their master either.

They did not have far to go, a march of not more than an hour and a half. Soon they saw the gentle line of hills behind which lay Nabal's house. And there in front of the house, beneath the palm trees, something was moving. Could the old miser have gathered other farmers together and set a trap for them? But no, what came toward them was an ass—no, twenty, thirty asses accompanied by only a few servants. And the asses were heavily laden.

"Halt!" commanded David. Had Nabal at last come to his senses? It seemed highly improbable. Moreover, his remorse came extremely late. Then David saw another ass coming toward them, a rare and expensive white animal bearing a rider—a woman. Urging her animal forward, she rode ahead of the others until she was within ten paces of David. Then she halted, dismounted, knelt in the sand, and bowed to the ground. She was young and slender, perhaps sixteen or seventeen years old and richly dressed. Costly rings sparkled on her hands. Her palms and fingernails were stained with henna, and countless little pearls were woven through the silky black hair that curled out from under her veil. Then she raised her head and David saw her face. She had the light brown skin of desert dwellers, wistful eyes, and a saucy upturned nose. "You are David, son of Jesse," she cried. "You must be."

"And who are you?" he asked.

"Your unworthy handmaid Abigail, lord, and, to my misfortune, the wife of a churlish fool."

"Nabal's wife?" asked David, amazed.

"Yes, lord. I did not see the messengers you sent, but his servants told me how shamefully he treated them. Pay no attention to him, I beg of you, for he is not worth it. Look, I have brought a present for you and your people." She pointed to the heavily laden asses. "Perhaps the Lord Himself has sent me to keep you from bloodshed." She did not see David's slight start. "Forgive Nabal's offense," she went on. "Look, I take it upon myself. Forgive *me!* For the Lord will surely make for you a faithful house because you fight His battles. When He has made you king over Israel, you will not have to reproach yourself that you have shed innocent blood. And then, in your good fortune, remember your handmaid."

David looked at her, wide-eyed. "The Lord has truly sent you to me, blessed be the name of the Lord," he said in a tense voice, "but also blessed be you and your wisdom. For if you had not come, no man of Nabal's household would have been alive by morning."

Big Ruben pushed forward. "The asses are carrying two hundred loaves of bread, lord," he whispered, "two leather bags of wine, five cooked sheep, five or six measures of parched corn, a lot of dried grapes, and two hundred fig cakes."

David scarcely heard him. The young woman's lovely, intelligent face was beaming at him. He would have liked to take her with him, for she was the best and most appetizing of all the gifts. But she was the wife of another man, even though she hated and despised her husband. He took a deep breath. "Thank you," he said, somewhat stiffly. "Return in peace to your house."

Abigail obeyed. She found her husband still at the table and so drunk that he could scarcely speak. There was no use telling him anything now—he would not understand a word—and she withdrew in disgust. An hour later two servants carried the heavy man to his room and laid him on the bed. He was unconscious. All night long Abigail sat beside him and stared into space. The sun was already high in the sky when Nabal awoke, yawning.

"Can you listen to me now?" asked Abigail sternly.

He turned on her peevishly: "What do you want of me?"

"I learned that you had turned away the messengers who came from David, son of Jesse," she said. "And the way in which you refused their plea, although he has protected us and our herds."

"David—what do I care about that yellow dog? I—"

"He was on the way here with hundreds of his men," she broke in, "and if I had not acted quickly, you would not be alive now, neither you nor your servants—"

He stared at her out of his red-rimmed eyes. "What have you done?"

"I rode out to meet him with thirty asses; I brought him what he wanted."

That drove the miser to his feet. "What have you done?" he roared. "You miserable extravagant woman—you viper—I'll break every bone in your body! I'll—"

The blood rushed to his head. He gave a hoarse rattle, his face twisted, and he fell full length on the floor. Abigail called her maids, who gathered about him and lifted him back on the bed. But he did not regain consciousness. For ten long days he lay there stiff and motionless, his eyes glassy, a rattle in his throat. Then he died.

Several weeks later Joab and Abisai came to the young widow.

"You are welcome," said Abigail. "What may I do for your lord and mine? Just tell me what he needs."

Abisai laughed; he was pleased. "David has not sent us for bread," he said. "Nor for dried grapes and fig cakes. This time he craves something better—you yourself, Abigail. He would take you to wife."

Immediately she stood up. Her cheeks flamed and she bowed very low. "His handmaid is ready to be his slave and to wash the feet of my lord's servants."

"You are much too good for that," Abisai burst out, and his brother gave him a hard punch in the ribs.

"We shall give him your answer," declared Joab with great dignity. "When will you come to him?"

Abigail clapped her hands and one of her five maids entered. "Have an ass brought to the door," she commanded, her upturned nose held high. "And you and the other maids, make ready to go with me." Then, turning to Joab. "When, you ask? I am coming with you now!"

Once more the long, snake-like column came crawling through the desert, and the manhunt was on again. Huzal's spies reported that there were nearly three thousand men in Saul's army. "And this time not only the king is with them, but Abner also."

David sighed. With his men's wives and children there were now more than nine hundred people for whom he was responsible. And in addition, there were the herds, increased by thousands of sheep and goats which Abigail had brought him at marriage. It was impossible to hide, they could only flee—or fight. He sent the women, children, and herds under heavy escort to the nearest oasis and watched from a rocky height as Saul pitched camp for the night. It was done in the usual way. The baggage wagons were drawn up in a square, and in the middle the king's tent and the tents of the army commander were raised. That gave David an idea.

"Who dares to go with me tonight to Saul's camp?"

"I, I!" cried Abisai hastily, warding off a blow from his brother.

"I too," said Joab.

"I can take only one with me," David replied, "and Abisai spoke first."

"He always speaks first," growled Joab.

Tufiah and Ruben were horrified when they heard of David's plan and they tried to dissuade him. "It's absolutely senseless," snorted Tufiah. "You'll never come out alive. And what becomes of us without you? If you would at least tell us what you intend to do down there?"

"I don't know myself and yet I'm going with him," laughed Abisai.

"I myself don't know exactly," David admitted frankly. "But I feel that this is what I must do."

Ruben shook his thick head, Tufiah groaned, and even Joab looked worried. "I thought you had a plan," he said.

"I do have one." David smiled. "But you can't always figure it all out beforehand."

He waited two hours until all sounds in the enemy's camp had died away. The moon rose—a young moon, a pale thin sickle in a sky studded with stars. In the distance jackals howled. The night would be chilly, even cold.

Slowly, silently David and Abisai stole forth. About two hundred paces from the camp David halted. "From now on keep right behind me and do everything I do," he whispered. Abisai nodded, and David walked on, keeping behind him the shadow of the mountains whose spurs reached as far as the camp. Abner was in the camp; that meant they had to be extremely cautious. Twenty steps before the barricade of wagons David stretched out flat on the ground, and behind him Abisai followed suit. Inch by inch they crept forward. For almost a quarter of an hour they lay side by side under one of the wagons, until David had discovered the intervals at which the sentries made their rounds. Then he crept forward, stood up, and walked upright to the king's tent, neither quickly nor slowly, but as though he were one of the sentries. Feverish with excitement, Abisai followed him. They passed hordes of sleeping men and they had to be careful not to step on a hand or foot.

In front of the king's tent lay seven bodyguards. David slipped quietly around the tent, drew his dagger, made a long slit in the linen wall, and peered cautiously inside. Saul lay there alone— and asleep. Silently David slipped into the tent; silently Abisai followed. At the king's head stood his spear, thrust upright in the ground, and beside his couch a pitcher with water or wine. "I hope it's wine," thought David. "Then he will sleep more soundly." Deeply moved, he gazed on the king's large, powerful face. His beard was now quite white, his features, even in sleep not peacefully relaxed, were as rugged and worn as the rocks of Ziph.

Putting his face close to David's ear, Abisai whispered, "You've done it! The Lord has given him into your hands. Now I'll run his own spear through his heart. One blow is enough, there will be no need of a second. He will not make a sound."

But David seized his hand in an iron grip. "Never!" he said under his breath. "Would you lay hands on the anointed of the Lord? No man can do that and go unpunished."

"But—then why are we here?"

"Hush! The Lord will decide between him and me. Take the spear."

Shaking his head, Abisai obeyed and they stole out again into the open. Slowly they made their way to the barricade, lay down as if they were sleeping, and after the sentries had passed on their next round, crept out from under the wagons. Then they ran back as swiftly as they had come, keeping constantly in the shadows. "How is a man ever to understand you?" Abisai burst out when they had reached the protection of the rocks. "One blow with the spear—and the whole war would have been over."

David took Saul's spear from Abisai, the spear that had so often threatened him. "Never," he said again. "The Lord Himself will decide whether He will strike Saul down, let him fall in battle, or live his life to the end. Never will I raise a hand against the anointed of the Lord." Suddenly, to Abisai's horror, he shouted in a loud voice: "King Saul, King Saul!"

"What are you doing?" Abisai whispered harshly. "Now they will—"

"King Saul!" shouted David again. From the camp below came sounds of wild confusion. A sharp voice commanded quiet. David recognized it. "Abner! Abner!" he called loudly. "Abner!"

The sharp voice came out of the darkness. "Who are you, who disturbs the king in sleep?"

"You are a great man, Abner," called David. "There is no better in Israel. But why do you keep such poor watch over your lord the king? Someone stole into his tent. He could easily have killed the king. Truly you all deserve death for guarding him so poorly. Now where is the king's spear? Go and look for it!"

Then Saul's voice roared. "Is that you, David?"

"Yes, my lord and king. Why does my lord pursue his servant? What have I done? What evil is there in my hand?"

Nothing but silence came from the camp.

In the pale starlight David's face seemed to shine. "If the Lord has stirred the spirit of hatred and enmity in you against me, then let Him accept sacrifice," he called in a resounding voice. "But if the sons of men have inflamed you against me, cursed shall they be who forced me to go to other lands where they serve strange gods! For here in my native land I would live and die. Know that I will never raise my hand against you. And the Lord judge between you and me."

Silence. A long silence. Then came Saul's voice, deep and hollow as the grave. "I have sinned against you. And I will no more do you harm. For you have repaid evil with good and have spared my life."

"Here is the king's spear," called David. "Let one of the king's servants come over and fetch it. And the Lord deliver me from all distress."

"He will send a thousand servants," whispered Abisai. "Flee!"

David did not move.

One lone man strode across the sand to the rocks. It was Abner. David handed him the spear and Abner took it from him without a word. His eyes were full of wonderment and—sympathy.

"Peace?" asked David softly.

Abner shrugged his shoulders. "Now, yes—until the evil spirit comes over the king again." Then he turned away quickly, as though he had said too much, and went back to his camp.

One hour later the king broke camp and marched north. From his rocky hideaway David watched them go. Behind him stood Joab and Abisai, Tufiah and Ruben, but not one of them dared to address him. They had never seen him like this. He stood motionless, spellbound, and his eyes shone with a strange light. When the last of Saul's troops disappeared over the horizon, he said in a dull voice, "Now we must go too."

Tufiah drew a deep breath. "Where shall we go, lord?" he asked. "Back into the mountains?"

"No. Into exile."

"But why?" Abisai flared up. "We've just—*you've* just won a

111

great victory. Your generosity has forced the enemy to withdraw. Why must we flee?"

"You heard what Abner said," David said between his teeth. "Shall we wait till the evil spirit comes over the king again? Shall we let ourselves be driven and hunted till he finally tracks us down and kills us?"

They were silent, deeply shaken. None of them was gifted with foresight.

"Where will you go, lord?" asked Tufiah again. "To Moab?"

"No. The king would not take us in. And even if he did, Saul would use that as an excuse for a campaign against him. No, we must go where he cannot follow us. To the west."

"To the Philistines?" asked Tufiah, in dismay.

"Yes. To King Achis. To Gath. Give the signal to break camp."

9

ABNER ENTERED the royal antechamber. "Is the king awake?"

"No, lord," replied Chusai. "And you bring bad news, I fear."

Abner shrugged his shoulders. "You get accustomed to it, at this court. Can you always tell what kind of news people bring?"

"Generally," was the calm reply. "Especially when they try to hide it."

Abner gave a short laugh. "If you were more ambitious, you would be a dangerous man, Chusai."

"It's well that I am not," said the secretary.

Abner nodded. "You are a councilor, but no commander. And you are right. There's a storm brewing."

"The Philistines, of course," said Chusai.

"Right again. What made you think of that?"

Chusai smiled. "Moab is weak. Amalech has contenders for his throne. The robber bands in the south have been decimated. The people of Gessur are happy to be left in peace. That leaves the Philistines. And they have not troubled us for over three years and a half. That was too good to last."

"This time, however, it doesn't seem to be the usual raid," said Abner earnestly. "They are mobilizing in all five cities."

Chusai glanced anxiously toward the curtain hanging before the king's bedchamber. "And—David?" he asked softly.

Abner stroked his pointed beard. More than ever he looked like an old fox. "He must have made a good deal when Achis took him into his service," he said. "And Achis is also much too intelligent not to realize that an additional six hundred doughty warriors was a very useful reinforcement for him, all the more so as other Philistine princes control many more troops than he. Six hundred men under a leader like King Saul's sworn enemy was an unusual stroke of luck! Naturally, David was fully aware of this and made good use of it. Had himself given the city of Siceleg, far down in the south where they couldn't keep an eye on him all the time. A masterly stroke!"

"How so?" asked Chusai eagerly.

Abner laughed. "One of my best informers came back last night from Gath. At Achis's court everyone is full of praise for David's raids against the south of Judah."

"Against Judah?" cried Chusai in astonishment. "But we would have heard of that here!"

"And we haven't," Abner nodded. "And why not? Because those raids were never made. Your friend David preferred to pillage Gessuri, and Gerzi, and even the Amalecites. He took a lot of booty, but never brought back any prisoners. Well, they are all thieves and Achis dislikes them as much as he does us. But David gaily informed his new lord that he had raided in Judah."

Chusai's ugly face relaxed in a smile. "Then he has never shed the blood of his own people," he said softly, "even though he is in the service of the enemy."

"Yes, yes that's the way it is, my good Chusai. But it won't be that way long. David has been called to Gath with all his men. This time he cannot help himself. He has no way out. He will have to fight against us. For what threatens us is a mass attack of all the Philistine tribes."

From the next room came a deep, long-drawn-out groan.

"The king is awake," said Chusai gloomily.

Abner sighed. "Announce me."

David and his six hundred men were marching north and the mood was anything but cheerful. The men had grown accustomed to the life in Siceleg and most of them had wives and children. For almost two and a half years they had worked industriously and made a good life for themselves, and their modest fortunes had been amply replenished by the successful raids they had made under David's leadership. A full-scale war was by no means to their taste. Only a little group of young men, above all Joab and Abisai, looked forward to the coming campaign. "This comfortable life in Siceleg has made us fat and lazy," Abisai scoffed. "Stealing cattle from a few poor Amelecite farmers—that was all there was to it! But a real war . . ."

"Be quiet, young man," Ruben snapped at him, "I was wielding a sword when you were still feeding at your mother's breast. What great thing have you done, anyway? Stolen a spear from a sleeping man . . . That's all you can do. And then we had to give it back again. The cattle, at least, we could keep."

"We'll soon see which is the better man," said Abisai, laughing.

"Ruben is right," said Tufiah. "As long as we were by ourselves, everything was good. But this time we are only part of the army, and the least important part at that."

"The least important?" Abisai growled. "What does that mean?"

"We are not Philistines," Tufiah informed him. "That means, we are auxiliary troops. And *that* means, we always get the smallest part of the booty, the part the others don't want. If you want to perform heroic deeds for that, go ahead and do it."

Furious, Abisai ran to David. "Is it true that they look upon us only as auxiliary troops because we aren't Philistines?"

"Don't get excited," said David calmly. "Many kings have bodyguards of foreigners, whom they trust more than their own fellow countrymen."

Abisai sighed with relief. "I knew they were only talking nonsense! Did you see the war chariots go past early this morning?"

"Of course," replied David seriously.

"Hundreds and hundreds of them!" Abisai was all enthusiasm. "It must be marvelous to drive a chariot like that right into the midst of the enemy."

"You're looking forward to the war?" David asked slowly.

"Yes, of course. Aren't you?"

"To a war against our own people?"

Abisai looked down, embarrassed. Then he cried angrily, "And how did they treat us? They drove us out of the land, they pursued us from one place to another. My family had to go into exile. Now, at last, we have a chance to hit back."

David shrugged his shoulders and said nothing. "Abisai is young," he thought. "Scarcely twenty years old. He and his family —he can't think beyond that. Was I like that too?"

From over behind the dunes another column marched past, men from Accaron probably. The war chariots came from Ascalon. And they were all heading for Aphec, the ideal assembly point for a great war drive. War chariots—that seemed to indicate that the decisive battle would be fought on level terrain, if they succeeded in forcing the Israelites to it. From Aphec, to be sure, that could not be done; they would have to strike farther to the north, as far as Sunam, or possibly Endor. The old army road over which an Egyptian king had once marched ran through there; Chusai had told him about it. What was the Pharoah's name? Thutmose—Thutmose the Third! That was long ago, many hundreds of years ago, but it was better to think of that than of what the next weeks might bring. King Achis had given him asylum and presented him with a city; he had a right to his services. And this time one could not throw dust in his eyes as he had about the raids in the south of Judah. This time they had to fight, fight under the king's eyes against Saul and Abner, against Jonathan . . .

Was that really what the Lord wished? Had he, David, acted against the Lord's will when he escaped to Gath the second time? Perhaps then, too, he should have asked the advice of the Urim and Thummim stones. Why hadn't he done so? Because he had come to the end of his rope and the end of his patience, because he had felt with a terrible clarity that he would not survive the king's next attack; in the very moment of victory, he had felt it, and Abner's words had merely confirmed his premonition.

Now, however, the hour of shame had come. As a lad of sixteen he had conquered Goliath and the Philistines. Now, as a man of thirty, he was nothing but a junior officer compelled to fight at the command of the Philistines against his own homeland. Yes, he had to fight. To refuse would be suicidal. King Achis had the right . . . These thoughts ran in a sharp, painful circle through his mind. There was no way out, none that he could see. "You have only one help," the old prophet had said . . . He prayed, not fervently or with lamentation, as in his songs, but simply, quietly, as though this was not young Abisai by his side, but the Lord Himself, so near and yet so inaccessible. "Lord, I see no way out. If there is one, show it to me."

In Aphec, where the great army mobilization was held, a platform had been set up for the five *serenim*, the rulers of Accaron and Ashdod, of Ascalon, Gath, and Gaza; and there they now sat, stiff in their armor, leaning on their swords. And each prince, proud of his own might, cast stolen glances at his neighbor as he took the salute of his troops. The lord of Gaza made a show of his new bodyguards, Nubians in bright red coats, with huge brass rings around their necks and on their arms. The lord of Accaron was confident that his contingent was greater than those of all the other princes, and the lords of Ascalon and Asdod paraded their war chariots. Achis of Gath leaned back in his seat. "In all these things I am no match for you," he said. "But I have something none of you has: I have won the most powerful of our enemies to my side." And with an elegant wave of his hand he pointed to a little group of well-armed men. One of them, with red-gold hair, walked in front. "By Dagon!" exclaimed the lord of Ashdod. "Those men are Hebrews!"

"Quite right," nodded Achis. "And their leader is the conqueror of the strongest man Gath has ever produced, and not only Gath —David."

"The red devil," growled the lord of Ascalon. "What's got into you, Achis! What's to prevent him from stabbing us in the back at a crucial moment?"

"No danger," Achis smiled. "He is in the greatest disfavor with his former lord. He has been in my service a long time and has made many raids on the territory of Judah. His name stinks in Israel."

117

"Send him back home!" cried the lord of Ashdod. "Once a traitor, always a traitor, I say."

"Right," the ruler of Ascalon agreed. "That's all we need, to have a traitor in our own ranks. We're simply giving him a chance to get into his former lord's good graces. Send him away—as fast and as far as possible."

Achis shook his head in astonishment. "You want me to send six hundred helmets away? To send the conqueror of Goliath away? I'm only too glad to have them."

The king of Gaza leaned forward. "This is the man they sang of in Israel: 'Saul slew his thousands and David his ten thousands.' Get rid of him, I say, and as fast as you can."

"You can't mean that seriously!" cried Achis incredulously.

The prince of Accaron's face was scarlet. "Listen," he said and his voice was hoarse with rage, "my troops were there that time in the Valley of Elah. This man cost me two thousand of my men. Either he goes back where he came from, or I'll pull out."

The king of Gaza said softly, but very emphatically, "*I* won't draw out. But I don't think this David and his men will get very far—certainly not past the first night camp."

That same evening Achis sent for David. "I'm sorry to have to say this, but you and your men cannot take part in the campaign. The other princes are against you."

David looked as though a thunderbolt had struck him. Unconsciously he shut his eyes. This was the way out for which he had prayed to the Lord, a way he would never have thought of. He prayed silently. But now it was up to him to play his part to the end. "What have I done?" he asked in a tone of deepest injury, "that I may not be allowed to fight against the enemy of my lord, the king?"

"Nothing—since you have been in my service," replied Achis. "But my royal allies have not forgotten the past and I was outvoted. Early tomorrow you must go back to Siceleg. Otherwise . . ." He shrugged expressively.

"As my lord commands," murmured David, and he left the king's tent the picture of despair.

* * *

Abner stood beside the king on the first, gentle height of Mount Gelboe and looked down with him on the broad plain below. It was early in the afternoon. "What you see there is only the advance guard," he explained and pointed with his sword. "It will take two or three hours before the whole army is assembled."

"You are right," said Saul. "They intend to roll up all Israel like a carpet. That explains the long march to the north."

"Yes, we dare not let them break through here," agreed Abner. "And that is our greatest problem."

Saul frowned. "What do you mean by that?"

With an effort Abner repressed the shrug he usually had for those who could not follow his strategic thinking. "They far outnumber us," he explained. "Therefore the obvious thing for us would be to occupy Mount Gelboe and calmly let them come on. But we can't do that. They would simply march past us and Israel would fall into their laps without a struggle. Therefore we have to fight down there, with the mountains to protect us at our backs. And on the plain they can outmatch us. Moreover—" Now he did shrug.

"What else?" asked Saul roughly. "Speak, man! What else is there?"

"This time they have brought their war chariots with them," said Abner. "And here on the plain they can make good use of them. Look over there, lord, there they come. That is far too much dust for marching troops. If we had only come here two days earlier—or even one day—I would have had time to have pits dug."

"That doesn't take so long," Saul said. "Give the command."

"Not much use now, lord," Abner replied. "Pits must be covered. Now they will see us digging and know where the pits lie. See? Over there come more chariots. But they won't attack today. They must be tired and in a few hours it will be dark."

"I'm going to my tent," said Saul suddenly. Abner looked at him anxiously. "Lord, you have not taken any food all day long. Let them give you something to eat. Tomorrow you will need all your strength."

Saul smiled a sickly smile. "I cannot eat," he said softly. "But you mean it well, I know." And he walked away. In his tent he let his servants take off his heavy armor. A man appeared bearing a dish of cold meat and a little bread, but Saul knocked it out of his hand. "Wine," he commanded. The man brought it, but Saul did not drink. Instead he ordered: "Send Achimelech to me."

"Lord?"

"Didn't you hear?" Saul cried angrily. "Achimelech. The priest with the ephod."

The man trembled. "Lord," he stammered. "There is no priest with the army."

Saul stared at him. "No priest?" He ran his hand over his forehead. "You are right," he said almost humbly. "Forget what I said. Go."

Blood red the old man's white beard had become when Doeg brought down the sword on his head. And all the others . . . But the Lord spoke not only through the Urim and Thummim stones of the priest. He also sent dreams, dreams that pointed the way. Saul laughed bitterly. His nights were an endless waking, with a few moments of leaden sleep. No dreams came to him, for many years now no dreams. There was still a third way—but that was contrary to the law of Moses. "I have obeyed Thy law, Lord," he cried aloud. "I have driven all soothsayers and mediums out of the land. Speak now to Thy servant, Lord, and tell me what I *must* know." He held his breath and waited. But there was no sound in the tent. Only from outside came the confused rumble of voices and a rhythmic hammering. "Tent poles," thought Saul mechanically. The Lord was silent. To Moses, to Samuel, He had spoken. To Saul He did not speak.

The king clapped his hands. To the servant who entered he said sharply: "Find me someone who has a divining spirit, whether man or woman." The servant vanished. Saul paced back and forth. After a while he stepped out in front of the tent and looked down on the plain again. It was now shortly before sundown and the broad plain, bathed in a ruddy glow, looked as if it were bleeding. On the other side, however, among the enemy, rose a forest of tents, so many and so close together that one could not count them. "They are at least twice as strong as we are," thought Saul and shuddered. Then he went back into his tent and flung himself down on his couch.

After a while the servant returned. "I found a man who knows where there is a woman that has a divining spirit, lord."

"Send him in."

He was a soldier, a skinny fellow with restless eyes.

"What is your name?"

"Joel ben Obed, lord."

"And you know where there is a soothsayer?"

"Yes, lord, in my native village. It is not far from here, in Endor."

Endor. Ten miles north.

The king nodded. "You shall lead me to her."

"Lord," said the man, embarrassed. "Will you go just as you are?"

Saul looked down at his purple garment. "I shall put on other clothing. Can you find the way in the dark?"

"Yes, lord. But it is a walk of two hours."

Saul nodded. "Wait outside for me." He clapped his hands. The servant came in with a little oil lamp. "Bring me an ordinary garment and a dark cloak," commanded the king. "And send me one of my armorbearers—send me Isaac. He is to lay aside his arms and dress simply."

Half an hour after nightfall three plainly dressed men left the camp and made their way north. They kept close to the edge of Mount Gelboe, where they were in no danger of meeting enemy spies, and they spoke not a word on the way. Not until they came to Endor did Saul ask, "Does the woman live in the village itself?"

"No, lord, the village elders will not permit it because she is a woman with a divining spirit—an *ōbh*. She lives outside, in the hut over there on the little hillock between the rocks."

A woman with a divining spirit—perhaps only some old witch who could easily fool the credulous. But there was nothing else. Saul clenched his teeth and went up to the hut. "Go inside and wake her, Joel," he ordered. "Tell her there is gold for her if she does her work well. But as you value your life, do not tell her who I am! Go."

But before Joel reached the door, it opened and a woman appeared on the threshold. She was hunchbacked and no bigger than a ten-year-old child. It was too dark to make out her features. "Who are you? What do you want?" she asked in a trembling voice.

"These two are my servants," said Saul. "Who I am does not concern you. Divine to me by your divining spirit and I will pay you with gold." He held out a bracelet to her.

The woman reached behind her and suddenly held a lighted torch in her hand. "It is truly gold," she murmured. "Ahi—gold is rare. Gold is good. But life is better. Don't you know the king has forbidden soothsaying and calling up the dead? You will not tell me who you are. Perhaps you are one of the king's men and are only setting a trap for me. Go on your way." And she stepped back.

"Wait," commanded Saul quickly. "As the Lord liveth, no evil shall happen to you. I *must* know the truth." The wild anxiety behind his words sent a shudder over the two men with him.

The woman's head swayed from side to side. "There is truth in your voice," she said slowly. "But if you betray me, I shall curse you and leprosy shall eat your bones. Come in."

Saul entered after her, Isaac and Joel following hesitantly. The woman thrust her torch into a holder. And now at last Saul could see her face. She was much younger than he had thought—perhaps in the middle forties. The coarse black hair that hung down from under her headcloth to her high shoulders was only slightly tinged with gray. Her large, deeply-shadowed eyes were the most prominent feature in the pale face, and her full mouth was colorless like the mouth of a corpse. The hut was roomy, with a floor of hardened clay, and in one corner was a couch, a jumble of covers and goatskins. Aside from that there was only a rusty hearth and a door that led to a room beyond.

"Who is with you?" asked Saul sharply. "I heard a jingling."

"The stable is next door," replied the woman calmly. "I have a cow and a calf. What you heard were their chains. Now speak. What would you know?"

"Nothing you can tell me. But let your divining spirit bring me back a man from the dead, the only man who knows the answer to my questions."

She raised her black eyebrows. "Who is this man?"

"Samuel of Ramatha," said Saul.

"The prophet," she whispered. "Yes, yes, he was a great man. But will he come? My ōbh will certainly be afraid of him. I will try," she added hastily as she saw her visitor's face darken. "But step back, lord. The place where you stand is the spirit's place, when he comes. And be patient. Magic like this takes time—at least half an hour, perhaps more." She seized a piece of chalk and made a mark in the shape of a pentagon on the spot where Saul had just stood. Then she took a pitcher from the hearth and poured a dark fluid in the middle of the figure. "Sacrificial blood," thought Saul. The fluid promptly seeped into the earthen floor. Now the woman crouched on the floor and crossed her long arms over her deformed breast. Her colorless lips moved silently. But the next moment she screamed.

"Saul! Saul! You have deceived me. You are Saul!"

"Yes, yes," said the king breathlessly. "But have no fear. I have sworn that no evil shall come to you. What do you see?"

"Beings from beyond," panted the woman. "They have come without waiting for my ōbh to call them. That has never happened before. Oh, oh, great, mighty beings, they keep murmuring your name and oh—there is another one coming up—"

"What form has he?" asked the king quickly.

"It is still not clear—wait—the others are fading—he is the only one still there, an old man covered with a long mantle—ah!" Her eyes rolled up so that only the whites were visible. Flecks of foam appeared on her lips. She twitched convulsively. Then Saul suddenly stepped back. With his own eyes he saw the tall, gaunt figure, the white flecked beard. The eyes under the bushy brows were expressionless.

"Samuel," groaned the king. "Samuel!" Then he heard the high-pitched, throaty voice he had feared so long.

"Why hast thou disturbed my rest?"

"I am in great distress," Saul burst out. "The Philistines fight against me. And God is departed from me and would not hear me—neither by the hand of prophets nor by dreams. Show me what I shall do."

Cold and hard as a hammer blow came the answer: "Why asketh thou me, seeing that the Lord has departed from thee? For the Lord will do to thee, as He spoke by me, and He will rend thy kingdom out of thy hand, and will give it to thy neighbor, David. Because thou didst not obey the voice of the Lord. And the Lord also will deliver Israel with thee into the hands of the Philistines. And tomorrow thou and thy sons shall be with me."

Saul staggered, put his hand to his face, and fell to the ground like a fallen tree.

When he came to himself again, he saw the three anxious faces bent over him. He tried to sit up but could not.

The woman watched him sharply. "Is it possible that a king suffers from hunger?" she asked in astonishment. "You must eat something at once. I will bring bread."

"I—cannot—eat."

"I have done all you asked of me, dangerous as it was," said the woman earnestly. "Samuel was so strong that my *ōbh* could not even get near him. The prophet came through his own power. It could have cost us all our lives. Now do what I ask you and let me give you something to eat."

"Lord, I beg of you do what she says," Isaac the armorbearer pleaded. "Otherwise you will not be strong enough for the journey home."

"Eat something, lord," begged Joel.

"Very well," Saul yielded, and the woman immediately went out of the room. Again he tried to stand. Isaac helped him and he managed to take a few weak steps, then sank down on the woman's couch. "Did both of you hear what the old man said?" he asked in a thick voice.

The two men looked at each other. "Which old man, lord?" asked Joel fearfully.

"Samuel, of course, who else?"

Isaac said, "The witch, or whatever she is, cried out something about an old man with a long cloak, but I neither saw nor heard him. Did you, Joel?"

The soldier shook his head silently. From next door came a short, frightened bleat, then a dull thud.

"I heard that," said Isaac. "I think she's killed her calf in your honor, lord." And it was even as he said. The woman came back with a wooden platter on which lay enormous pieces of meat, and she began to roast them. She kneaded meal and baked some unleavened bread. Then she watched to see how the three men liked it.

When he noticed that she was looking at him, Saul stopped eating. "What are you thinking of?" he asked.

Her eyes shifted. "I'm thinking that all men are poor—even kings," she said.

"Did *you* hear what Samuel said to me?"

"No, lord," she replied calmly. But he knew that this time she did not speak the truth.

He stood up. "Here is another gold bracelet," he said and tossed it on the couch. "That is for the calf you killed for me. No, don't speak, you do not owe me any thanks. We must go."

They journeyed back in silence, as they had come, reaching the camp two hours before sunrise. Saul lay down on his couch, stared into space, and waited for the fate he could not escape.

Abner, in command of the center, held off the enemy's first attack, but he looked anxiously toward the left wing. There the Philistines had sent in their war chariots, and Abner knew at once what their purpose was. If they succeeded in overrunning the king and his men, then would come the push on his unguarded flank. "This accursed plain!" he thought.

"Not so fast!" he shouted to the spear throwers. "Keep calm and take careful aim." There was a breach on his right, and he stopped it with five hundred men of the three thousand he had prudently held in reserve. Above the wild battle cries and the shrieks of the wounded, he could hear the clatter of war chariots. Two years before this he had tried to persuade the king to get some of them. One could buy plenty of horses in Egypt. But Saul would not hear of it. Two arrows pierced Abner's leather shield and he cut them down with an angry stroke of his sword. Yes, there it came—the first fugitives from the left wing. Fugitives! But why no message? The dust cloud behind the fleeing men was full of thunder and clatter and much too close, and over to the left men were scrambling up the mountain heights. They, too, were fleeing! That meant the left wing had been broken through. He called up the commander of the reserves. "The king is in danger," he said hastily. "You must immediately—"

He got no farther. Out of the dust cloud broke not hundreds, but thousands of men, Israelites, wild-eyed, in panic flight; they, and not the war chariots of the enemy, were stampeding his flank and dragging his men along with them. "The chariots are coming!" voices screamed. "Save yourselves, the chariots are coming!"

Abner raised his sword in an effort to check their mad flight, but he was swept along by a dense mob of fleeing men. On the left the first war chariots were already breaking through the dust cloud.

Saul, on the left wing, saw them racing madly along, shadowy ghost chariots and ghost horses. Though he stood between the bodies of two Philistines, an arrow struck him so deep in the groin that not much more than the feathered end showed above the wound. It hurt like the bite of a wild beast but it was not as terrible as the dead eyes of Jonathan, who lay at the foot of the rock. The other two sons out there on the farthest end of the left wing were certainly no longer alive. Samuel did not lie . . . No, neither in life nor in death. The day was lost, Israel was lost, the army, the camp, the crown, his life, all, all lost! The Lord demanded obedience. Long, long years he had fought against the punishment, but now it was here, inescapable and final.

"Isaac," he called.

The armorbearer looked up at him, but he had a gaping wound in his head and could no longer see clearly. "Lord?"

"Draw your sword and kill me," commanded the king. "The enemy will be here any minute. They shall not take me alive."

Isaac looked at him in horror. "How can I do that, lord?" he stammered. "You are the king—the anointed."

Saul raised his eyes to heaven. "The anointed of the Lord," he wailed. "That does not count in the underworld. Or—or does it?" He dropped the royal spear, drew his sword, thrust the hilt in the cleft of a rock at the foot of which lay Jonathan's body, and threw himself on the broad blade.

"Lord!" shouted Isaac in despair. "Lord!" He reeled toward Saul. The king was dead. Then Isaac, too, drew his sword, thrust it firmly in the ground, and fell upon it.

A few minutes later a crowd of fleeing men ran past the spot. One of them stopped, an Amalecite in the Israelite service. "By the gods," he cried, "that is the king! That is, it was the king." He looked around hastily. His comrades were already out of sight. Quickly he unfastened the royal circlet from the dead king's helmet, then the heavy gold armbands. Immediately afterward wild cries rang out behind him and he fled in haste.

David and his six hundred men were nearing their homeland; only a few more dune hills separated them from Siceleg. Seldom had a war party made such a jolly retreat. Most of the six hundred were overjoyed not to have to take part in a war which at best did not concern them, which offered them, as reserve troops, little booty, and bade fair to separate them for a long time from their wives and children. Only the small group of young daredevils was dissatisfied; they had dreamt of great victories under the eyes of five kings, of daring deeds they could talk about in years to come. Now they were returning without glory, without booty—sent home ignominiously like a pack of women whose services are no longer needed when the battle is joined. That, at least, was what Abisai maintained loudly and clearly.

David was happy. The Lord had shown him a way out, a way of which he himself would never have thought. Samuel was right, there was only one help for him—but what a Help! And this Help was always there, always within reach, always dependable—as long as one obeyed Him. That gave one a feeling of security and protection a hundred times stronger than the walls of a fortress and the spears of ten thousand heroes. Nothing could happen to him save what the Lord willed.

A long, wailing cry from the vanguard brought his thoughts to an abrupt end. Five, ten, twenty voices joined in. The men around him suddenly fell silent, and as though on command, they ran forward. And now the cry became one vast almost animal-like roar. Then it died away and there was silence, as though all those six hundred men had been swept up in a sandstorm and carried away. David rushed up to them. As he reached the height, he saw that where Siceleg had stood, a pleasant, flourishing little town, there was only a blackish heap of ruins. Every house had been leveled to the ground.

The six hundred men ran to save what they could, but David stood as if rooted to the spot. Achinoam—Abigail—what had become of them? He clenched his teeth. "But nothing can happen to me save what the Lord wills," he said aloud.

Then he followed his men. He found them, howling and crying in the midst of an indescribable tangle of ruins and charred household effects. Within a few seconds they had been plunged from happy expectation into sudden fright, from fright to horror, and from horror into deepest grief. Now, when they saw David, their mood changed again. "That's what we get from your leadership!" roared big Ruben. "My wife has been stolen, and my son—and all that was mine!"

"And why?" cried Tufiah. "Only so we could march to Aphec and back again, six days on the march."

In that moment David decided that not only Ruben, but also Tufiah should never have command over a larger group. The next moment he had to throw up his shield to ward off stones flung at him by a few men, half mad with rage. "That's right," howled big Ruben. "Stone him! It's all his fault!"

But already Joab and Abisai were there, holding their shields before him and drawing their swords, and after a brief hesitation, other men joined them, not only young fighters, whose losses were not grave, but even men who, like Ruben, had lost wife and child.

"He who throws another stone, dies by my hand!" Abisai's eyes blazed with fury. "To hell with you, you thankless dogs!"

Then David raised his hand. "Has any one of you seen a dead body?" he asked in a loud voice.

Silence. Ruins they had seen, broken dishes, charred cushions—but no bodies.

"No one? Then the robbers have carried your wives and children off alive—my wives too—and all the herds. The more they have carried with them, the better, for it holds them back. Huzal!"

"Here I am, lord."

"Take your men and find out in which direction they have gone."

"Lord, the trail may be seven days old."

"Yes, at the worst. Probably it's only two or three—first the robbers had to hear that we had left Siceleg. And the trail must be very broad. Abiathar, I want to consult the Lord."

He asked only two questions: "Shall I pursue after those robbers?" and "Shall I overtake them or not?" Two white stones were the answer.

"Eat and drink of the provisions we brought with us," commanded David. "We set out as soon as Huzal returns."

Huzal came a quarter of an hour later. "You were right, lord. The trail is there; it is broad and leads south."

David sighed with relief. The raid did not come from Judah, but from Amalec. "Forward!" he commanded.

It was a hard and pitiless forced march. David constantly urged the men on, driving them as never before. When they came to the swollen Besor torrent, two hundred of the men were so exhausted they could not go any farther. "We'll leave the baggage with you," David decided. He crossed the torrent with the four hundred men left him and with freshly filled water gourds. After that the ground became stony and they lost the trail. "Search, Huzal," said David grimly, "and find it!"

Two hours later Huzal found a man, dark-haired, with slender limbs and long slanting eyes. He was lying on the ground, groaning. Huzal set him on his feet but he was so weak that men had to support him or he would have fallen.

"Give him something to drink," David ordered as soon as the

prisoner was brought before him. The man drank so greedily that the water ran down over his chin onto his breast. "Hungry," he groaned. "I'm starving." He spoke a harsh, awkward Amalecite dialect and he spoke it badly. "Bread," said David. "Give him some raisins too, and a fig cake," he added hastily. The man ate and ate. Then he looked up and smiled gratefully. "Who are you?" asked David in a kindly tone. "An Egyptian, aren't you?"

"Yes, lord, but my master is Bisu, a junior leader. He deserted me when I fell ill."

"When was that?"

"Three days ago, lord."

"Were you with them at the raid of Siceleg?"

"Yes, lord, with the baggage. And before that at the raid on Cerethi and in Caleb and in the south of Judah."

"Then you have taken a lot of booty everywhere, I suppose?"

"Oh, yes, lord, very, very much booty."

"For such large raids one needs many men," said David. "How many of you were there?"

"Very many, lord, more than I can count."

"More than my men here?"

"More than twice as many, lord."

That meant perhaps a thousand men. "And where are they camped now?"

The Egyptian looked worried. "If my lord learns that I have betrayed him, he will have me cut to pieces, ears, nose, lips and all, and then he will bury me up to my neck in sand and the vultures will come and—"

David cut him short. "I will not betray you."

The Egyptian looked at him imploringly. "Lord, will you swear that by the gods in whom you believe?"

"I swear it by the only God," replied David earnestly. "How far is it to your people?"

"They intended to stop for rest in an oasis called Mersah."

David did not know this oasis. "Lead us there. You shall have your freedom and a good reward in addition."

They reached the neighborhood of the oasis late in the afternoon. Huzal stole into the oasis and came back in high humor.

"Lord, they have a booty camp such as I have never seen! And they are eating and drinking and making speeches. Most of them are already drunk and they are still drinking."

"The prisoners?"

"They are chained together, men and women separately. The children are with the women."

"How many robbers did you count and how many of them are in condition to fight?"

"It is hard to say, lord. They have scattered over the whole oasis and that is fairly large. But there must be at least a thousand, and most of them are drinking."

"Sentries?"

"Four at a time, two hundred steps apart. But they are drinking too."

David had heard enough. He beckoned to Abisai and Joab and gave them his orders. Then the four hundred moved cautiously toward the oasis. In all Israel, Judah, Amalec, and the land of the Philistines there were no troops so skillful at taking advantage of the terrain. Sixteen sentries fell before they had even sighted an enemy. Then four storm columns pushed forward to the heart of the oasis, spears and swords ready. What now followed was not so much a battle as a slaughter, and only the great number of robbers prevented the slaughter from being over by nightfall. Instead they fought the whole night through under the light of a bright full moon; in fact, around midnight the opposition of the Amalecites became heavier. David had ordered his men to take no prisoners and his command was obeyed. But not until he saw in the early light of dawn a large group of camel riders fleeing to the south—there were several hundred—did he know that the battle was as good as won. However, as a few small groups of robbers were still making a bitter stand, it was late afternoon before the oasis was completely cleared of the enemy.

Meanwhile countless tender reunions had taken place. Achinoam and Abigail knelt at the feet of their liberator. Big Ruben, clasping his son in his arms and with his wife clinging to him in tears, danced for joy. The prisoners had not been harmed, but all of them were exhausted and they suffered from bruises and abrasions as the result of being so long in chains.

David stationed sentries at well-planned intervals to guard the camp and let his people sleep. The next morning he took stock of their losses. They were astonishingly light—eleven dead and about thirty wounded. The dead were buried on the spot; Abiathar, who as a priest knew something about medicine, tended the wounded, and a number of women helped him as far as he would permit.

When at last David inspected the booty, he opened his eyes in astonishment. The Amalecites had stolen and accumulated a tremendous fortune. What was at hand here in herds, household provisions, gold and silver jewelry, materials, and costly weapons was six times more than they could store in Siceleg.

"We're all rich!" exclaimed Tufiah, completely staggered, "rich as the Phoenicians."

"It's too bad about those camels that got away from us," complained big Ruben. "How can we take all that stuff away now?" But there were oxen and asses enough on which the booty could be loaded, and the next morning an enormous caravan set out peacefully on its way home. Every man had not only recovered his own property, but had received in addition booty amounting to many times its value. After they had crossed the Besor torrent again, they came upon their own baggage wagons and the "weary two hundred"—as they were called to the end of their lives. Ruben and a few other men wanted to deny them a share of the booty, other than their own wives and children.

David quickly put an end to that plan. "That is not the way one acts with what the Lord has given," he said in a loud voice. "We have Him to thank for our victory and the booty. The commander of an army decides who goes into battle and who guards the baggage. If you had your way there would always be strife. No man will be deprived of his share of the booty, and every man shall receive an equal share." The "weary two hundred" were won over to him forever, and the others comforted themselves with the fact that they had hardly known what to do with that gigantic amount of material anyway. But none of them forgot the haughty dignity with which David had made his decision.

It was the dignity of a lawgiver. And "an equal share of the booty for all" became from then on an unwritten law.

In Siceleg there was intense activity. Everyone lived in a tent until the city was rebuilt. From his own share of the booty David sent presents to his friends in Judah, to all those who had stood by him and his men and to the elders of many cities, including Bethel, Ramoth, Jether, Aroer, Sephamoth, Esthamo, Arama, Bor Asan, Athach and Hebron—the last a city he particularly loved because Achinoam and Abigail came from the vicinity.

Three days after the return from their pursuit of the robbers, a man was sighted coming from the north. The sentries arrested him, but he proved to be unarmed. His clothes were torn and he had strewn dust on his hair as though he were a mourner or the bearer of sad news. He insisted upon being taken to David.

David looked at him sharply. "You are no Philistine," he said. "And you are no Israelite. Who are you?"

"An Amalecite, O Father of Keen Eyes, only an Amalecite. But I have served in the Israelite army."

"Your clothing shows that you do not bring good news. What has happened?"

"We have been defeated, lord," said the man with a long face. "Badly beaten. It was up on Mount Gelboe, O Master. The army was cut in two and put to flight. The king is dead."

David turned pale. "The king, you say?"

"Yes, lord, he and all his sons."

"Jonathan?" David cried aloud.

The man nodded. "Prince Jonathan fell beside the king."

David hid his face in his hands. It was too much, too much at once. He would never get over it. "Is it—is it certain?" he asked groaning. "How do you know this?"

At that the man straightened up. "I myself killed the king," he said proudly.

David stared at him in horror. "You—killed him?"

"Yes, lord. He was seriously wounded and begged me to kill him. I did as he wished. Here is the proof." From his torn clothing he pulled out Saul's diadem and the two heavy gold armbands,

and he held them out to David. "Your enemy is dead, O Master,"
he said, "and with him all his sons. Now there is no one between
you and the crown. Take it, lord—and remember your servant,
who has brought this to you."

David's eyes stared sightlessly like those of a bird of prey.
"You dared to lay hands on the Lord's anointed!" he raged.
"Ruben! Come here! Strike this man down!"

Ruben drew his sword. The Amalecite fell on his knees, his
face contorted with fear. "Lord, lord, what are you doing? I—I
did not tell the truth, I lied! I didn't do anything to the king. He
was already dead when I came by. I only wanted—" Ruben's
sword pierced his breast and he fell on his side, kicked the ground
with his feet, and died.

"His own mouth spoke his judgment," said David. Then at last
he gave way and wept, wild, unrestrained weeping. He rent his
garments and strewed dust on his hair, and all those with him
followed his example, even Ruben, though he whispered to
Tufiah: "Can you understand that? His worst enemy, our worst
enemy, is dead—and he weeps?"

"Prince Jonathan is dead too, and he was his friend."

"But Saul? Why—"

"He was the king, you dunce!"

Alone in his tent David sat hour after hour without saying a
word, frozen in deepest anguish. But in his heart and brain
thoughts ripened into immortal words and melodies, and finally
he began to sing softly to himself, a song of mourning for a great
king and for the dearest of friends:

> The illustrious of Israel are slain upon thy mountains: . . .
> Tell it not in Gath, publish it not in the streets of Ascalon;
> lest the daughters of the Philistines rejoice, lest the daughters
> of the uncircumcised triumph. Ye mountains of Gelboe, let
> neither dew, nor rain come upon you . . . swifter than eagles,
> stronger than lions . . . are the valiant fallen in battle . . . I
> grieve for thee, my brother Jonathan: exceedingly beautiful,
> and amiable to me above the love of women.

Later, when the song had taken form, he gave orders that all boys should learn it. The great king and the truest of friends should never be forgotten.

For days he took no nourishment. Again and again he lived over the strange tangle of events which, at the beginning and entirely without his volition, had bound his fate with that of the king, the kings' son, and the king's daughter. The anointing by Samuel, the sudden summons to the royal court, then the conquest of Goliath, his marriage to Michol, Saul's dreadful jealousy, the many years of being hunted down, and finally the exile in enemy land. How good it was that he had never raised his hand against Saul! And behind all his deeds and far above them and all through them was something like an invisible net in which all happenings were collected, but of which one was aware only at rare moments—and yet it was always there. God had been his help from the very first hour. He had sent Samuel to anoint him. He had rescued him from his pursuers, that time in Ramatha on the height of Najoth. He had shown him the way. He had let him liberate Ceila and win Achinoam. Through Abigail He had preserved him from blood guilt, and through the Philistine princes from the even heavier and greater sin of having to fight against his own people and his true king. And when the Amalecite robbers burned down Siceleg, He had given him back the plundered booty sevenfold.

Suddenly David straightened up. Siceleg! The Lord had allowed Siceleg to be destroyed. Was that a sign? He had never thought of that possibility before. And now this news of the death of the king and his sons, the collapse of the whole north under the yoke of the Philistines! Could there be a message for him in all that, too? "Long enough hast thou dwelt in exile, return home to thy people!" And on top of that came a thought, sharp and swift as an arrow: There was no man alive in Israel and in Judah who had been anointed by the prophet but him. Had the time come for that too? The Lord had allowed Saul to fall. The Lord had given David victory over the robbers. And who had given him the idea, only day before yesterday, of sending gifts to the cities of Judah?

"Abiathar!" he called in a loud voice. "Send Abiathar here."

He came at once, and again David had only two questions to ask the holy oracle: "Lord, shall I go up into one of the cities of Judah?" The answer was a white stone. So, back to Judah! But he must have a definite goal, a certain region, a place where he could settle down, a center. He thought of the city which was his favorite. "Lord, shall I go to Hebron?" And again the stone was white. "The Lord has spoken," David rejoiced. "We set out immediately."

The news caused boundless rejoicing among the six hundred and their families. No one thought of the dangers that might await them in the homeland. It was as though they had all been waiting for this moment, and it was a band of singing, dancing, laughing people who crossed the borders of southern Judah with their household possessions. Everywhere they passed, men laughed and rejoiced with them, even men who were old and bitter.

"Who is marching into the town?" asked an Edomite slave. "Is it a god?"

"Silence, thou fool of Edom! There is only one God in Judah and Israel, and no man's eye can see Him. This is David, son of Jesse—David, the conqueror of Goliath, and he is coming home."

In Jezrahel the entire population came out from the gates to welcome them, the women and young girls sang and danced as for a returning conqueror, and the song they sang was: "Saul slew his thousands and David his ten thousands."

Thousands accompanied the procession as far as Hebron. When David and his people entered the city they found a great crowd gathered at the marketplace, and in their midst such a group of city elders as was seldom seen even at the great receptions at Gibeah.

Sobak, the honorable chief elder of Hebron, embraced David. "The Lord bless your coming," he said. "See, almost all the cities of Judah have gathered to welcome you. We have considered much and long and this is what we have to say to you: King Saul has fallen in battle. The north is in the hands of the Philistines. We in the south are helpless. We need a strong arm to protect us from danger, a royal eagle who will take us under his wings.

136

Who could do that better than the conqueror of Goliath and the Philistines, the man Saul and his army could never conquer, though they were ten times stronger? So I ask you, David, son of Jesse, and all those gathered here ask it with me: Will you be king over Judah?"

Then the six hundred and their families broke into deafening shout of triumph.

David waited awhile. Then he raised his hand and the happy uproar ceased. "Yes, I will be your king," he said. "Hebron is from now on my capital. And may the Lord bless our covenant."

Abiathar, radiant with joy, stepped forward. In his hand he held a little horn containing balsam.

10

HEBRON WAS FLOURISHING. The whole south was flourishing. It was hard to imagine that in the north the enemy held the land in his clutches, harder still to understand why he made no move to push south. It almost seemed that Israel was separated from Judah by an invisible abyss which the enemy could not cross. The young king was the idol of his people. Songs appeared celebrating his victory over Goliath and over countless other giants, his marvelous escape from a thousand dangers, his justice, and his leniency. And the Lord was quite obviously with him; one could see that plainly from the beginning of his reign by the way one good harvest followed another.

The whole land rejoiced when news came that his first son, Amnon, had been born. Achinoam, the mother, was beside herself with joy. The young beauty, who had been the first to accompany David on his campaigns—she never tired of reminding Abigail of that fact—was now also the first to give her lord a son! That alone would have been joy enough. But wasn't the eldest son of the king the heir to the throne? That little crowing bundle she held in her arms would one day wear a crown! Achinoam was in seventh heaven, and she was not offended when, shortly thereafter, Abigail presented her lord and master with a boy who was given the name Cheleab. In fact she even congratulated

Abigail graciously on the health and beauty of her little son. Abigail thanked her with charming courtesy and praised the merits of little Amnon in glowing terms. Abigail's sole desire was to please David by serving him. She knew he hated quarreling in the women's quarters and she herself had lived through too many wild scenes during her first marriage not to long for peace and quiet. At first Achinoam had received her with distrust and ill-concealed jealousy, but she soon realized that Abigail was not a serious threat. When, however, in the second year of his reign, David brought home a young princess—Maacha, the daughter of King Tholmai of Gessur, a marriage that was almost like an alliance—the two wives joined forces against the newcomer. But not for long. Far from asserting her rights as a princess, as Achinoam and Abigail had feared, Maacha proved to be so amiable, so warm and natural that they could not maintain a stiff and reserved attitude toward her. But neither Achinoam nor Abigail were aware that Maacha practically always had her own way. Not that the pretty young princess lorded it over them; on the contrary, she was and remained the personification of gentleness. But she managed to instill her wishes so cleverly in the minds of the other two women that Abigail and Achinoam mistook those wishes for their own. Among the rugs a merchant was displaying was one that Maacha had particularly liked. She begged the king to buy it because it suited Achinoam's personality so well, and, touched by Maacha's way of always thinking of others, David bought it. A jeweler showed the royal ladies three pieces of jewelry, a pearl necklace, a ruby ring, and a bracelet of marvelous turquoises. Maacha immediately decided that the turquoises would look charming on Abigail's light brown skin, and that nothing was so expressive of Achinoam's fiery temperament as the glowing ruby. She would be satisfied with the pearl necklace. To be sure, pearls brought bad luck—everyone in Gessur knew that—but she had an amulet against that and with two such dear friends by her side nothing could happen to her. (In Gessur they not only had amulets—they also knew that a pearl necklace like this was worth twice as much as the ruby ring and three times as much as the turquoises.)

Maacha, too, gave birth to a son, and she herself suggested the name he should be given. "No son has ever had a better father," she said to David, gazing at him with admiration in her beautiful eyes. "With him I am as safe as if I were in God's pocket, and so will the child be. Therefore he shall be called 'My father is peace' —Absalom." The flattered father naturally agreed.

In the years that followed David took three more wives: Haggith, Abital, and Egla. "I have founded a new dynasty," he said smilingly to Abiathar, who, in the meantime, had also had a son. "I must therefore make sure that it does not die out." Within five years six sons and four daughters were born to David, and when he went to the women's quarters, in the palace he had built for them, he spent some time with each of his children, but he lingered longest by Maacha's son, whom she had named in his honor.

"He looks more and more like you every day," the young mother said softly, "Don't you think so?"

Smiling, David shook his head. "He has inherited his mother's beauty," he answered. "From me he has only the red hair."

"It is curly, like yours," flattered Maacha.

Thoughtfully David gazed at the child's lovely face with the large, dreamy eyes. "Strange," he murmured, "sometimes he reminds me of . . ." But he did not go on.

"Of whom, Beloved?" asked Maacha calmly.

"You never knew him, Maacha. He was the best, the truest of all friends, the noblest man I have ever known, and in his heart a child, an innocent child—like Absalom. When I first saw him, he was in his early twenties . . ."

"So it was a man! How can your little son remind you of him?"

"His eyes, his expression—and the smile. True resemblance probably comes from within."

"And who was the man?" asked Maacha lightly.

"Prince Jonathan, King Saul's eldest son."

Maacha was surprised to see that David had tears in his eyes.

"That would perhaps be the greatest gift the Lord could give me," he went on in a choked voice, "if Absalom were to be like Jonathan." He turned away abruptly and left the palace.

From that day Maacha began carefully and systematically to gather whatever information she could about Prince Jonathan—how he looked, how he wore his hair, how he dressed, the sound of his voice, but above all, what part he had played in David's life. And she learned a great deal.

The only painful news David received during the first years of his reign was word of the death of his parents. They had learned of his ascension to the throne of Judah with the greatest joy, but they were not strong enough to undertake the journey home. Soon after that Father Jesse died, and only a few months later David's mother followed him. Like their ancestor Boaz, Eliab, Abinadab, and Shammah had married women from Moab, and even David's sisters had made new marriages. The only one of David's family who came to Hebron was his nephew Asael; he was still very young, but already eager to fight. To his great joy David allowed him to enter the bodyguards, which were commanded by Abisai.

"I hope I shall soon have a chance to show you that I am just as good as my brothers," cried Asael with blazing eyes.

"I hope not," replied David earnestly, "but it might well be." A whole network of spies worked for him in Israel and he knew fairly well how things were going there. After the crushing defeat on Mount Gelboe the country had been forced to accept the despotic rule of the Philistines. But the Philistines were not capable of ruling an enemy people for long. They did not even have the desire to do so. They plundered, murdered, destroyed by fire, chose the prettiest women and girls and made slaves of them; but they did not build strongholds, they did not even put regular garrisons in the cities, and there was soon no possibility of an orderly rule over the subject land. And gradually individual Philistine tribes moved back to their own land. Now let the Israelites work and till their fields in peace again, until they were so well re-established that it was worthwhile for the Philistines to make another raid against them.

Now it appeared that one of Saul's sons was still alive; he was, to be sure, the least capable and the most simple-minded of all, and so weak that he had not taken part in the last war. Esbaal was already forty years old. In Judah people shrugged their shoulders scornfully when it became known that he had been anointed king. That the people of Israel were willing to let themselves be ruled by such a weakling showed that they did not deserve better, Abisai thought. But David sensed that there was danger brewing, and this feeling became a certainty when he learned through his spies that Abner had engineered the choice of Esbaal. For years nothing had been heard of Abner and there was even a rumor that he had fallen in the battle of Mount Gelboe. Now the old fox was back again, and it was clear that he was the ruling power: Esbaal was no more than a puppet in his hands—all of which meant that war between Israel and Judah was almost inevitable. With Abner as his chief councilor, even Esbaal must hit on the idea of trying to win Judah back again.

And that was exactly what happened. David, however, had had time to build up an army such as neither Judah nor Israel had ever known before. The forces that marched against Abner and his men were no longer, as in Saul's day, humble farmers who had been called from their plows to have a sharpened staff or club thrust in their hands, with a "There, now go and fight!" They were men who had been trained in the use of weapons by the best detachments among David's six hundred, and David had managed in devious ways to get hold of good weapons. Moreover, through his spies he had learned that Abner could command no more than a few thousand men. In those conditions he thought he could venture to entrust young Joab with the chief command. "You have the best troops," he said, "and six men to every four of Abner's. We have also discussed Abner's ideas on strategy often enough. Nevertheless, be cautious. He is an excellent leader. And don't take unnecessary risks."

"If I do not defeat him, you shall not entrust me with even a hundred men," replied Joab. "But let me take my brothers with me."

"Abisai, gladly. But Asael? He is still very young—"

"You were even younger when you conquered Goliath," Joab

reminded him. "Don't shame him by making him stay behind."
David relented.

Five days later a battle was joined at the great pool of Gabaon.
When Abisai and the other captains asked Joab about the plan
of battle, he answered curtly: "Craftiness and tricks are poor
strategy whe one is dealing with a fox; he knows them all better
than we do. This time the impact of the attack will be the decid-
ing factor—and in that we are superior to the fox." He waited until
Abner had brought up all his troops into position, and then he
directed a massive frontal attack against the center and both
wings at the same time. As a result Abner had no chance to
maneuver. The impact was too much for the Israelites, and when
David's guard broke through the center under Abisai, both wings
fell back.

Realizing that he could not force his men to make a stand,
Abner tried to organize a somewhat orderly retreat. But even that
was only partially successful. He himself had great difficulty in
shaking off a young pursuer who seemed to be after him per-
sonally. "May the devil take this young whippersnapper!" he
cursed. "How can I give sensible commands when he is always
underfoot?" The face of the young warrior was familiar to him.
He looked like Joab—no, Abisai—no, like both of them. Abner had
his spy service too, and now it occurred to him who the young
hothead was who was so determined to stab the enemy's commander-in-chief. Here he came again, as swift as a panther.

"Are you Asael, Joab's brother?" Abner called.

"I am," shouted Asael, and he brought his sword down with
such force on the helmet of an Israelite who was blocking his
path that the man staggered.

"Then kindly pick another opponent!" Abner shouted to him.
"Today we are enemies, tomorrow perhaps no more. How shall
I sit at the same table with Joab if I have killed his brother? Be
off, and do not follow me!" he added angrily as he parried a
well-aimed sword thrust.

"Certainly not!" panted Asael. "Here—parry that if you can—
and that—"

Four times Abner parried the young man's thrusts. Then he

thrust his spear so deep in Asael's groin that it came out at the back; jerking the weapon out of the wound, he continued to organize his men's retreat.

Beside themselves with rage and anguish over the death of their brother, Joab and Abisai dashed after him at such speed that only a few hundred men were able to keep up with them. They escaped death by a hair's breadth, for Abner had managed to collect his men and take possession of a hill. "Halt!" he cried to Joab. "Shall my sword never cease to kill? The end would be dreadful for all of us."

Joab stopped short. Grimly he measured the enemy troops and the peak of the hill. He would willingly have slain Abner and all his troops and laid them at the feet of his dead brother. But the sun was setting, the enemy was now in a strategically strong position, and Joab knew that his men were tired. He sounded the trumpet to call off the pursuit.

Abner had no desire to continue the battle the next morning. That same night he set out in haste, marched through the Valley of Jordan, and crossed the river. Not until the next day at noon, when they came to Mahanaim, did he allow his tired troops to rest. He had lost three hundred and sixty men; that was more than a mere reverse, and he knew now that it would take a major campaign to win back Judah. Moreover David would certainly make political use of the result of the fighting at Gabaon, and finally Abner had to face an unpleasant meeting with the Israelite king. He was in a very bad mood when he presented himself before Esbaal.

The meeting was decidedly unpleasant—but in a wholly unexpected way. For the report of the unfortunate battle of Gabaon, Esbaal had only a shrug of the shoulder. "I never wanted this war," he declared angrily. "One would think we have enough to do here in Israel. Why should we stick our heads into David's wasp's nest? But you are ambitious, Abner, much too ambitious. And that reminds me: A very dubious matter has come to my ears. How do you happen to have furnished a house for Respha? You know as well as I that she was one of my father's concubines. Very unseemly, to put it mildly."

Respha—"Glowing Coal"—was a beautiful woman, and Abner loved her with all the passion of an aging man. Esbaal had taken over only his father's chief wives, as was customary, and had paid practically no attention to the concubines. When he saw Abner's face pale, he foolishly mistook it for a sign of fear. "Yes, yes," he cried threateningly, "you didn't expect to be found out, did you? Too much pride has brought many a good man to a fall. With one of my father's women by your side you thought you could rule, rather than serve! We shall have to put a stop to your ambition. He who grasps a 'glowing coal' burns his fingers!"

"You dare say that to me?" Abner thundered. "To me, who saved the throne for you? Have you lost your mind? Because of a woman you dare to reproach me—me, the only one who can hold the throne for you? Now you have gone too far! I have had enough!" The courtiers and servants in the antechamber listened in horror. The expressions of the angry general became more and more violent, and when Abner finally came out, he looked neither to right nor to left but strode angrily past them.

Three days later David heard about this scene, and he calmly waited for further developments. When, a week later, he was told that an ambassador from Abner wished to speak to him, he let the man wait twenty-four hours.

"Dekar is his name," Achitophel reported, a pale, thin man from Gilo whose intelligence had caught David's attention and to whom for the time being he had handed over the post of master of ceremonies. "He begs to be allowed to speak to the king alone. Those are exactly his words."

David understood at once. Abner's ambassador had called him "king"—not "king of Judah," but simply "king." With Abner the fox, every nuance had a meaning, and Achitophel wanted to call David's attention to it. David nodded. "The messenger is a courteous man," he said. "And you are a slyboots. I shall receive the man alone. And you are not to stand behind the curtain and eavesdrop."

Achitophel grinned. "The curtain does not reach quite to the floor," he said. "I thought at once that the king had not arranged that to save money, but because he is wise. A man cannot stand behind the curtain and eavesdrop without showing his feet."

Dekar proved to be a polished courtier. He bowed to the ground, wished the king a happy reign of a thousand years, excellent health and many brave sons—

"Your message," David interrupted curtly. "My time is limited."

Dekar bowed again. "So says Abner, the son of Ner, the first minister in Israel," he began. "The question arises: To whom does the land belong? Not to Judah alone—to Israel, too."

"The question to whom Judah belongs does not arise," David corrected him sharply. "It has recently been very clearly answered."

Dekar bowed a third time. "As the king commands," he said. "The question arises therefore: To whom does the land of Israel belong? Never did Abner raise his hand against King Saul—"

"Nor I either," David interrupted. "And Abner knows that."

"Of course, lord. And he often sought to dissuade King Saul from his pursuit, which was as senseless as it was wrong, but always in vain."

That was credible. David thought of Abner's warning, that time, when he returned the spear to him.

"But King Saul is dead," Dekar went on, "and with him his best sons. Certainly he would have loved to leave his throne to his son Jonathan, but Jonathan died with him. Esbaal, however . . . Do you know what people secretly call him in the cities and villages of Israel? Isboseth—'Man of Shame.' He thinks only of himself, his wives and his concubines. He has no interest in the fate of his land."

"All you have told me so far I already knew," said David gruffly.

Dekar's gesture asked for indulgence. "Abner feels that Israel, like Judah, needs a strong hand," he went on. "And therefore he is ready to make a treaty with you and will bring all Israel to you."

David's face was stiff and expressionless. Did Abner really mean what he had told his messenger to say? Could one be Abner and not think of the crown for himself?

"Before it can come to an alliance," he began slowly, "a serious injustice must be rectified."

"Command us, lord," Dekar bowed eagerly.

"King Saul gave me his daughter Michol to be my wife," said David. "Later he withheld her from me. I demand that she be brought back to me."

Dekar was embarrassed. "The Princess Michol has become in the meantime the wife of the noble Phaltiel of Gallium—"

"She is my wife," declared David grimly. "She must come back to me. Not till then will I listen to what Abner has to say." He stood up as a sign that the audience was over.

Dekar did not dare to add anything, but bowed again and withdrew. The same day he departed for Israel.

He had been only a few hours on the way when David sent a messenger to—Esbaal, demanding the immediate return of the Princess Michol. Esbaal flew into a rage, wept hysterically, ordered the messenger to be killed, recalled the order in the same breath, and sent for Abner. The latter had, in the meantime, received Dekar's report.

From Esbaal's behavior Abner realized that David had not betrayed Dekar's mission, and from that Abner understood that David had smoothed the way for him in a really masterly fashion.

"David's demand is only reasonable and just," he declared flatly.

Esbaal rumpled his thin hair, which was prematurely gray. "If he gets Michol back from me, that means I am recognizing him as king of Judah," he wailed.

"What does that matter?" asked Abner shrugging. "He is that anyway. Whether you recognize him or not makes no difference. You can always push him off the throne—if you can."

"But Phaltiel! What will Phaltiel say to that?"

"No one cares what Phaltiel says," replied Abner roughly.

"Oh, there's no use talking to you!" Esbaal cried in a rage. "You do as you please anyway."

And that is what Abner did. Not only did he hold a number of secret conversations with leading dignitaries from all parts of the land, but he also outfitted a comfortable traveling coach, and taking twenty men with him, appeared at Phaltiel's house. "Order of the king," he said dryly when Phaltiel protested wildly.

"She is the mistress of my house," shrieked Phaltiel, "the light of my eyes, the joy of my soul!"

"Order of the king!" repeated Abner. "The princess's coach is waiting in front of the door."

"I'll kill myself!" wailed Phaltiel. He was a rather effeminate man, with an almost beautiful face and hands that were far too well cared for.

Abner looked at him scornfully. "What you do with your life is your business," he answered. "Now send for the princess."

Phaltiel jerked out a slender, bejeweled dagger. "I'll kill her before I'll hand her over to you!" he shouted.

Abner grabbed his hand, twisting it so hard that Phaltiel dropped the dagger with a cry of pain. "If even one hair of her head is touched, I'll have you skinned and then put to the stake," he threatened. "Send for the princess—no, you stay here. One of your servants can go for her and you will give him the order in my presence."

Phaltiel obeyed, and a few minutes later Michol appeared, accompanied by Nossu, who had become enormously fat. Phaltiel fell at her feet: "Michol, my sweet, adorable Michol, tell him you refuse to go with him! Tell him you are my wife and will belong to no other man."

"What does all this mean?" asked Michol, raising her eyebrows. "What do you want of me, Abner?"

"Your brother Esbaal is sending you back to David, Princess," Abner explained curtly.

Michol's eyes lighted up. "To the king of Judah, you mean," she answered, breathlessly. "I'll be ready to leave in an hour. Come, Nossu." And she swept out of the room, followed by the beaming maid.

"Michol!" Phaltiel screamed. "Michol!" And, weeping, he flung his forearm over his eyes.

"Like a boy," thought Abner scornfully. He disliked having to stay with Phaltiel until Michol returned, but he dared not let him out of his sight. Phaltiel wept quietly almost the whole time.

Even before the hour had passed, Michol appeared. She had ordered a second coach made ready. "I have a few things I want to take with me," she explained to Abner, "and six of my maids. Nossu will ride with me in the first coach."

"Michol," howled Phaltiel, "you can't really mean—"

"Farewell, Phaltiel," she interrupted him coolly. "I thank you for your—hospitality." And she swept past him. Nossu laughed in the unhappy Phaltiel's face and followed her mistress.

Immediately afterward the little caravan set off. But very soon one of the guards reported: "The husband is following us, lord."

Abner looked around. There rode Phaltiel, alone, on an ass. "The fool," growled Abner.

"The fool my father handed me over to," corrected Michol harshly. "But I have made a tame fool of him."

Abner shrugged. "He is alone. If he insists upon accompanying us for a while—he'll soon get tired."

But Phaltiel held out, hour after hour, until finally Michol lost patience. "Do you want to take him to King David, too?" she asked angrily. "I scarcely think that will please the king."

Abner sent for Phaltiel to come up, and he turned on him. "Now this is enough! Leave us and go home!"

"Michol," wailed Phaltiel. "Michol!"

The princess laughed. Snatching up a gown that was spread out in the coach, she tossed it at his feet. Nossu turned up her flat black nose and shouted with laughter. Abner frowned. Michol's gesture was a severe insult: It meant that she counted Phaltiel among the women. Now at last the man might hurl his dagger . . .

Instead Phaltiel dismounted, picked up the gown, and weeping, kissed it. Then he mounted the ass again and rode homeward with bowed head.

11

THE WOMAN DAVID SAW stepping from the coach no longer resembled the picture his memory had retained of her. The years had left their mark: her features were sharper and there were faint lines around the corners of her mouth. But she was still very beautiful. "I have kept my word late," he said, "but not too late. Welcome, Michol."

Michol, too, saw a new David before her, a man of over thirty-five years, broader and stronger, self-assured and accustomed to command. She smiled proudly. "My lord and my king," she said with a charming curtsy, "I knew you would send for me."

David nodded to Abner in approval. "It was a good idea of yours to escort the princess yourself," he said. "I thought you would think of that."

Abner bowed. "I am the king's servant."

"The only question is, which king's?" said David lightly.

"There is only one king," declared Michol, "and he is the lord of us all."

David turned Abner over to the dignitaries of his court who had assembled to welcome the princess, and he himself accompanied Michol to the women's palace, where Achinoam, Abigail, Maacha, and the others bowed before her. She was now the mistress. To be sure Maacha was also the daughter of a reigning prince, but Gessur was of less importance than Israel, and besides, Michol was the king's first wife and the daughter of his predecessor on the throne.

"We are friends—all of us," declared Michol. But her tone sounded a little reserved. Custom demanded that David now leave her. Moreover, he was eager to wind up the arrangements with Abner quickly.

Previously, as soon as his spies had reported that Abner's caravan was approaching, he had sent Joab and Abisai hunting. "Bring me a great victory over four-footed enemies," he had said in jest. He did not want them to see Abner; they had taken the death of their younger brother too deeply to heart, and he was anxious to avoid a meeting that might lead to awkward political consequences. The two brothers had gone off unsuspecting.

But now he had to bring Abner to the point before they returned. As their conference progressed, David was astounded to learn how far Abner had already gone with his negotiations in Israel. "Everything is as good as done," David said approvingly. "But there is still one point: What is to become of Esbaal?"

"Esbaal is not Saul," replied Abner with a shrug. "He doesn't amount to much anyway. These events will make no impression on him; he would scarcely outlive them."

David shook his head. "I, too, am not Saul," he said. "I fear no rival. Esbaal shall live. I insist upon that."

"With any other man I would say it was a sign of weakness," replied Abner. "With you, I know it can only be strength. It will be a pleasure to serve you, my king." Two hours later he set out on his way home and David went to Michol.

The next morning, when David came into the palace hall, he met Joab and Abisai. "Back already?" he asked pleasantly.

"Yes—and just in time," replied Abisai.

David looked serious. "What do you mean by that?"

"We have brought back rich booty," answered Joab in his brother's stead. "Twelve antelopes and an old fox who was once called Abner."

"Joab! What are you saying?"

"The truth, and nothing but the truth," said Joab grimly. "Abner was with you and you let him go in peace. How could you do that? He came, of course, only to spy. He wanted to learn your plans. But we have seen to it that he can't talk about them."

"What have you done?" cried David beside himself.

"I sent a messenger after him, on the swiftest ass we had," Joab said, "and told him you wanted to speak with him again. He was already at the Sira oasis, but he turned back like a lamb. At the gates of Hebron I greeted him—with this!" And he slapped his sword. "I struck him exactly where he struck my brother Asael —in the groin."

David raised both arms to heaven. "The Lord is my witness," he cried, "I am innocent of his blood! On your head be it, Joab, and on your race." He looked around. There stood Achitophel, Tufiah, his new chancellor Jehosaphat, Abiathar, and many others. "Rend your garments!" he ordered loudly. They hesitated. "Don't you understand?" he raged at them. "A prince, a great man of Israel, has fallen. Do as I say!"

As they began to mourn he turned back to his two nephews. "What were you trying to do?" he asked softly. "Were you trying to avenge Asael's death? He fell in honorable battle. If one death could be avenged only by another, there would never be peace. Or were you trying to show me that you were stronger and wiser than I?"

The brothers were unrepentant.

"I should have you both killed," he went on, still so softly that only they could hear. "Should I then have to take my own life to avenge your blood? And what good does it do the country which has now lost Abner if I send you after him? You acted like fools, like wicked fools. The union of Israel and Judah was all arranged, settled, and you have now jeopardized the arrangements. I need you—unfortunately—for the things that will now come. But you must learn to obey and not to act on your own initiative and upset my plans. You, too, must rend your garments and mourn with me, with all Judah and all Israel, both for Abner and for your own folly and crime."

Abner was given a magnificent burial. David himself, in mourning garments, walked behind the bier, followed by all the nobles of the court. Even Joab and Abisai were obliged to take part in the funeral procession.

A great number of political agents were sent to Israel to explain to the elders of the tribes and clans that the king was innocent of Abner's death. Nevertheless it looked very much as though the war would be resumed. David's agents and spies reported a general unrest in the land, but Esbaal issued countless orders only to revoke them the same day, and it was impossible to get a clear picture of the situation.

Then two brothers, officers in Esbaal's bodyguard, appeared in Hebron and demanded to be taken before the king. As far as could be discovered, they had no weapons on them, but a short knife, perhaps poisoned, could easily be concealed, and David, prepared for an attempt at assassination, received them in the presence of twenty guards. One of the officers carried a small, carefully wrapped bundle.

"Hail and long life to the king!" he cried. "I am Baana, son of Remmon, and this is my brother Rechab. We bring you a gift, lord, such as you have never received before." And opening the bundle, he took out a human head. "This is the head of Esbaal, whom they called Isboseth," he announced triumphantly. "We have killed him."

Deeply shocked, David gazed at the tragic head. He knew Esbaal from Gibeah; he had been an effeminate man with a soft, flabby face. Now, pale in death, and with the prominent hooked nose, he looked like his great father. "How did you do this deed?" David asked. His own voice sounded strange to him.

"We two entered his house alone," declared Baana proudly. "We killed him as he lay on his couch. Since then we have walked without stopping, day and night, to bring you this."

David nodded. He thought of Siceleg and the messenger who had boasted of killing Saul. "You have murdered an innocent man," he said slowly, "in his house, on his couch. You must die. Strike them both down!"

The guards rushed forward. Two piercing cries and it was over.

"Hang up their bodies," David commanded, "outside on the

pool so that every man may see the reward for murdering a king. Esbaal's head shall be laid in Abner's grave."

Joab and Abisai urged the king to take advantage of this favorable moment. "Just think how things must look in Israel now!" urged Joab eagerly. "There is no one to take command, everything is in confusion. Give the order to march in quickly, before they have found a leader, and the country will be yours."

"No," David answered firmly. "That would imply that I had planned Esbaal's murder, and the Lord is my witness I did not. They must come to me of their own accord."

And they came. One week later all the heads of the tribes of Israel appeared in Hebron. At their head strode a tall, thin man with a tousled black head of hair and eyes such as David had seen only once before, eyes before which even a brave man must lower his own, eyes like Samuel's. "I am Nathan," said the tall man. "You do not recognize me, but I know you."

"You and I cannot have met before," replied David, examining him carefully. "You are not a man one forgets."

Nathan smiled. "And yet we have met. I saw you in Ramatha. On Najoth. I am a pupil of Samuel's."

David embraced him. "You are most welcome, no matter what brings you. Stay with me, that I may always know the will of the Lord."

"I cannot stay with you," Nathan replied, "but I will come when you call me—and possibly sometimes without being called. These are the tribal leaders of Israel. They have their own requests." He stepped back.

"Lord," cried the ancients of the tribes, "all those you see here are your own flesh and blood. Even when Saul was still our king, you were the one who led Israel in battle—and came back victorious. We know now that the Lord has chosen you for our prince."

Again it was Abiathar who performed the ceremonial anointing, the third in David's life. And the men from Israel had brought quantities of provisions and many herds with them to celebrate the king's festival worthily.

"King of Judah and Israel," growled Joab. "And no more enemies far and wide! Now it will be boring."

"That's what I thought, too," replied Abisai, "when I saw him wailing over Abner and when he could not look at Esbaal's head. And when he rejected your suggestion to invade Israel."

"On that point he was right," Joab admitted. "They really did come of their own accord. I would never have thought it possible."

"All very nice and fine, but we didn't have a chance to get any plunder. And from now on we are all courtiers and will have to ask the king every morning how he has slept. He isn't the same any more, Joab. He's grown soft and sick of it all and cautious. He has everything he wants. He won't fight again."

That same evening they were summoned to David. "Hebron is a city I love as no other," began the king. "And not only because the father of us all, Abraham, lies buried here. It was a good capital for me as long as I ruled over Judah only. Now that has changed. I must have a capital from which I can reach Israel just as quickly as Judah."

"That'll be difficult," said Joab. "Up there they have only little dens, holes in the wall—unless you follow Saul's example and take Gibeah."

"And Gibeah is only a little hole in the wall," replied David. "No, the only city that is fit for a capital is Jerusalem."

"Not bad," grinned Joab. "But it's a pity—"

"—that Jerusalem belongs neither to Judah nor to Israel," Abisai broke in. "The Jebusites rule there."

"Today, yes," said David dryly. "But not much longer."

Joab gave Abisai a poke in the ribs. "Shut your mouth," he laughed.

However, the attack on Jerusalem had to be postponed. Scarcely three weeks after the leaders of Israel had returned home, messengers covered with dust came to Hebron, one after the other.

"Lord, the Philistines from Ashdod are back again!"

"The Philistines from Gath are on the march, lord."

"The Philistines from Accaron are gathering at the border."

David grasped the situation at once. As long as Israel was governed by a weak, incapable ruler, the archenemy had had no reason to attack prematurely; they could allow themselves to wait until the land was rich enough to warrant an invasion. Now, however, the news that David had been anointed king of Israel had reached the five cities, and the *serenim* had decided to attack before the conqueror of Goliath had time to mold Israel and Judah into a strong power.

His commanders were also quick to grasp the point. "You are the evil that must be nipped in the bud," grinned Abisai. "But even the sprout could prove to be too strong for their sickles."

"It's too bad we aren't in Jerusalem now," said Joab. "It is stronger than Hebron."

"No news from the Philistines of Ascalon and Gaza," said David thoughtfully. "Perhaps the others think they can get along without them." He stood up. "We must go away," he decided.

"Away from Hebron?" asked Joab in astonishment. "We can't begin the war by leaving the principal city to the enemy."

"That is exactly what the enemy hopes we will think," replied David. "Nothing would suit him better than to shut us up here. We must go."

"But where?"

"To the rocky desert. It is like old times again. The enemy must seek us. That way, sooner or later, he will give his game away. And then—"

"Odollam!" cried Abisai eagerly. "And from there an attack on Gath."

"Odollam, yes. But the time is not yet ripe for a counterattack. The only important thing now is for them not to be able to find us."

And they did not find them. Small groups, led by the old fighters from the time of Saul's pursuit, would suddenly appear in the midst of the Philistines, to capture transports, cut down stragglers, and make life as difficult as possible.

To the three Philistine princes the enemy was a mystery. They held a council of war. "This David is a fox," declared the prince of Ashdod. "If we march south now we won't find him, and the terrain there is utterly unsuited to war chariots." The princes of Accaron and Gath agreed with him. They therefore decided to take possession of the plain of Raphaim, close to Jerusalem. By that move the Philistines drove a wedge between north and south and David could not get reinforcements from Israel. To be sure, by that move the Philistines lost the initiative.

As soon as David learned where the enemy stood, he himself seized the initiative. Orders were quickly sent to countless little groups that had remained in hiding in the rocky country. All were to march to the north, but only by night. Baal Pharisim was the meeting place, a scant mile and a half north of Jerusalem and therefore to the rear of the enemy. Here there were gentle ridges behind which they could hide; moreover, it was now possible for the divisions from Israel to join the army and bring up provisions.

With the supply column there appeared a man David had not expected, the prophet Nathan. He was unarmed and bareheaded. "I bring you the help of the Lord," he said simply.

The air was heavy and oppressive. The birds flew low. "Before the sun rises, help will be here," Nathan announced.

During the night the stars disappeared behind heavy clouds. Then the storm broke. The men could not see their hands before their faces. It began to rain, harder and harder; great torrents poured from the sky. Everyone was wet to the skin, and the men waded in mud. As the sun rose, the entire plain of Raphaim was a single morass, in which the Philistines' war chariots were stuck like stranded ships. The enemy's best weapon had been rendered useless.

David ordered the attack along the whole line—in the enemy's rear. The Philistines' tents went up in flames. Their terrified priests tried to rescue the statues of Dagon and Astarte, but the wagons on which the gods' statues stood were held fast in the mud. The priests were killed and the gods flung from the wagons while the war chariots tried in vain to work free.

Attacked from the rear, their gods stolen, their tents a mass of flames, and their war chariots rendered useless—it was too much for them! The Philistines fled.

"The Lord has helped," said Nathan calmly.

"We are so near Jerusalem," said Abisai, "how would it be if we took advantage of the opportunity?"

But David thought of the princes of Ascalon and Gaza, who were nowhere to be seen. "No," he declared. "This victory was too easy. The Philistines will come back. We must first avert that danger—and once and for all."

Events proved him right. Four months later the enemy was back again, and this time in full force. Again they advanced into the plain of Raphaim.

"What will you do this time?" Abisai asked. "At this season the Lord can scarcely come to our help with a storm."

"He can do anything," David retorted. "But why should he repeat himself? He has so many ways and means."

Abiathar's Urim and Thummim stones answered yes to the question whether the Philistines would be defeated. But it was Nathan who added the decisive word which the Lord had given him in a dream. "Attack from the baka trees as soon as you hear the steps of the Lord in the treetops."

From the baka trees! There were baka trees only in the east. That meant that an attack could be made from cover.

Again David's army marched only by night. From the woods he watched the enemy draw up in battle array. This time, too, he had managed to get into position without their knowledge. Abisai was holding in readiness the eighty war chariots they had captured in the last battle. He had trained crews to use them and could scarcely wait to turn them loose against the Philistines.

"It will soon be midday," Abisai complained angrily.

"Eat," commanded David. "But do not light any fires. And the moment I give the sign, every man must be ready immediately." Another hour passed, a second, then a third.

Then David raised his head and listened. He looked up at the trees.

"Do you hear it?" he whispered to Joab.

"What?"

"The rustling! There is a rustling in the treetops!"

"I don't hear anything!" replied Joab, shaking his head. "And the treetops aren't moving. There's not a breath of wind!"

"It rustles," whispered David, "as if from ten thousand footsteps, from ten times ten thousand steps. The Lord is here. Give the alarm signal. We attack immediately."

This time the signal to attack was not given on the horn but by word of mouth, and the men had orders to advance noiselessly until the enemy heard them. Breaking out of the woods, the first wave advanced a hundred paces before the Philistines saw them.

"Swing your men into line!" shouted Achis of Gath to the prince of Ashdod. "The attack is coming from the east."

"That's probably only a feint. But I'll stop them." And the prince of Ashdod ordered his war chariots to attack. However, the chariots needed time to get in motion, and before they could move, the first salvo of arrows rained down on them. At the same time Abisai's eighty chariots tore out of the woods and attacked them on the flank.

"That is no feint!" shouted Achis. "The whole wood is alive with them. We must—" An arrow struck him in the throat and he crashed to the ground.

In close formation the Israelites and the men from Judah broke through the flank of the Philistine army. The princes of Ascalon and Gaza did not have time to swing their troops into line before a flood of fugitives broke on them like a gigantic wave, for the men from Gath, discouraged by the death of their king, could not withstand the impact of the enemy's attack. For a few minutes there was frightful chaos. Then the Philistine army scattered in all directions.

"The day is won!" Joab shouted triumphantly.

"That is not enough," said David. "The *war* must be won, and for all time. Pursue the enemy and give him no quarter."

"That's the way I like to hear you talk." Abisai grinned.

Sixty of David's war chariots were still available, and he ordered that each charioteer take two archers with him. Then he let them race after the fleeing enemy, and he himself followed at the head of the king's bodyguards.

"When he can smash something to pieces, he is happy," growled

Joab, and he gave the order to advance. David, with six thousand men, swerved to the left and marched quickly to the northwest to cut off the fleeing army from Accaron. By Gezer he managed to stop them. The king of Accaron fell, and only about two hundred of his troops reached the gates of their city.

"We have slaughtered more than half of their whole army," declared Joab when he joined David late in the night. "Darkness came between us, otherwise we would have finished them all off. If you had only let us attack a few hours earlier!"

David smiled strangely. "Don't worry. This time they will not come back. And now it is time to think about Jerusalem."

Jerusalem was an ancient city. More than seven hundred years before, when the wild Hyksos tribes overran Egypt, it had been an old city. The Amurren and the Mitanni had captured it, and after them the Jebusites, who made a first-class fortress out of it.

"It is impossible to scale the walls," declared Joab, who had inspected them thoroughly. "The city cannot be taken by storm. They have collected enough provisions to last them for many years. And they have their own drinking water system, an underground spring."

"If that were not so," retorted David, "there would long since have been no Jebusites left."

Joab nodded gloomily. "Looks fairly hopeless."

"That's why they're so impudent," raged Abisai. "Do you know what they called down to us yesterday from the walls? 'David will never come in here. Even if we were all blind and lame we could hold the city against you. And whether we are or not you can find out whenever you wish."

"We must dig an underground passage," said David thoughtfully.

"That would take years of work," objected Abisai. "At least, let me try to make an attack on the walls. I will have ladders built with room on them for three men side by side. Perhaps then it will work."

David shook his head. "What we need is a new idea," he said. "One thing I promise you: the man who enters Jerusalem first I will make a prince and commander-in-chief of the army." He smiled. "King Saul said something like that when he needed a man. Only he also offered the hand of his daughter as a reward. Unfortunately I have no daughter of marriageable age. And yet— at that time there was a man who earned the prize. Perhaps there will be one this time too."

"Yes, *I* will," declared Joab, "and you don't know it, but you have just given me an idea." With that, he walked out of the tent. Two weeks later he reported that his preparations were finished. "I will open a gate from inside the city for you," he declared casually. "Only, I still don't know which one. Early tomorrow morning by sunrise I shall be in Jerusalem. Hold yourselves in readiness."

In the night, with three hundred picked men, he forced his way into the drain shaft. With the help of ropes and wooden planks, they crossed the wildly foaming underground water source and swam through the broad canal pipe as far as the well. Now they came out at the foot of the city overlooking the citadel of Zion.

By dawn the guards were killed and two gates were opened from within. Outside, David ordered an attack. Seven thousand men broke into the city, just in time to rescue Joab from ninety-five guards who were still alive.

"You are prince and commander-in-chief of the army," cried David to Joab, and he flung his spear at a Jebusite who was taking aim.

"Then my first command is: The king must not again run into danger," retorted Joab, holding his shield before David.

Later, when a Jebusite prisoner asked Joab how he had managed to force his way into an impregnable city, he answered dryly, "You were not lame, but you were blind and that was enough. And the city was not impregnable—but from now on it will be."

Two hours later Abisai could report that all resistance was at an end. "Our work is over," he reported.

"On the contrary," said David. "Now it begins."

12

As DAVID HAD FORETOLD, the Philistines did not dare to attack again. But that did not save them from Israel's attack; for the first time war was carried into the Philistines' territory. David captured Gath—not only the city, but the whole realm—and the enemy to whom they had for so long been forced to pay tribute now had to pay tribute to them. But the king managed to make friends, even among the conquered. Six hundred of their best warriors—three hundred Cerethi and three hundred Phelethi—entered his service, and out of them he formed a new bodyguard —much to Abisai's resentment, for he had considered himself and his men indispensable. The king opened the harbors of Philistia and initiated a steady commerce with the Phoenicians.

In a series of swift drives, one after the other, the Edomites and Moabites were conquered, and they too were forced to pay tribute. Tremendous treasures of gold, silver, and bronze flowed toward Jerusalem, where thanks to the cleverness of Phoenician architects, the king's palace had been transformed into a truly magnificent building. "No other ruler within many thousands of miles has a palace like yours," wrote the king of Tyre in admiration.

The army was reorganized and the royal court considerably enlarged. The most experienced and cleverest minds in the kingdom now belonged to the Crown Council, among them Achitophel and Chusai, whom David called to his side shortly after the capture of Jerusalem. The little lame man was radiantly happy.

"With me life won't be as difficult as under King Saul," David promised. "You can wake me at any time without having to fear that a spear will whiz past your head."

"That's important," said Chusai gravely. "You have your moods, lord, of course—what prince doesn't? But at least I can guess at them."

Chusai got on excellently with the other members of the Crown Council, but to David's great surprise, with Achitophel he was somewhat reserved. It was jealousy, no doubt—more and more Achitophel was proving to be the keenest mind at court—and perhaps that was just as well. In that way one good mind could watch the other and neither would gain too much influence. One had to be cautious—not mistrustful, but cautious. A king could not trust fully in any man—only in God.

Princess Maacha stood at the palace window and looked down on the street below. "The whole city is empty," she said. "In half an hour I have seen only two old women and a couple of children."

Achinoam nibbled at a raisin cake. She glanced over at Michol, but the latter sat stiff and bored on her highbacked chair, staring into space. Finally Abigail spoke. "That's not surprising. Everyone has gone to meet the king when he brings home the Ark of the Covenant."

"That what?" asked Maacha.

"The Ark of the Covenant," said Michol suddenly in a loud voice. "Don't they know in Gessur what the Ark of the Covenant is?"

"Oh, but of course," Maacha's voice was as soft and pleasant as ever. "Only *I* do not know. Forgive an ignorant woman—"

"Why should she know it," Achinoam intervened, "when so many of us in Judah and Israel have almost forgotten about it? My parents talked about the Ark of the Covenant when I was a child. That was many years ago and no one has mentioned it since. By the way, where has it been all this time?"

"The priests had it in safe keeping," explained Michol. "In Nobe, I think, or in Kirjath-Jearim. The king insists upon having it here in Jerusalem, why, I do not know. In any case it would have been sufficient to have sent for it. He really did not need to go himself." She drew a sharp breath as always when she was annoyed. Achinoam and Abigail exchanged a knowing look.

"Now I have learned a great deal," said Maacha, smiling. "I know that the Ark of the Covenant has been forgotten a long time, that the king wants to have it here, and that he should have sent for it instead of going after it himself. But what *is* the Ark of the Covenant?"

"The great shrine of the Chosen People," said a beautiful woman who so far had been silent. "And very ancient. The great Moses had it built exactly as the Lord commanded him. It is a shrine of acacia wood, lined inside and out with gold and covered with a sheet of heavy gold. At the four corners are gold rings through which the staffs on which it is carried will be inserted. Two cherubim, also made of gold, are attached to the ends and their wings protect the shrine."

"And what is in it?" Maacha inquired. "Or may one not ask that?"

"The tables of the law that Moses received from the Lord on Mount Sinai," said the woman. "And the Lord himself is always there, where His shrine is. The shrine is His throne on earth. That is why David wants—why the king wants to have it where he himself is. There is a great blessing on it."

"Very nicely said, Haggith," praised Michol, and the other women looked at her searchingly as if they were not quite sure she had meant what she said.

"If that is the way it is," said Maacha, sweetly, "then I don't understand why Princess Michol objects when our lord wishes to bring home the shrine himself."

"Neither do I," said Haggith calmly.

Michol pressed her lips together, but she said nothing.

"There will be a ceremonial entry very soon," said Abigail,

changing the subject. "Unfortunately we can see it only from the window. I wish we could go out among the people."

"You don't mean that we should mingle with the common people, do you?" said Michol scornfully. "You should be glad you can't. The masses smell bad, and one who has a nose that turns up like a duck's bill could not miss any stench."

Abigail wrinkled the insulted nose. "You are the *gebira*," she retorted. "It is not for me to speak of *your* imperfections."

"I am glad you know your position," said Michol coldly. "So far, at least, I have not had to complain of you." At this half-veiled threat there was silence in the large room. For a while the only sound was the splashing water of the delicately chased fountain.

Then from a distance came a very different sound, deep and solemn and always in the same rhythm.

"The shophar," said Haggith. "They're coming!"

Immediately Achinoam and Abigail rushed to the window, followed by Maacha and Haggith. Michol did not stir. "Let me know as soon as you see something," she commanded, and she tapped her slender fingers nervously on the arm of her chair. How boring these women were, she thought, how ignorant and stupid! Not one of them was capable of a single intelligent thought. Abigail was not much better than a peasant, Achinoam had become a fat little cat, Maacha was falsity personified, and Haggith was a religious zealot who listened to the king for hours at a time when he talked of Jehovah. Egla and Abital were stupid geese. How could the king waste his time on these miserable women? How could he have chosen them? The only explanation was that he himself came from the people.

The ceremonial procession was still far away; it was only now passing the city gate, where the guards bowed their helmeted heads and beat their spears against their shields with a clatter. A tremendous crowd ran ahead of them. Five hundred men of the king's bodyguards led the procession itself. Then came the ancients of the tribes and clans, then the priests, Abiathar and Sadoc, and the six heads of the Levites, Uriel, Asaia, Joel, Semeia, Eliel, and Aminadab. Then the singers with their musical instruments, harps, zithers, and cymbals, and behind them the Levites with the shophar—the trumpet of ram's horn. Then the guardians of the shrine, and finally, borne by Levites, the Ark of the Covenant, protected by cherubim and shimmering with gold.

Directly behind it walked the king. For this day he wore the threefold emblem of king, priest, and singer—the purple mantle around his shoulders, the crown on his head, the ephod around his loins, and the harp in his hand.

The singers sang the song the king had composed and had set to music for the great day:

> Give glory to the Lord, and call upon his name:
> Declare his deeds among the Gentiles.
> Sing to him, yea sing praises to him:
> Relate all his wondrous works.
> Glory ye in his holy name:
> Let the heart of them rejoice that seek the Lord.
> Seek ye the Lord, and be strengthened:
> Seek his face evermore.
> Remember his marvelous works which he hath done;
> His wonders, and the judgments of his mouth.
> O ye seed of Abraham his servant;
> Ye sons of Jacob his chosen.

The king raised his eyes high above the golden wings of the cherubim to the throne of the Lord above the clouds. He felt as though he himself were suspended in air, light, light as a feather, as though he were floating above the clouds, his heart overflowing with joy and happiness and gratitude. He was one with every word with which he had praised the Lord; yes, he *was* each of those words and his very life itself was a song of praise.

He began to dance, though he was hardly aware of it, for he swayed to a completely natural, God-given rhythm. The purple mantle hindered his movements, and unhooking the clasp, he let it fall from his shoulders. One of the Levites following him picked it up respectfully and carried it in outstretched arms as though it were a sacred treasure. The singers sang:

166

He is the Lord our God:
His judgments are in all the earth.
He hath remembered his covenant for ever:
The word which he commanded to a thousand
generations.
Which he made to Abraham; and his oath to Isaac:
And he appointed the same to Jacob for a law, and
to Israel for an everlasting testament:
Saying: To thee will I give the land of Canaan, the
lot of your inheritance.
When they were but a small number: yea very
few, and sojourners therein:
And they passed from nation to nation, and from
one kingdom to another people.
He suffered no man to hurt them:
And he reproved kings for their sakes.
Touch ye not my anointed:
And do no evil to my prophets.

From time to time the king plucked the strings of his harp and
sang one or the other of the verses with the singers. But the
powerful body, more like an athlete's than a dancer's, swayed
constantly to the rhythm of an ecstatic triumph, and wherever he
passed, leaping, singing, and playing, the breath of an almost
superhuman joy swept over all the people who thronged the
streets, and they began to sway in time to the music, back and
forth and up and down. Among them were thousands who knew
little about the meaning of the Ark of the Covenant or the importance of the fact that it was now to dwell in their city. They
merely felt that something great and good was happening, that
the king was very happy about it, their king who wanted them
to be happy too. They followed along with him, swaying back
and forth, and where there was room, they danced along with
him.

Joy itself danced through the city and laid its special mark on
it, the sign of a deep bond with God, a thousand-year covenant
with the Creator of heaven and earth. Through the street it went,

past the palace where all the wives and concubines stood at the windows. The song of jubilation continued:

> Sing to the Lord, all the earth:
> Shew forth from day to day his salvation.
> Declare his glory among the Gentiles:
> His wonders among all people.

Now the procession went uphill to the square, where the new tent that was to hold the Ark of the Covenant had been erected.

The precentor sang loudly: "Who shall ascend into the mountain of the Lord? . . ."

The answer came in a thunderous roar: "The innocent in hands, and clean of heart!"

Then the solemn call of the rams' horns rang out again. So the horns had blown when the Ark of the Covenant had been carried around besieged Jericho, and after the seventh time the walls of that great place had fallen. Now, however, they announced that the Lord of Hosts had taken possession of his very own city. And the singers sang:

> For he hath founded the world immoveable.
> Let the heavens rejoice, and the earth be glad: . . .
> Say among the nations, the Lord hath reigned.
> Let the sea roar, and the fulness thereof;
> Let the fields rejoice, and all things that are in them.
> Then shall the trees of the wood give praise before
>   the Lord:
> Because he is come to judge the earth.
> Give ye glory to the Lord, for he is good: for his
>   mercy endureth for ever.

On the square where the tent was set up stood the bodyguards. With lowered spears, they saluted the holy shrine that had accompanied the people on all their wanderings. Slowly the bearers moved into the tent.

Then the king offered holocausts and peace offerings before the shrine—and from now on Abiathar, Sadoc, and the other priests must sacrifice regularly mornings and evenings, as the law prescribed. The royal storehouse distributed bread, meat, and cakes to every dweller in the city.

"Your cloak, lord," Abiathar reminded David when the latter had finished sacrificing. The king ran his hand over his forehead. He felt as though he had returned from a far land. Oh yes! The cloak, the purple cloak. He was wearing only the ephod. Wrapping himself in the cloak, he returned to the palace.

Achinoam, Abigail, Haggith, Egla, Abital, Maacha, and the concubines knelt as he entered the women's quarters. Only Michol remained standing.

"How glorious was the king of Israel today!" she said, and the biting scorn in her voice startled David. "Uncovering himself before the handmaids of his servants, he was naked, as if one of the buffoons should be naked."

The silence that followed was unbearable. Michol went on, "If my father, King Saul, could have lived to see that—"

David raised his hand, and so imperious was his gesture, so threatening his glance that she fell silent.

"Before the Lord, who chose me rather than your father," asked the king icily, "and rather than all his house? And commanded me to be ruler over the people of the Lord in Israel? I will both play and make myself meaner than I have done: and I will be little in my own eyes: and with the handmaids of whom you speak, I shall appear more glorious. You, however, have never understood me. Leave the room. I will not see you again."

Michol went, pale as death. And David never sought her again.

It was a wrench, an end, a break with the past and almost like a death. Long ago Michol had tried to protect him against her own father. And yet she had never really belonged to him; she had always been more Saul's daughter than David's wife. She had never understood that, when all was said and done, neither Saul nor David were the rulers of Israel and Judah, but the Lord. "The Lord is thy only help." Samuel's last words were engraved in David's heart and mind. They were the key to his being and the cornerstone of his royal reign.

And now he lived in a palace such as Israel had never seen before, and the Ark of the Covenant, God's throne on earth, stood in a tent. David sent for Nathan, Samuel's pupil. "I want to build a temple for the Lord."

"Do so," replied Nathan. "The Lord is with thee." But the next morning he returned unsummoned. "I answered you with the mouth of a man, before the Lord had revealed Himself to me," he said. "In the night, however, the Lord came to me, saying: 'Go and say to my servant David: Thus saith the Lord: Shalt thou build me a house to dwell in? Whereas I have not dwelt in a house from the day that I brought the children of Israel out of the land of Egypt even to this day; but have walked in a tabernacle and in a tent. In all the places that I have gone through with all the children of Israel, did ever I speak a word to any one of the tribes of Israel whom I commanded to feed my people Israel saying: Why have you not built me a house of cedar? And now thus shalt thou speak to my servant David: Thus saith the Lord of Hosts: I took thee out of the pastures from following the sheep to be ruler over my people Israel: And I have been with thee wheresoever thou hast walked, and have slain all thy enemies before thy face: and I have made thee a great man, like unto the name of the great ones that are on the earth. . . . And when thy days shall be fulfilled, and thou shalt sleep with thy fathers, I will raise up thy seed after thee, which shall proceed out of thy bowels, and I will establish his kingdom. He shall build a house to my name, and I will establish the throne of his kingdom for ever. I will be to him a father and he shall be to me a son . . . my mercy I will not take away from him. . . . And thy house shall be faithful, and thy kingdom for ever before thy face, and thy throne shall be firm for ever!' "

David listened with bowed head. Involuntarily he folded his hands as in prayer and tears ran down his cheeks. Long after Nathan was silent, David still could not speak. Instead he embraced the prophet and hastened on swift steps to the holy tent. Before the Ark of the Covenant he prostrated himself and prayed aloud. Nathan had followed him silently and he heard the king's words. His memory, sharp as a knife from years of practice, retained every word as if it were engraved with a pencil of bronze, and later he wrote it all down. It was the most moving prayer of thanks a man had ever prayed to God out of the fullness of his heart.

"Who am I, O Lord God, and what is my house, that thou hast brought me thus far? But yet this has seemed little in thy sight, O Lord God, unless thou didst also speak of the house of thy servant for a long time to come . . . Lord, there is none like to thee. . . . And now begin, and bless the house of thy servant, that it may endure for ever before thee; because thou, O Lord God, hast spoken it, and with thy blessing let the house of Thy servant be blessed for ever."

When David returned to the palace, he found Chusai waiting for him.

"A word with you alone, lord," the little man murmured.

David nodded mechanically. "Come with me," he said, and he strode through the great audience hall, greeting people to right and to left. Chusai limped along beside him; with age his lame left leg grew more painful. The king's study was roomy and the doors were so far from the middle that from outside it was almost impossible to hear a word.

"It's about Ammon," began Chusai.

"Ammon? But that's Achitophel's business. Why doesn't he report it himself?"

"Because he is clever," replied Chusai. "His official reason is a slight fever and he has asked me to take his place because the news is important—in other words, because it is bad."

"Bad news from Ammon?" David shook his head. "A neighbor with whom we have had good relations? Old King Naas was like a personal friend to me, although I never saw him—"

"He is, unfortunately, dead, as you know."

"Yes, and I sent ambassadors to his son to convey my sympathy to him. Is he dead too?"

"Not yet," replied Chusai, "but if I know you, he probably won't be alive much longer."

"What does that mean?"

"That means, lord, that young King Hanon has let his old but

171

unwise advisers persuade him that you sent your ambassadors only to spy around his capital Rabbah and then to turn an army loose against him."

"That's a lie!" cried David angrily.

"But not such a bad one," replied Chusai. "It sounds plausible. After all the Ammonites, with the exception of the Aramaeans, are the only neighbors who do not have to pay tribute to you."

"I shall write to him at once," declared David firmly. "He must be made to understand that I have no such hostile intentions towards him. By the way, how did you hear all this?"

"From your ambassadors, lord."

"What!" exclaimed David. "They are back and did not report to me?"

"They are not back, lord, that is, they are not yet in Jerusalem, but still in Jericho. Poor old Sekal could not go any farther. I have taken the liberty of sending them messengers and urging them, in your name, to remain there for the time being."

"How dare you do that?" cried David, beside himself with rage. "Why didn't you ask me first?"

"Lord, today was a very solemn day and a very beautiful one for you and for us all. It would not have been right to disturb you. But it was important that your ambassadors should not travel here at once. For had they done so, war would have been unavoidable. And that I really could not decide without you."

"You talk in riddles. What has happened?"

"Hanon played an ugly trick on our ambassadors," Chusai said. "He ordered half their beards shorn and half their clothes cut off as far as their thighs. And in that condition he sent them back. If they had entered Jerusalem in that state and had been seen by the people, you would have been forced to act at once. Now you can still do what you please."

"You are right, Chusai," said David. His face was like stone. "I can still do what I please. But who brought you the news from Jericho?"

"It was brought to Achitophel by Huzal, the spy."

"Then it is true," said David. "Write, Chusai! To Sekal and his fellow ambassadors in Jericho: 'Stay where you are until you can come back without causing any stir. The king will avenge the insult given him through you.' That is all. Now send me Huzal and—Joab and Abisai."

"The war dogs," murmured Chusai.

David smiled grimly. "The Ammonites will have to seek allies for themselves. Perhaps they have already found them and are courageous on that account. While we are talking here, they are already making their preparations."

"So it is war," sighed Chusai. "I might just as well have let the ambassadors come. But no! You want to save Sekal and the others from being seen in that condition—for your own sake. I might have thought of that myself. Stupid of me."

This time David's smile had warmth.

King Hanon of Ammon had actually succeeded in winning the help of King Adarezer of Soba and several other Aramaean princes. To be sure, it cost him the handsome sum of a thousand talents of silver, but it seemed to be worthwhile, for his allies appeared with a strong army.

In a two-pronged battle before the gates of Rabbah Joab conquered the Aramaeans, while Abisai held the Ammonites in check. The Aramaeans tried a second time, in even greater strength. This time David himself took the field and slaughtered them. But King Adarezer did not yield; he had ambitious plans for a pan-Syrian kingdom. David crushed them in the battle of Hemath. In addition to thousands of war prisoners, almost all the war chariots of the enemy fell into his hands, but he kept only a hundred and had the others destroyed. To celebrate his victory the royal poet wrote: "They were strong in war horses and chariots, but we in the name of the Lord our God."

The Edomites seized this opportunity to fall upon the tribes in the south. Within six months, after very hard fighting, Joab drove them out again, pushed them back to Edom, destroyed their army, and killed all the male members of the Edomite royal family with the exception of one single prince, who succeeded in escaping to Egypt. Edom then became a province of the kingdom. Now Israel had access to the Red Sea over the Gulf of Elath.

Then at last Joab turned back to the city from which all three wars had had their beginning. He appeared with strong forces before Rabbah and began a systematic siege of the city.

13

Soft carpets covered the flat roof of the palace, where a broad canopy, shielding the king's couch from the rays of the midday sun, cast its shadow over a little table of marvelously wrought bronze on which stood the golden fruit bowl, the wine pitcher, and the king's gold cup. Here the king rested during the heat of the day. And here he drew up many of his plans. It was almost the only place where he was certain not to be disturbed. The servants had strict orders not to let anyone up the little stairs, not even his closest councilors or his highest ranking officials. For two hours, often even three, David was alone here every day, as alone as he had been on the sheep pasture, before the Lord, through Samuel, had wrought such changes in his life. He had never lost his love for solitude; it was a necessity for him even today—and perhaps today more than ever before. To get away from all of them—clever councilors, clanking army captains, suave ambassadors, servile courtiers, and the ever sweet, ever loving world of the women's quarters. Up here on the roof things looked different to him; he was not harassed by the cupidity of men who expected from the king praise, honor, recognition, and above all, power and riches. Here not only could he rest, he could also think—and there was so much to think about.

The kingdom had become a vast realm, feared and respected,

independent of aid from outside, owing nothing to any other land. War with the Ammonites, the only war that was still going on, had dwindled down to the siege of one city. To be sure, Joab still had much hard work ahead; Rabbah was strong and well fortified. But its fall was really only a question of time. It was good not to have to think about these things for awhile. Strange how one became indifferent to so many things which earlier one had found highly exciting! Was that a sign of age? Day before yesterday he had discovered the first white hairs in his beard. The servant had wanted to take them out. What nonsense! "There will soon be many others. You can't pull them all out. Shall I end by being bald and beardless merely because I would deny the silver of old age?"

The silver of old age—he had said that so carelessly, never thinking that perhaps it was really on the way! One sign of old age was that people to whom you had become accustomed died. Jacob, his former enemy, had died, at the last a puzzled old man, content to be left unmolested. But Jacob had been twenty years older than he. Michol had died—just as the news came from Joab of the end of the Edomite war. But she had been very ill for a long time, no physician knew the cause. She had grown very thin; at the last she had been not much more than a skeleton covered with a brownish skin, and she had suffered great pains in her body that had once been so beautiful—and yet had never brought forth a child. Michol—she had long been a stranger to him. And the only one who mourned her was her slave—now what was her name?—Nossu, a black horror of a woman. She had thrown herself out of the palace window. Well, there had been at least one person who loved Saul's cold, haughty daughter to the end of her life! Even kind Chusai, who had once loved her so deeply, had become estranged. Only Nossu had not been able to live without her—and David had given orders to have her buried at the foot of her mistress's grave.

Suddenly a thought came to him, a harsh, provocative, thought: Would there be anyone who would refuse to outlive King David's death? He made himself consider the question objectively, without any illusions. The women? Achinoam was no longer the ro-

mantic little dreamer of Ceila; since the birth of Prince Amnon
and her two daughters, she had grown fat and indifferent. She
comforted herself with raisin cakes and with the new Syrian
pastry made of almonds, eggs, milk, and honey, a lot of honey.
Even Abigail had not retained her beauty, though she had not
lost her dignity. To be sure, her gaiety had vanished since the
death of her son. Maacha was completely absorbed in her children: Thamar was really a beautiful girl and Absalom—ah,
Absalom was a great joy, constantly renewed, a gifted boy, clever
and warmhearted. Another year and the hearts of all the girls
would be his for the asking; he had only to smile at them! Jonathan must have looked like that when he was a boy. And Absalom
adored his father. But follow him in death? It was foolish to
think of such a thing—and wrong. The young wanted to have
their own life and they had a right to it. Haggith—she would
mourn long and sincerely, and Abital would weep too—she wept
easily anyway. But she and Egla would soon hope that his successor would take an interest in them. The concubines—how many
were there? All specially chosen beauties, highly honored if the
king visited them once, but for the rest of the time sunk in
apathetic boredom. No woman would take her life when David
died.

And the men? Joab—sometimes it seemed as though he were
already looking around to select the prince with whom he should
curry favor. Abisai thought only of soldiers and war. Neither of
the two brothers knew what love was. True, they had been beside themselves over Asael's death, but not so much on Asael's
account as because he was their brother, a member of their clan,
and therefore part of themselves. They avenged themselves by
avenging Asael. Chusai—yes, he would mourn, in his own dry,
cool fashion. As Chusai was cool, so was Achitophel hotheaded;
where Chusai was witty, Achitophel was malicious. The man was
a brain and nothing more. To Nathan the king was a servant of
God to whom one brought messages now and then. To the soldiers, a leader who had never been defeated. Many of them
would be ready to die to win a battle for the king, to protect the
king. But not one of them would follow him in death—certainly

none of the court officials and courtiers. With all her arrogance, Michol had had her Nossu, thought David, and he smiled ironically. "Would I be richer if I had someone? And I myself—is there any human being whom, for love, I would follow in death?"

That whole line of thinking suddenly struck him as unworthy. Perhaps one had to be an individual without rank and without attainments, and moreover grotesquely ugly, to do what Nossu had done—an individual who, like a parasite, shared the life of a popular hero. He shrugged his shoulders, poured out a beaker of wine, and drank. How did he happen on such thoughts anyway? Because life on the throne was lonely. And it was not the loneliness of the pasture, in which you were one with earth, air, sheep, and sun. It was an isolation, a cold solitude, that left much unfulfilled. A king bore the sorrows of all, he made the decisions for all. But he himself could go only to the Lord, to the black and white yes or no of the Urim and Thummim stones, or the guidance of dreams and the faces of prophets. There were moments in which he could understand how Saul could not endure the terrible loneliness of sovereignty. But that was the way it was and so it would remain, until old age came and after that—death. He drained the beaker to the last drop and was about to set it down on the little table when his eye fell on the roof of the next house, which lay somewhat below his eyrie; he paused with his hand suspended in air.

A young woman was standing there alone, and she was in the act of taking a ritual cleansing bath. She had apparently no suspicion that she could be seen from the palace roof. Her skin was milky white and when she loosened the two large combs that held her hair, it fell in a reddish-brown wavy flood over her shoulders and back. Her figure and movements were so wonderfully beautiful in their natural comeliness and high dignity—how was it he had never seen her before? He tried to recognize her features, but the distance was too great. She was like a remote, unattainable dream.

Slowly David set the beaker down on the table. Then he struck a bronze tray with a little hammer. A servant appeared from the staircase leading to the terrace.

"The woman down there," said David casually, "do you know who she is?"

The servant looked down. "No, lord."

"Then find out and tell me."

The man disappeared again. That she could only be a woman of some rank was revealed not only by her appearance but by the house in which she lived. Now she had finished her bath and was trying to pin up her hair again, but she could not manage it. Perhaps she was accustomed to the help of a maid, whom she had not brought with her. Laughing, she shook back the reddish-brown flood and picked up a light wrap; it was as though she had wrapped herself in a cloud. The cloud glided toward the stairs and disappeared.

The servant came back. "Lord, the woman is Bathsheba, the daughter of Eliam. Her husband is Urias, the Hittite."

Eliam—the commander of thousands and brother of Achitophel! Urias? A leader of hundreds. Both were at the front under Joab. A king must have a good memory. Nothing makes him more popular with the army than for him to remember the names and deeds of his officers. Bathsheba! Was she alone in the house?

"Who else lives over there?"

"Only a servant, lord."

She was alone. "Go over there," David commanded. "Say that the king wishes to receive her in audience."

"Yes, lord. On which day?"

"Today, you fool," said David angrily. "Now. And here!"

The man, very much flustered, withdrew. David bit his lip. It was unwise to hold the audience here. It was unwise to receive the woman anyway: She was married and the niece of Achitophel. But he was not Esbaal, who countermanded his own orders.

She came a few minutes later, tall and slender and so beautiful that David had difficulty in hiding his admiration before the servant who had brought her up to the roof. But the finely cut face was pale and fear shone in the large, dark eyes. She threw herself down before the king as custom demanded, and he forced himself to speak calmly as he gave her permission to rise. At a motion from the king, the servant withdrew.

"Forgive your handmaiden, lord," she begged, "but if you have bad news to tell me, do not keep me waiting longer. Has my father Eliam fallen, or my husband?"

"Neither one," he replied. "Do not worry, I have no bad news for you."

She drew a deep breath. But the sudden relief after the tension was too much for her and she swayed. Immediately he was beside her, supporting her.

"My king," she said softly, "I must beg your forgiveness, but I was so greatly afraid . . ."

He led her to the couch. "Sit down," he commanded. He filled the beaker. "Here—to give you strength." She hesitated, but he held the beaker to her lips and she sipped a little. He sat down beside her. "It is not fitting that I should sit in the presence of the king," she murmured, and she made a move to rise. He held her back, kindly but firmly. "It is fitting when it is my will," he said. "Do you feel better?"

"Yes, lord. You are very kind to me."

"Am I?" he asked half to himself.

A shimmer of fear came into her eyes again, but curiosity shone there too and—he recognized it at once—admiration.

"You were worried about your father and your husband," he remarked casually, "and you mentioned your father first. Are you not happy with Urias?"

"Oh, yes, lord." The answer came promptly but without much warmth, and David's heart beat faster.

"Have you been married long?"

"No, lord. He had to go to the front soon afterward. But he was glad to go, he is happy to be a soldier. That is what my father liked so much about him. Since then, I have not seen him for almost a year."

"Drink a little more wine," David urged and, with a shy smile, she obeyed. "What are you thinking?" he asked suddenly, and he watched with delight as a light red flushed the delicate white face.

180

"I'm thinking how strange it can seem when a wish is fulfilled," she replied hesitantly.

"What do you mean by that?"

The flush deepened. "I have so often wished to be allowed to meet the king," she said softly. "My father stood before you twice and I made him tell me about it again and again. How could I ever think then that one day I would be permitted to sit beside the king and speak with him as I do now! You the ruler over Israel and Judah and so many other lands, the victor over all our enemies—Urias says there is no king in all the world to compare with you."

David frowned. Then he laughed.

"It is unbelievable," she continued. "The hand that slew Goliath has held the cup to my lips."

"For the king, too, this hour means the fulfillment of a wish," said David. "I wanted to see the most beautiful woman in my kingdom."

"The king mocks his handmaiden," she murmured. At that he seized both her hands.

"Do you really think I am mocking you?" he asked softly. The man who held her prisoner was the king, the all-powerful, of whom the people sang songs, the hero who had made his people great. How could she withstand him, whom the strongest could not withstand? Her lips opened under his kiss and her whole being surrendered to him.

The news was brought to him by a slave of Bathsheba's—only a few words scratched on a clay disk. David's face was stony as he read them. He dismissed the messenger, a very young girl who certainly could not read, and lost himself in angry and gloomy reflections. Urias was at the front; he had not seen his wife for a year. And the punishment for adultery was stoning. Stones flung by brutal hands on the most beautiful body among women, her face—that magical work of Nature—bruised, crushed, a mass of bleeding flesh and broken bones. No, no! It must not be! And what of him? Was there a woman who would not call out the name of her lover when she looked death in the face? "It was the king himself, the king!" But him they could not stone. They could not even call him to account, no, not him. He laughed maliciously. He was the supreme judge in the land, he had to provide for justice. He! They could do nothing to him except the worst, the double sorrow: to let him suffer under the terrible fate of his beloved, and under the realization that they knew of his guilt. No! It must not be.

He wrote to Joab. His letter was very short.

"Send Urias, the Hittite, to me."

Six days later the man was there and the king received him alone. A big, strongly-built man with rough-hewn features as if carved out of wood. No Israelite, no man of Judah—a Hittite. He held himself like a soldier; he moved like a soldier. Not a talented man, a little clumsy, inept. Not too bright either—but a man.

David began to question him. "How is my commander-in-chief, Joab?"

"He is in good health, lord, and confident."

"His brother Abisai?"

"He is well, lord."

"And the troops?"

"They are in good health, lord."

"No sickness in camp?"

"Only a few cases of fever, lord."

"Our losses in the last four weeks?"

"Up to the day I left the army, thirty-four dead, one hundred and twenty wounded, and about half of them are well again."

"So, then, no attack was made in the last weeks?"

"No, lord, we are working our way slowly into the City of Waters."

David nodded. The City of Waters was the original Rabbah which lay on the river, a tributary of the Jabbok. Behind it lay the citadel. "How much longer does Joab think it will take?"

"It may take quite a long time, lord. Nine months, perhaps a little less, the commander thinks."

"And what do you yourself think?"

"The captain of a hundred has the same opinion as his commander," replied Urias with unshaken earnestness.

Again David nodded. A good man, but stupid, he thought. It will work. Aloud he said. "I thank you for your report. Now go and visit your wife."

Urias hesitated a second. Then he saluted and strode clanking from the audience chamber.

David clapped his hands. "I shall attend the banquet today," he told the servant who entered. It was the first time for days that the king had not dined alone. To his table companions—all high officials and officers—he appeared to be unusually talkative, but nervous. He went to bed early, but for a long time he could not sleep. He thought of Urias, who now, only a stone's throw away, was spending the night with his wife. Of course he was her husband. But how did this good dolt ever manage to get such a wife? Not till the early morning hours did he fall asleep. A few hours later he was up again, making the rounds through the palace. When he came to the guards at the main gate, he stopped suddenly. He had recognized Urias.

"What is that man doing here?" he asked the commander of the guards. "Has he just come?"

"No, lord, he was here with my men all night long. Four hours he stood guard and four hours he slept like the rest of us."

David went up to Urias. "You have had a long journey," he said in as kindly a tone as he could muster. "Why did you not go home?"

Urias smiled, embarrassed. "I couldn't bring myself to, lord," he said apologetically. "The holy Ark of the Covenant lives in a tent. My commander Joab and my comrades sleep in the open fields. And should I go to my house and lie with my wife? By your blessed life, lord, I could not do it."

"You are a good man," said David in a husky voice. "Stay here today. Tomorrow you can go back to your comrades."

"As the king commands," said Urias and struck his spear against his shield in salute.

David turned away. The clumsy fool, he thought angrily. The good, honorable, seven times cursed fool! He ordered Urias to attend the banquet that day, and at the table plied him with wine. The man drank just as obediently as he had stood guard or fought. David watched sharply to see how the wine affected him, and when the right moment had come, he nodded to him: "You are excused, Urias. Now go home to your wife."

Urias saluted respectfully and awkwardly, strode stiffly from the banquet hall—and lay down again with the guards at the main gate.

That night David did not sleep at all. In the morning he sent for Urias. "I am giving you this letter to my commander Joab," he said, and he did not look at the man. "See to it that it does not fall into other hands. It is important."

"I shall die before I let anyone take it from me," replied Urias calmly. Then, taking the letter, he saluted respectfully and awkwardly and went away.

David smiled bitterly. "Before?" he said to himself. "No. But certainly very shortly after."

Two weeks later a young officer in command of a hundred, by the name of Zettur, stood before the king. "Your commander Joab reports: 'The enemy tried to attack us and we repulsed them, though the Ammonites far outnumbered us. We pushed them back as far as the east gate of the city. This brought us within range of the archers on the wall and we lost sixty-one men.'" Zettur paused.

"Is that all?" asked the king hoarsely.

"All, lord, except for one thing; among the dead was Urias, the Hittite."

The sun shone brightly through the huge palace windows. In the silence that followed ghosts walked through the room.

"It is well," said the king. "Have them give you food and take a rest. When you go back, say to Joab: 'Let not this thing discourage you, for indiscriminate are the events of war and sometimes one, sometimes another is consumed by the sword. Fight on. Conquer!'"

"Yes, lord." Zettur saluted and left the room. His step was light and lithe, not clumsy.

David sent for Achitophel. "I have just received word that a relative of yours has met an honorable death in the battle for Rabbah," he said. "It is the son-in-law of your brother, Eliam. Urias was his name. I knew him only slightly. Will you inform his widow?"

"Urias was no Israelite, but he believed in the Lord," said Achitophel. "I will go to my niece." He spoke, as always, without any trace of emotion. Not a man but a brain, and a good one.

"Present my compliments to her and my sympathy," commanded David. "And inform her that the king will receive her in the royal women's palace as soon as the seven days of mourning are over."

"The king pays my niece great honor," replied Achitophel. Was that the same cool tone as usual, or was there a hint of reserved hostility in it? It was probably only the king's imagination.

"That is all, Achitophel."

"I thank the king."

Saved, thought David when the gaunt man had left. She was saved. She was the widow of an honorable officer who had fallen in battle. No one could point the finger of scorn at her. The child, too, was saved. Two lives for one, the one a brave but very mediocre man. It was the only possible solution.

Immediately after Bathsheba had been brought into his palace, one week later, David went in to her and she lay in his arms happy, released—and unsuspecting.

Seven months later word was brought to the king that Bathsheba had borne him a son. To be sure, the birth was premature, but the child seemed to be very strong. David went to her immediately. She was pale and exhausted and strangely sad. The child was beautiful and full of life.

14

WHEN HE RETURNED TO THE PALACE, the visit of Nathan the seer was announced. He had not sent for him—that meant it was something important. Nathan, tall and gaunt, the first white strands in his tangled black hair, entered silently. "Lord, I come to invoke the king's justice," he said.

"I promise you now, you shall have it," replied David.

"It is a case which only the king can settle," Nathan began. "There were two men in the same city, the one very rich and powerful, the other poor. The rich man had exceeding many sheep and oxen. But the poor man had nothing at all but one little ewe lamb, which he had bought and nourished up and which had grown up in his house eating of his bread and drinking of his cup, and sleeping in his bosom; and it was unto him as a daughter. And when a certain stranger was come to the rich man, he spared to take of his own sheep and oxen, to make a feast for the stranger . . . but took the poor man's ewe and dressed it."

Outraged, David leaped to his feet. "As the Lord liveth, the man that has done this is a child of death! And he shall restore the ewe fourfold."

Then Nathan looked him square in the eye. "Thou art the man," he said.

The king was speechless. Nathan's simple tale had taken him back to the days when he was a shepherd. The greedy rich man who would rather rob the poor man of his last possession than sacrifice the smallest portion of his own property—the poor man's grief—all that had so carried him away that it had never occurred to him to connect the story with himself. And now he had pronounced his own sentence. Suddenly his wrath boiled over. "You misled me!" he cried.

"Your passion misled you," replied Nathan. "Do not try to take that attitude toward one who speaks to you in the name of the Lord. Thus saith the Lord: 'I anointed thee king over Israel and I delivered thee from the hand of Saul. And gave thee thy master's house and thy master's wives into thy bosom, and gave thee the house of Israel and Judah, and I shall add far greater things unto thee. Thou hast despised the word of the Lord. . . . Because thou hast killed Urias with the sword, therefore the sword shall never depart from thy house. . . . Behold, I will raise up evil against thee out of thy own house, and I will take thy own wives and give them to thy neighbor. . . . For thou didst it secretly; but I will do this thing in the sight of all Israel, and in the sight of the sun.' "

And as suddenly as it had come, so David's anger fell from him. He hid his face in his hands. "I have sinned against the Lord," he groaned.

The prophet's fixed eyes softened. "The Lord has forgiven your sin. Your judgment was more severe than his. You will not die. But the child born to you shall surely die."

When the king managed at last to look up, the prophet had gone, silently as he had come. Then the curtains rustled and Jehiel, the head guard of the women's quarters, entered. "Lord, Bathsheba sends word that your son is ill with a high fever."

David fasted. He slept on the ground instead of in his bed. In vain his people tried to persuade him to take a little nourishment, to allow himself a cushion and a cover. And this went on for seven days.

On the eighth day toward noon Jehiel came again. Chusai

received him, took his report, and whispered it to the other high officials. No one dared to tell the king. But when David saw them whispering he asked in a weak voice: "Is the child dead?"

Chusai gave a great sigh. "Yes, lord, it is dead."

But the terrible cry of sorrow they expected from the father did not follow. David rose, went into the bath, let them give him clean clothes, and went to the holy tent to pray. When he came back, he asked for food. Reading bewilderment on every face, he said, "While the child was yet alive, I fasted and wept, hoping the Lord would take pity on me and the child would live. Now he is dead. Fasting and weeping will not bring him back. One day I shall go where my son is, but he will not return to me." After he had taken food, David went to Bathsheba.

A message came from Joab: "Rejoice, lord, we have taken the City of Waters. Now come with fresh troops and lead us to victory over the citadel, that the name of the king may be shouted throughout the city, rather than the name of your servant, Joab." This sign of loyalty from his commander-in-chief was the first joy the king had had for a long time. He called up his bodyguards, marched on Rabbah, and stormed the citadel at the head of his troops. The garrison offered desperate resistance, but after a battle of five hours David's elite troops forced their way in. King Hanon of Ammon was quickly killed and Abisai brought the royal crown out of the treasure house; it was made of heavy gold and set with innumerable precious stones. David put it on, and with that act Ammon ceased to exist. The male population of Rabbah was led away and sent to the king's mines and brick kilns. Then, at last, the army returned home.

Even before the year was out, Bethsheba bore another son. According to custom she should have chosen a name for him, but she begged the king: "Do it for me. It will bring him luck."

"Israel has no hostile neighbors left," said David. "He shall be called Solomon—rich in peace."

Prince Absalom bit his lips angrily when a messenger reported that his mother wished to see him at once. His mother had been sickly for some time; she complained much and at great length about all sorts of grievances, and when she was not complaining, she bored him with endless tales of court life in Gessur where she had grown up—he knew them all by heart. Moreover he was expecting friends with whom he intended to go hunting. He would have liked to send the messenger back with an excuse, but it was just as well not to cross his mother. She still had great influence with the king and she was very clever about managing him . . .

Instead Absalom sent a message to his hunting friends, explaining that they would set out somewhat later, and he himself went to the palace. He was kept waiting in the antechamber of the women's apartments—grown sons were not allowed to enter the rooms themselves—and this did not improve his temper. But when his mother was carried in by two strong dark-skinned maids, his anger vanished. This time she seemed to be really very ill. How deep her eyes were sunk in their sockets! The last time he had seen her, she had been able to walk quite well. "She won't last much longer," he thought. But he smiled at her.

"Leave us alone," Maacha ordered, and the servants waddled out of the room like clumsy wading birds.

"Absalom," said Maacha, "I shall not live much longer."

"What are you saying, Mother! You are sick, but if you take care of yourself and—"

"Hush!" the soft, still melodious voice interrupted him. "You yourself don't believe what you are saying."

"Mother!"

He sounded so honestly hurt that Maacha had to smile.

"You can fool all the others, Absalom, but not me," she said. "No, don't contradict me. I am too ill to quarrel with you over such foolish things. We have more important matters to discuss." She paused. A slight spasm shook her; she coughed and quickly held a handkerchief to her lips—quickly, but not quickly enough.

"Blood!" he said, deeply moved.

"Yes—and for some time now. Wait . . ." A few breaths later she went on. "I am nearing the end. But I have not lived in vain. You have become the man I hoped you would be."

189

"Thank you, Mother," he replied earnestly, and she smiled again.

"You are like most young princes—thoughtless, vain as a peacock, and thinking only of your pleasures . . ."

"I thank you again!"

"But you have a keen mind, and enough sense not to let people know it . . ."

"You shouldn't talk so much, Mother; it tires you."

"I must speak. For it is the last time." She breathed with difficulty. "The king loves you dearly," she went on.

"Nevertheless Amnon is still the firstborn," objected Absalom in a casual tone.

"Amnon is a fool. He is what you only pretend to be."

Absalom looked at her sharply. "You are clever, Mother."

She smiled painfully. "I, too, have had to hide it. Your grandfather, King Tholmai of Gessur, taught me early in life that while it is good for a woman to be clever, it is very foolish to show it. That was the mistake Michol made; in her stupid pride she always had to *show* that she was cleverer and stood above the others. And what did she get for it? She wrecked herself."

"Amnon really is a fool," said Absalom. "He thinks only about women. But he's still the firstborn."

"Amnon will not live long," said Maacha very softly. "Khodad saw it in the stars. I know you don't believe in the stars, but we in Gessur know more about those things. Amnon will not live long. Even without the stars—he is wild and erratic; he will do something foolish that will destroy him, believe me."

"Let's hope so," said Absalom with a shrug.

"Keep away from him," warned Maacha, "or he will drag you into misfortune. And never forget who your father's ideal man was."

"Jonathan," sighed Absalom. "How often you have preached him to me, Mother! Wear your hair long like Jonathan; practice archery—Jonathan was a master at it. Be courteous to all men like Jonathan; tell the king how much you have always admired the great Prince Jonathan—I could spit when I so much as hear his name!"

"Spit as much as you please," said Maacha, "but only when you are alone."

He laughed heartily and she watched him, her heart brimming over with love. Nothing was more becoming to him than merriment and gaiety; his whole being glowed and sparkled, and all, men and women alike, took him to their hearts. And he was beautiful—almost too beautiful for a man, and yet there was nothing feminine about him.

"The Jonathan game has been very useful to you, even if it was often a nuisance," she said. "It has had much to do with the fact that the king prefers you over all his sons. The only one who sometimes worries me is the son of this Bathsheba. I hated her from the beginning."

"Solomon?" Absalom laughed again. "But he is still only a little boy! Besides, he is too far down the line of succession to the throne. If your stars tell you the truth and Amnon dies early, I would come first in line, and after me Adonias."

"Bathsheba!" repeated Maacha and the name sounded like a curse on her lips. "He has fallen in love with her—at fifty! Late loves are always dangerous." She coughed again. "I can't say any more," she murmured, "but now you know my thoughts."

"Solomon doesn't worry me," said Absalom scornfully. "And— I may as well tell you, Mother, there are people who would rather have me succeed to the throne than Amnon. Important, influential people."

"Who, for instance?"

"Achitophel is one."

"Clever," said Maacha. "Cold. Ambitious. Use him. But don't let him use you."

"No fear, Mother. Joab is another of my friends."

"That one thinks only of war."

"Yes, and that's why he says that if Amnon became king, there would be only women's affairs and a life of luxury. He looks upon me as a man from whom one could expect better things. He is thinking about war with the Phoenicians and I pretend to go along with his theories."

Maacha nodded. "You will be king," she murmured. "And then

take a princess from Gessur as your wife and unite the two king-doms."

Absalom looked at her in sincere admiration. "You have thought far, Mother. Farther ahead than I."

"I have had more time for it," she said in a low tone. "Now farewell, Absalom, my son, my beloved son. We shall not see each other again . . ."

"Mother, you must not talk like that—"

"No, don't kiss me," Maacha cried, and raised her thin arm to ward him off. "Oh, what would I give if I dared to kiss you! But my illness is contagious. Farewell. And when you wear the crown, think of me sometimes . . ."

She clapped her hands and the two servants appeared. "Carry me back," she commanded.

So heartrending was her last look at her son that tears came to Absalom's eyes. "Mother," he stammered. "Dear mother . . ."

The heavy curtain closed behind the servants and their burden.

Slowly, deep in thought, Absalom went back to his house. The friends who came to take him to the hunt found him grave and not very talkative. Not till he had brought down three splendid gazelles with an arrow apiece did he recover his usual gaiety.

Maacha died five days later in the arms of her daughter Thamar, whom she did not recognize. Her last word was the name of her son.

Thamar, the "palm," was an unusually beautiful girl. Her long black braids made a piquant contrast to her light skin, and her figure was slender and willowy. Her mother had never paid much attention to her—girls meant little to Maacha—and besides, Thamar had little understanding of the subtleties of feminine intrigue. She was simple and quiet and totally unaware of the effect she had on Prince Amnon.

Prince Amnon, twenty-four years old and already a little paunchy, was insatiable and not accustomed to opposition, but Thamar bore herself with such dignity that he could not show her too frankly how much she attracted him. Her quiet, steady friendliness roused his growing passion for this half sister of his until it became unbearable. Pretending to be sick, he begged the king to give him Thamar as a nurse. The king never liked to refuse any of his sons' wishes, particularly when they were ill and in need of help. He gave his permission and Thamar came. Amnon's eyes blazed with fever, but it was not the fever of illness.

That same evening Thamar dragged herself to her brother Absalom's house. Her gown with the long sleeves, which only princesses of the blood were allowed to wear, was torn; she had strewn ashes on her hair, and she wept hysterically. "Amnon," was all she could get out. "Amnon . . . Amnon . . ."

Absalom understood at once. He turned deathly white. "Against your will?" he asked sharply.

"Yes."

"With . . . force?"

"Yes." Thamar fell on her knees and hid her face in her hands.

Absalom did not move a muscle. For a long time there was no sound but the girl's sobbing. At last he said between clenched teeth: "Marriage between half brother and half sister is against the law. But perhaps our father would make an exception when he learns—"

"No!" Thamar jumped up. "No! No!"

"What does that mean?" cried Absalom. "Don't you want to? You have to, do you hear? You have to marry him!"

Thamar tried to answer, she struggled, her features became distorted, but she could not utter a word.

Then Absalom realized that he had not heard the worst. But what could be worse than this most scandalous of all crimes? Things like that might happen in war against another nation, but not in Israel, not even among the roughest men here. And that was not all. Was it conceivable that Amnon . . .

"He hates me!" cried Thamar.

Absalom could hardly speak. "How can that be?" he whispered hoarsely. "He can't—out of hatred—I don't understand . . ."

"He hates me," repeated Thamar shrilly. "Because he has done that to me, he hates me!" She tried to go on, but her words were lost in an unintelligible stammering. Absalom rushed to her, seized her shoulders, and shook her. "Speak!" he roared. "I want to know everything! Speak!"

But she jerked away from him, fled to a corner of the room, and went on stuttering. The words "driven out" were among the few Absalom could understand.

"He drove you out?" he cried incredulously, as he drew a sharp breath.

Thamar nodded. Suddenly she said in a perfectly clear voice: "He ordered his servant to put me out . . . to put me out . . . on the street . . . and . . . bar the door . . . behind me." She burst into shrill laughter, clutched her throat, and fainted.

When she regained consciousness she was lying on a couch and Absalom sat beside her. "Hush," he said very gently. "Keep very quiet, dear sister. From now on you will stay with me in my house. No one will ever harm you again."

She stared at him. Absalom's beautiful face was still and relaxed, he seemed almost gay. "Forget, Thamar," he said softly. "Forget there is such a person as Amnon. Forget what happened. Forget . . ."

Prince Amnon stood before the king and wrung his hands. "I'm quite beside myself," he whined. "I don't know what came over me. I was sick, Father, that is the only explanation I have and the only excuse."

"You lie!" the king raged at him. Amnon's servant had confessed that the prince had only feigned illness. "You are a weakling, a woman chaser, a licentious cad, and a liar to boot! Do you know what the sentence for your crime must be?"

Amnon was silent. "Let him get it out of his system," he thought. "He'll have to stop sometime."

"Death!" cried the king. "And a blot lies on your whole family, on the whole royal house! I am the supreme judge in Israel. It is for me to pronounce sentence on you." The ruler's blazing eyes had daunted men ten times stronger than the spineless young man before him.

"Father," stammered Amnon, startled, "you won't . . . you won't do that to *me* . . ."

"How can I ask an ordinary man to keep Moses' command-ments and respect the king's law," David interrupted him, "if a prince of my own house tramples them underfoot? Shall it be said: The king has two sorts of justice—strict for the people, but lenient and mild for the great? You have deserved death."

Amnon drew in his head. His pretty face twisted in a grimace. "And who judges the king?" he asked in a choking voice. "No one! Bathsheba's first son is dead. But the second is growing up. Solomon is a prince like all the rest of us."

David turned ash-gray. He had long suspected that Urias' death had not remained his and Joab's secret, but never before had anyone dared to speak of it. For a long time father and son faced each other in silence. "May the day never come in Israel," said the king finally, "when the son sits in judgment over the father."

Suddenly Amnon broke down in tears. "Forgive me, Father— I did not mean to insult you. It was a madness that came over me, an evil spirit. Never again shall you hear ugly words from me, Father, I swear it by my life and yours."

"Get out of my sight," commanded David. "You are exiled from the capital for six months. Remain on your country estate. If you are seen in Jerusalem before that time, you shall die. Now go!"

Amnon slunk out like a whipped dog.

The king sank down in an armchair and closed his eyes. Straight through the great room marched Urias the Hittite, stiff and ungainly—the loyal, faithful soldier, the brave man, the incu-bus of so many nights. Amnon knew about it, and if he knew, many others also knew. Could the sin never be buried? Must he always read it in angry, accusing eyes?

David thought of Nathan's prophecy: "Through your own house evil will come over you." Was this what the seer had meant? Or was it only the beginning? Amnon was weak, not the man who would rise up openly against his father. But he was also the firstborn, the heir to the throne, and that was a heavy anxiety. How could one entrust the destiny of the people of Israel to a man who had compromised his own half sister? Moreover, the people did not like him. Active, busy men resented his dissolute life, his love of pleasure. David thought of Isboseth, the "Man of shame." Amnon had more right to that epithet than the unfortunate man who had been murdered in his own bed. Absalom and Adonias, too, thought only of pleasure, and Solomon was still a child, a little boy. The king shivered. Must a man be guilty himself before he recognized that guilt was a living thing, a monster that never left your side, that stared at you out of sightless eyes day and night, until the moment when it bit with jaws dripping with poison? "I should have been stricter with Amnon," was his tormented thought. But it was no use sitting here, reproaching himself like a helpless old man—yes, an old man!—for a bungled life. He must do something, he must at least see that this scandal did not spread too far.

He sent for Achitophel and Chusai. They must see to it that the men who knew did not talk.

"Using *all* means?" asked Achitophel casually, and the king suddenly looked into an abyss.

"No!" he burst out. "It is godless—and foolish—to try to cure evil with evil."

"You are right, lord," said Chusai earnestly.

Achitophel shrugged. "The best doctor for such things is time," he said. "There will, of course, be some talk, but the talk will die away."

And apparently he was right. Beautiful, reserved Princess Thamar had few personal friends and acquaintances. No one found Prince Amnon's absence from court particularly regrettable, and when he returned after his exile, no one seemed to be scandalized. It was remarked that Absalom did not speak to the heir to the throne, but young princes often quarreled among themselves and Achitophel spread the rumor that Absalom and Amnon had quarreled over a young woman with whom they were both in love, but who, meantime, had married another man. For a time there was curiosity about the identity of the beauty, but even that did not last long and soon court gossip turned to other matters.

15

THE KINGDOM PROSPERED and no hostile neighbor dared disturb its peace. It seemed incredible that Israel and Judah had ever paid tribute, for now rulers of other kingdoms paid tribute to them; and mighty rulers like the Pharaoh in Egypt and the king of the Phoenicians sent gifts whose value and splendor bore witness to their respect for the man who had never lost a battle and had made his kingdom great and prosperous.

"He is small in stature, but a great ruler," the ambassador from Tyre reported to his king. "His hair and beard are gray; only a few strands of red are left, like tongues of fire among the embers. But it will be a long time before that glow dies. King David's strength is unbroken. The years of peace have not made him soft. He still *is* Israel and Judah."

"Has he really no weaknesses?" asked King Hiram.

"Yes, All-Powerful One, he has one—his sons. It is a strange weakness."

"Why strange?" King Hiram stroked his silky beard that was bedecked with jewels. "Most fathers love their sons."

"David's love for his sons is blind," replied the ambassador. "They say a prophet told him that one of his sons, or a descendant of his, would accomplish something he himself could never carry out. What that is no one knows, but it must be something very great—and perhaps that is what he looks for in his sons."

"*One* of his sons, you say?"

"Yes. But I think he doesn't know which one."

"Prince Amnon is the heir to the throne."

"He is the firstborn, yes. But it is doubtful whether he is the one the prophet had in mind. Nevertheless, it is as though David saw in each of his sons his own final destiny. There is a secret here, a mystery I cannot solve."

King Hiram shrugged. "The Israelites are an incomprehensible people," he said.

"My king and father!"

On the way to the audience chamber David paused, and behind him Achitophel, Chusai, and the eight picked bodyguards who accompanied the king wherever he went also paused.

Prince Absalom smiled winningly. "Forgive your son and servant for daring to stop you," he begged. "I ask for a favor."

The king frowned. "What more can you wish for? You have everything a man can desire."

"I would be the most thankless of sons if I did not admit that," replied Absalom. "The Baalhasor estate alone, which I owe to your favor, is a treasure many a ruling prince might well envy me."

"I am glad you recognize that," said the king. "I gave it to you to atone for a wrong done to you through a close member of your family," he added softly.

"You are my father. My family is also yours," said Absalom gently. "Tomorrow at Baalhasor we shall celebrate the feast of sheepshearing. In the old style, Father, with all the pageantry and with folk dances. And the favor I beg of the king is that he will honor us at Baalhasor with his presence."

David was surprised and touched. He knew how much Absalom liked to be the center of everything he undertook, especially as host on his own estate before all his farm hands and servants. But with the king present, the prince must needs be content to play a secondary role. The king was never the guest of his subjects. Wherever he appeared, he was the principal person and all others were subject to his command. Moreover, he was always accompanied by his household troops. To invite the king to a feast meant feeding at least two thousand men all day long.

"You are a good son, Absalom, and I thank you," said David, "but it is better if I do not come. To feed so many mouths would be a serious burden on you."

"I will gladly assume that burden," Absalom assured him warmly. "Everything I own comes from you anyway, from your kindness and favor."

But the king smiled and declined. "No, no, you must celebrate your beautiful feast without such encumbrances. And I am pleased that you keep up the customs of our forefathers." He started to move on, but Absalom stood in his way.

"If you really won't come, let the princes come and send your eldest son in your place."

"Amnon?" asked David in surprise.

"Yes, Father," Absalom looked the king straight in the eye. "I am inviting all my brothers. If I were to make an exception, it would only cause more talk."

The king hesitated.

"No quarrel between brothers should last forever," said Absalom calmly.

David was relieved. "You are right," he said. "And I am glad. Very glad. Permission is granted."

Absalom bowed low. The king ran his hand goodnaturedly over the prince's beautiful hair and walked on.

At Baalhasor the festival was at its height. The shearing was over and the feast in full swing. The prettiest girls from the clan of Ephraim danced in honor of Absalom and his royal guests. No less than eight princes of the blood, and among them, Cheleab, Adonias, Saphathia, Jethraam, and Solomon, all Absalom's half brothers, sat at the richly bedecked, heavily laden table and regaled themselves with delicacies such as fat tails of young sheep and special sweetmeats from Syria. Behind each prince stood two servants: One held in readiness a silver bowl and a soft woolly towel, the other a richly ornamented jug of wine; after each course they handed him the bowl filled with water, which was poured over his right hand and gently dried; and his cup must never remain empty longer than four heatbeats.

Absalom proved to be a most courteous host. For each man he had a friendly word and he drank to each man's health. Several of the young princes drank more than was good for them, and twice Adonias and Jethraam quarreled openly. But Absalom smoothed things over with such charm that the two young fighting cocks soon calmed down again.

Prince Amnon occupied the seat of honor, which was his as the king's representative. At the beginning of the feast he had held himself rather shyly aloof, but Absalom's friendly and yet respectful manner had reassured him. "You have excellent wine, Brother," he praised. "Even the king has no better—to say nothing of myself."

Absalom bowed and smiled. "What is mine is thine," he replied and Amnon threw back his head and laughed. "Your courtesy could almost lead me into temptation," he said. "Baalhasor is incomparably more beautiful than my own estate."

"The king was gracious to his undeserving servant," murmured Absalom.

Amnon laughed again. "Neither one of us has had occasion so far to distinguish himself. Our only merit is the accident of birth." He drank with relish and the servant behind him promptly filled his cup again. "You have inherited your mother's charming courtesy," he went on. "And probably her cleverness too. It was clever of her always to keep on the king's good side. It is clever of you to keep on the good side of the heir to the throne."

Absalom smiled. He said nothing.

"In this life the deserving are seldom rewarded," Amnon continued. "You have to depend on yourself to get what you want— and I think you understand that to perfection, Brother. I know why the king gave you Baalhasor," he sniggered, by this time quite tipsy. "When you come right down to it, you might say you owe it to me."

"You have praised my courtesy," said Absalom slowly, "and that should keep me from contradicting you—and yet I must do so. I believe one does get what one deserves—though not always right away."

Prince Amnon shrugged, raised the freshly filled cup to his lips, and drank.

"But in one thing you are right," Absalom went on. "One must see to it oneself." Again he smiled his winning, radiant smile. "And I," he said, "will see to it that you get what you deserve." And still smiling, he ordered loudly: "Stab him!" One of the servants behind Prince Amnon leaned forward, and there was a flash of metal as his hand moved in an incredibly swift half circle.

The cup fell from Prince Amnon's hand; his eyes bulged out of their sockets. A dark red stream of wine and blood spurted from his slit throat. At the same moment the second servant thrust a long dagger into his back and Amnon fell forward heavily on the table. The young princes sat motionless, frozen with horror.

Six servants surrounded Prince Absalom, drawn swords in their fists, ready to protect him from immediate revenge. Amnon's blood poured over the broad table and into the lap of Prince Adonias, who sprang up with a loud yell. That brought the others to their senses. With one accord the princes fled from the table and out of the hall in such haste that they overturned tables and benches. No one made the slightest effort to stop them.

Absalom had remained calmly in his place. Now he leaned forward, seized Amnon's head by the hair, held it high, and stared into the glassy eyes. "Thamar sends you her greetings, brother Amnon," he said softly. He was still smiling.

A ruler must have many eyes and ears. In Baalhasor, a servant who saw Prince Amnon fall, ran to the courtyard, mounted the nearest ass he could find, and rode south like the wind. Less than an hour and a half later he dashed into the courtyard of the royal palace in Jerusalem, leaped down, gave the officer of the guard a secret sign, and was promptly taken before the king, who had just left a session of the Crown Council.

"I am Simmu, the ear of the king in Baalhasor," stammered the servant. "Prince Absalom has had the young princes killed."

David clutched his heart. He swayed and Chusai had to support him. "My sons," moaned the king. "All my sons!"

Achitophel pushed forward. "Are you sure of your facts, man?" he asked sharply. "Speak! What did you see?"

"I saw Prince Amnon stabbed, lord. Then many of Prince Absalom's servants drew their swords—"

The king cried out in a loud voice and rent his clothes. The members of the Council silently followed his example, even Achitophel, though it did not prevent him from asking "Is that all you saw?"

"Yes, lord. I then hurried here as fast as I could—"

"You have done well and will receive a reward," Achitophel cut him short. "Now go. Report to me early tomorrow morning." Then he turned to the king. "You have lost only one of your sons, lord. Not all. Prince Amnon only is dead."

David stared at him, perplexed. He still could not speak. But Chusai asked in his place: "How do you know that?"

"It is reasonable," Achitophel replied coldly. "Between Prince Absalom and Prince Amnon there was an unavenged wrong. Now it is avenged. There was no reason to kill the other princes."

"You may be right," Chusai admitted.

Ethai, the commander of the Cerethi and Phelethi, stepped forward. "Lord, shall I go to Baalhasor and arrest all those who are to blame for your son's death?"

But David had still not recovered enough to be able to give orders. Again Achitophel stepped into the breach. "You would not find them there, my good fellow. They have long since fled."

"But where to?" asked Chusai quickly.

"To the north of course," Achitophel informed him. "To Gessur. Has my learned colleague in the Crown Council forgotten that Prince Absalom's mother came from Gessur? If you want to find him you must go to King Tholmai's court."

"The cleverness of my colleague in the Crown Council is to be admired," declared Chusai. "He knows Prince Absalom's plans as accurately as if he had outlined them with him."

Achitophel gave him a sharp look and was about to answer angrily when Ethai, who was standing at the window, cried:

"Here come the young princes, lord. I see the white animals they are riding. Two . . . three . . . five . . . seven! Seven princes, lord, and their attendants. Only Prince Amnon is missing. His mule is riderless and a servant is leading it by the bridle."

"You see, I was right, lord," said Achitophel.

A few seconds later the young men rushed in the door. The king opened his arms and they crowded around him, weeping like children who are afraid of the storm.

It soon appeared that all of Achitophel's reasoning had been correct, when the king's spies reported that Absalom had fled to Gessur with a strong escort. The king did not send troops after him. He did not even send to Gessur to ask to have him returned. He knew that old King Tholmai would have to refuse such a demand. "Let Absalom stay where he is," he said wearily. "Tholmai cannot hand over his own grandson. And shall I wage war with Gessur only to punish my own son?" But when Absalom's numerous friends begged for mercy for him, they met stony opposition. "I forbid you ever to speak of him again. He has forfeited all mercy."

Not until three years later did Achitophel think he detected the first signs that the king had softened. He took Joab aside. "I think this is now the time to gradually remind the king that his eldest son has lived long enough in exile," he said.

"If that's what you think, why don't you do it?" grinned Joab. "No, don't say anything, my wise friend. I know the answer to my question. You are chairman of the Crown Council; that means you are the king's first advisor, and you intend to remain in that post. Therefore, you would rather have someone else burn his fingers. For example, a blunt, stupid soldier like me. Right?"

Achitophel smiled thinly. "For a blunt, stupid soldier you are astonishingly shrewd, Joab. But seriously: You and I have the same opinion about Prince Absalom. He is a talented young man, he has proved that he can keep a definite plan secret for years, and he has shown that he has courage. That is more than one could say about Prince Amnon. Just between us, it is not a pity about Amnon. The king himself had been aware for some time that he would not have a good successor in him."

Joab shook his head. "Beyond the life of the king I cannot and will not think," he declared morosely.

"The Lord spare him to us many years more!" Achitophel hastened to say. "But he himself is fully aware of the problem. And Absalom was always his favorite. So that now it is a question of *helping* the king."

"How do you mean that?" Joab asked distrustfully.

"I will tell you. In his first anger the king forbade us ever to mention Absalom's name again. Now he cannot bring himself to be the first to do so. He does not want us to think it is weakness on his part. And he knows very well that many people have noticed his weakness where his sons are concerned. Therefore one of us must begin to make it easier for him. If I were to do so, the king would be quite capable of getting rid of me and appointing old Chusai or some other dunce as my successor. You, on the other hand, are irreplaceable."

"Mice are caught with cheese," growled Joab. "You always flatter when you want something from someone."

Achitophel laid both hands in protest on his breast. "*Who* could replace you?" he asked. "Your brother Abisai?"

"No. Far too hotheaded."

"General Amasa?"

"The man is a fool and a lazy fool at that. I wouldn't trust him with any troop of a thousand men."

"Ethai?"

"What's the matter with you? He's never commanded more men than my six hundred bodyguards. Besides, the man is a foreigner, a Philistine by birth and a mercenary."

"There you have it!" cried Achitophel triumphantly. "There is no one to replace you. You and you only can dare to speak openly to the king. Moreover, the king trusts you completely. I—I confess to you frankly, I am not courageous enough for that. But if anyone has the courage, it is you."

No one had ever appealed in vain to Joab's courage. "All right then," he said sighing. "I'll see what I can do."

And this he did the very next morning. But after the first word the king became angry and forbade him to say any more.

"I was afraid of that," said Achitophel anxiously. "It is a pity. Now I really don't know what to advise. We shall have to give it up."

"Perhaps," said Joab and rubbed his nose thoughtfully. "And perhaps not." He began to whistle to himself softly.

"You seem to have an idea, Joab. What are you up to?"

But Joab refused to explain. He simply looked sly and went on whistling softly.

In the great courtyard of the palace the king was sitting in judgment, as he did every day in the week with the exception of the Sabbath. And as usual a number of higher officials participated, but only as observers. The king alone pronounced the sentence against which there was no appeal. Joab, Chusai, and the priests, Abiathar and Sadoc, liked to stand behind the king's judgment seat; Achitophel, on the other hand, seldom appeared, for he found it hard to attend a meeting in which he himself did not play the principal part.

No one knew the woman who flung herself on the ground before the king and begged for his help. The clerk read out her name and her home village: Basemath was her name and she came from Thecua, a little town in the mountains of Judah. She was dressed in mourning.

"What is your request?" asked the king kindly.

"Lord, I am a widow," said the woman. "I had two sons who both inherited their father's hot-tempered nature. They quarreled with each other in the field, and there was no one there to part them. And the one struck the other and slew him. Then the whole kindred rose against me, saying that I should deliver him who had slain his brother that they might kill him for taking the life of his brother. Then I would have lost both sons—and the inheritance would have gone to the kindred."

David nodded. A woman could not inherit. He understood the eagerness of the kindred. "The obligation to preserve the family is greater than the obligation to avenge the death of a relative," he decided. "Go home; as the Lord lives, not a hair of your son's head shall be harmed. Say that to the head of the clan. And if he will not believe you, bring him before my judgment seat."

The woman brightened. "Your wisdom has pronounced a sentence like one of God's angels," she rejoiced. "Permit me to ask one more question, lord; why is not your judgment valid also for your own son, who lives in exile because he killed his brother?"

There was absolute silence in the courtyard. David looked around. Behind him stood Joab, staring innocently straight ahead.

David looked the woman sharply in the eye. "Basemath of Thecua," he said, "tell the truth. Is General Joab behind this thing?"

The woman bowed her head. "By your life, lord, you are as an angel of God. I think you know all that happens on earth. It is impossible to pass you on the right or on the left. Yes, your servant Joab put those words in my mouth."

The king glared at Joab, who glared back stubbornly.

"You, too, must now go to Gessur," said David. The old soldier turned pale and David let him worry for a while before he continued: "I am sending you to the court of King Tholmai. Seek out my son Absalom. He is permitted to return to Jerusalem."

Joyfully Joab threw himself down before the king.

A few weeks later Prince Absalom returned. Joab had procured one of the famous white asses for his homecoming. He himself rode a dun-colored ass that had accompanied him on many a campaign. Behind him came six husky slaves, bearing a richly carved litter in which reclined a beautiful young woman with a two-year-old boy by her side. Prince Absalom had married a princess of Gessur as his dying mother had advised. Six wagons with the princess's handmaids and her household goods brought up the procession, along with the dozen armed soldiers who had accompanied Joab on his mission. The streets of Jerusalem were full of the usual cheerful, busy crowds, but Absalom noticed at once that no special preparations had been made to receive him; in fact, it seemed even as though no one had heard of his homecoming. Only the white ass he rode caused the people to look up and salute mechanically: One of the royal princes was passing by, one must be courteous. That was all. No troops were drawn up, no rugs hung from the windows. "The people seem to have forgotten me completely," he remarked with a touch of bitterness.

Joab looked embarrassed. "I sent a swift messenger day before yesterday to announce your arrival," he murmured.

Absalom nodded. "It's certainly not your fault. You have shown that you are a good friend. But if you had not told me about the woman from Thecua and described the effect it had on my father, I would think he had still not forgiven me."

They were approaching the royal palace, in front of which stood twenty of the bodyguards under the command of a young officer. Joab dismounted and was about to help the prince when the young officer stepped up to them. He saluted Absalom with a formal bow and turned to Joab. "Order of the king," he said. "You alone are permitted to enter the palace."   ,

"What does that mean?" Joab exclaimed angrily.

"It is clear enough what it means," Prince Absalom burst out.

The officer turned to him. "Order of the king," he repeated. "Prince Absalom is to take quarters in his own house in Jerusalem." He stepped back and took his place at the head of his men again.

"I had more freedom in Gessur than I seem to be allowed here," said Prince Absalom. "Farewell, Joab."

"Lord," stammered the old soldier. "Believe me I knew nothing of this decision of the king's."

"Of course not. For otherwise one would have to assume that you lured me here from Gessur under false pretenses. To be sure, the end result is the same. My thanks for your escort and your protection. Farewell." And the prince turned and rode slowly along the street to his house on the south side of the city.

16

Joab requested an immediate audience with the king, but David refused and did not receive him until the following day.

"You've put me in a bad position, lord," complained the soldier. "How could I know that you would not receive Prince Absalom? He must think I lured him under false pretenses from the freedom and security of Gessur to a prison here."

"You are a loyal man, Joab," said the king coldly. "Therefore I forgive you for something I would not forgive many others. I have allowed my son Absalom to come home. But by no word have I given him to understand that I have forgotten the past. His life is not in danger. He is free to go where he will. But I retain the right to receive whom I please. I do not wish to see Absalom. The shadow of his brother Amnon looks over my shoulder. No, do not speak, do not contradict me. And if you value the king's favor, do not mention Absalom's name in my presence."

Joab had known the king too long not to understand when it was better to keep silent. Without a word he left the room—and from that day on, he avoided Absalom.

For a long time Absalom lived quietly. He did not leave Jerusalem and seldom even his house. That none of his brothers came to see him did not disturb him. But that his friends of the old days, particularly Joab and Achitophel, gave no sign was, though understandable, exceedingly bitter. He needed them—needed them more desperately than ever before; for only through them and with their help could he obtain the one thing that mattered to him—a meeting with the king. He knew with an almost prophetic clarity that if he could meet the king face to face all would be well. But the king knew that too, which was why he refused to see him. "He does not want to appear weak," thought Absalom. He even played with the idea of slipping into the palace in disguise, but he knew that Ethai's mercenaries kept a sharp watch. Those Cerethi and Phelethi made no distinction between a common murderer and a prince whose sole purpose was to see his father again; any man who forced his way into the palace unauthorized would be slain.

The more time passed, the more impatient the prince became. Even the fact that his lovely princess from Gessur had meanwhile presented him with a second son, and finally with a daughter, made no difference. He named the son Jonathan and the daughter Thamar, and sent respectful messages to the king as head of the tribe, announcing the new additions to the royal family. There was no answer; in fact Absalom could not be sure that his message had ever reached the king.

This was more than he could endure. He sent messenger after messenger to his old friends, begging, even imploring them to arrange an audience for him. He offered them treasures, estates, precious jewels, enormous sums in silver.

Achitophel replied laconically that it would be undiplomatic to act in direct opposition to the king's clearly expressed desire. They must be patient and wait a little longer. General Amasa, with whom Absalom had often hunted in the past, sent word that he was ill. And Joab did not answer at all.

The princess tried in vain to comfort her husband. "I have become a leper," he cried. "People go out of their way to avoid me. If I could only talk with Joab for half an hour, I know I could convince him."

"Talk him into it, you mean," the princess said. She knew her husband and, in spite of all his bitterness, Absalom was forced to smile.

"You are right, my little dove."

They were sitting side by side on the flat roof of their house, looking out over the city wall to the fields where a great number of farm hands were at work.

"To think that Joab and I are neighbors!" growled Absalom. "His fields begin over there by the yellow border markers. He has had barley planted." He drew in a sharp breath and the princess looked at him attentively.

"You've just had an idea," she said.

He nodded. "Joab will come to see me and this very day."

She shook her head. "How will you arrange that?"

"Leave it to me. You will see." He clapped his hands, ordered the servant to send the overseer of the farm hands to him, took the man aside, and spoke eagerly to him. The princess saw that the man first looked at him incredulously, then with shock and surprise; finally he laughed, bowed and left.

"There," said Absalom and for the first time since his return to Jerusalem he looked inwardly content. "Now see what happens, my dove."

She asked no questions, though by this time her curiosity was aroused. Absalom looked closely at the fields below. "The wind is in the right direction," he muttered enigmatically.

After a while the overseer appeared on the field with about a dozen farm hands. The men all carried burning torches and they ran as fast as they could to the adjoining field.

"What are they doing?" cried the princess in horror. "That is Joab's field and if they are not careful they will set it on fire. There! There! Look! That is smoke over there—and over there, too! Absalom! They are setting fire to it deliberately! They are burning up Joab's corn."

"Quite right, my little dove," Absalom replied with the greatest satisfaction.

The princess was bewildered: "But why? Is this your revenge because he has not done anything for you? He will be beside himself. He will—oh, look! Now they are running away! And there come Joab's men! And there—there is Joab himself!"

"Yes, and he gives orders as if he were on a battlefield," Absalom chuckled. "They're trying to put out the fire, but it's a little too late for that. The field is done for."

"And you have one more enemy?"

"Wait, my little dove. If I'm not mistaken, Joab is coming to our house."

"Yes, that's true, but—oh, I begin to understand!"

He laughed and went slowly down the stairs from the roof. A few minutes later Joab burst into the house fuming with rage, his face black with smoke.

"What does this mean, Prince?" he roared. "Your farmhands have set fire to my fields—deliberately. All my beautiful barley is burned down. I insist that you pay for the damages."

"With pleasure, my dear old angry friend," replied Absalom smiling. "You yourself shall decide what your field is worth and I will pay you back seven times its value . . ."

Joab stared at him, dumbfounded. "But how—why—?"

"It was the only way I could get you here. I *had* to talk to you and I knew that in your well-justified wrath you would come in person to call me to account. Here, take this purse filled with silver. If that is not enough to pay you seven times over for your barley, tell me and I will add to it. You are here, we are talking together, that is the only thing that matters to me."

Joab burst out laughing. "By my life and the life of the king, no one but you would have hit on such an idea! I must tell this to the king. He doesn't have many opportunities to laugh nowadays. He is often lonely."

"Yes, do tell him," replied Absalom earnestly. "And ask him also why he let me leave Gessur if he didn't intend either to punish me or to receive me? And if in his eyes after all these years I have not yet atoned for my sin, he should kill me. Death is better than his displeasure."

"You are right," said Joab simply, "and I would feel as you do. I, too, have not always been of the same opinion as the king, but without him, without his favor, life holds no real joy. And even if he sends me into exile in Gessur for this, I shall tell him what you have charged me to say."

A few days later Ethai arrived with a letter from the king. It contained a single word: "Come."

Absalom went at once to the palace. The king received him alone. Throwing himself at his father's feet, the young man touched his forehead to the ground. But David put his arms around his son, raised him, and kissed him on both cheeks. The prince was deeply moved and he wept. As the king turned away, his heavy gold necklace clicked lightly. "It is too large for him," thought Absalom. "He has grown old . . . old and weak."

Absalom was not the only one who thought the king had aged. Never in their history had the people of Israel enjoyed so many years of peace. The days of war with the Philistines, of raids from the Moabites, the Ammonites and the Aramaeans seemed to belong to a different era. Only the middle-aged or very old could remember how greatly the land had suffered then. Peace and freedom had become a matter of course, and the desires of the people turned to other things. Not all the king's servants were just and not all honest work received its due pay. And the king seemed to have lost the firm hand that once had made a clean sweep of all evil.

For one thing, the king's chief councilor Achitophel had managed to come between the king and the people. In innumerable cases he was the one who made the final decisions. The army, like its commander Joab, had nothing or practically nothing to do; it was bored, and a bored army is fertile ground for the seed of rebellion. Many officers, particularly among the younger ones, were sure they would never have a chance to win laurels for themselves under the leadership of King David. The king was simply too old to take an interest in military deeds, they said. He no longer cared to enlarge his realm, he had grown narrow-minded, stubborn, an old man who wanted peace and quiet and who ruled Israel and Judah as though they were one huge farmstead.

It was significant that such talk almost never reached the king's ears. Now and then Chusai brought him word of dissatisfaction in the land, but even he was silent when he saw that his frankness only roused the king to anger; and from time to time gentle warnings came from another source. The king's visits to the women's palace had become less and less frequent of late. The company of young girls bored him, and the wives of his youth were either no longer alive or they lived in the past—with one single exception: Bathsheba. She, too, was no longer young, but her face still retained much of her former beauty and she had the gift of entertaining the ruler. Not for nothing was she the only one whose influence Maacha had feared—Bathsheba still had great influence over the king. Even now he came to her to unburden his heart, and she knew many of his most secret thoughts and many of his fears. For his part the king knew that anything he told her would be as safe as if he had not spoken. He was well aware that she herself had her own aims, or rather her one aim: her son's future. And more than once the king had to admit to himself that of all his sons Solomon was the most gifted. The boy learned easily and his judgment was surprisingly keen and accurate, far beyond his young years. Yes, during Absalom's exile, David had sometimes thought seriously that it might be best for the people of Israel if he were to leave Absalom in Gessur, and instead of Adonias, the next in line, make Solomon his heir to the throne . . .

Bathsheba had inspired the thought—which was only natural. He had told her that this would inevitably lead to a deadly enmity between Solomon and Adonias, and probably to civil war, and she had apparently been satisfied with his explanation. But to himself he had to admit that she was not wrong. In Solomon there was a real ruler. Adonias, on the other hand, was not much better than poor Amnon had been—lazy, caring only for a life of ease, women and pleasure.

Bathsheba knew instinctively what was going on in the king's mind. But she also knew she could not push him too far. That could spoil everything. And so she waited. Absalom's return was a heavy blow to her and her plans. Adonias was a hindrance that could be overcome. But Absalom, on the other hand, was a deadly threat to Solomon. As soon as Absalom knew that Solomon might stand in his way—and sooner or later he must notice it—not only was her ambition endangered, but Solomon's entire position, even his life. Bathsheba hated Absalom from the bottom of her heart.

The reconciliation between the prince and the king was a further blow which infinitely increased the danger. Absalom was now without any doubt the heir to the throne and from all she could hear he was very well aware of it.

One heard a great deal in the women's quarters if one had sharp ears, and Bathsheba eagerly gathered all the news she could. A few years after the hated reconciliation, she had enough information to open the king's eyes to the dangerous situation. Unfortunately she was not only obliged to wait until he appeared, but also until he was in a mood to listen to her. Often he came to her only to have a new song played for her, one he had composed in praise of the Lord; and at such times he would not listen to anything else. But at last her opportunity came. David told her about Absalom's new chariot. "That chariot he has had built for himself is a sheer miracle. If I were younger I could envy him. But I do not care much about driving fast any more."

"Yes, the chariot is said to be very beautiful," Bathsheba replied. "And very, very expensive. And the four horses he had sent from Egypt were even more expensive."

The king shrugged good-naturedly. "I know! He loves pomp and splendor!"

"Your son Amnon loved pomp and splendor too," replied Bathsheba, and the king gave a slight start. "Forgive your handmaiden for reminding you of the suffering Absalom caused you," she went on quickly. "But my anxiety forces me to speak of things a loving father does not like to hear. Amnon loved pomp and splendor for its own sake. Absalom, on the other hand, has a purpose in everything he does, an objective in mind. When he drives out he is accompanied by no less than fifty runners. He courts the friendship of the powerful of the land—"

"He has the friendship of the king," David interrupted dryly. "And the king is the most powerful of all."

She knew that the ruler was displeased, but she had waited so long that now she must seize her opportunity. "Lord, though I risk your anger, I must say it: Do not forget that Prince Absalom has waited silently all these years for the moment when he could carry out his revenge. And this time the most important thing of all is involved—"

But the king stood up and she knew that now she could not say any more. Kneeling before him, she crossed her hands over her breast.

"Absalom may be ambitious," said David sharply, "but he is not the only one. I know your ambition, Bathsheba." He turned away abruptly and left the room. Nevertheless she was not displeased with the result of his visit. That she was ambitious for her own son was only natural. A man even less clever than the king would have taken that for granted. And because the king was angry, he would think over her words. That was all she wanted.

"Achitophel."

"My lord and king."

"How does my son Absalom spend his time?"

"The prince enjoys life."

"Has he many friends?"

"Of course, lord. That is his temperament."

"Powerful friends?"

"Friends from all classes, lord. But he does not attach any special importance to them. Only recently he said to me: 'Since my father has taken me back into favor, I have as many friends as a cornfield has ears of corn. If he were to withhold his favor rom me again, tomorrow not one of them would appear at my house—just as before.'" Achitophel smiled. "He said that without any bitterness," he added.

David nodded. "Do you consider him ambitious?"

"No, lord," replied Achitophel calmly. "And I will tell you why not. Ambition is a characteristic of men who fight tenaciously for power. Prince Absalom is not the man for that. He is far too easygoing and too much accustomed to having the good things of life fall into his lap. That is why he does not have to climb. Why should he, who stands on the top of the mountain, try to climb?"

The king was silent for a moment. Then he said dryly: "Not quite on the top."

Achitophel raised his hands. "The prince is young," he said, "but not so young as not to know that the king is irreplaceable."

"You think so?"

"I am convinced of that, lord. But that is not all. I can bear witness to how much the prince suffered when you withdrew your favor from him. He had everything a man could desire: a beautiful young wife, lovely children, riches—and yet he was unhappy, so unhappy that even I could not bring myself to visit him—I could not bear to see how much he suffered. You have no idea how greatly you are loved, lord."

David bowed his head. "I know people say I have been weak with my sons," he said slowly. "And perhaps I have. But I do not regret it. Go, Achitophel, you are my best councilor and my most loyal friend."

"My king is very gracious," murmured Achitophel and withdrew. One hour later he stood before Absalom.

"The king has shown the first sign of distrust," he reported.

The prince was startled. "What is the cause of that?" he asked hastily.

"I don't know for certain, but I think it is Bathsheba. Last evening the king visited the women's quarters."

"The poisonous toad!" cried Absalom and scowled furiously.

"To be sure, her enmity is only natural, but she is beginning to be a nuisance," said Achitophel coldly. "I have done my best to pull the wool over the king's eyes, but when he begins to be distrustful, he will keep his eyes open."

"In other words, we must act quickly. It's a good thing we are so well prepared."

"I am waiting now for an important report," replied Achitophel. "It may come any moment. As soon as I have it, the messengers will go to the various cities of Judah with the password we have arranged. The south is almost completely organized. The riches you brought with you from Gessur have born fruit."

"And my own work also," retorted Absalom. "It was a bore trying to win over ordinary men individually."

"You mean the petitioners who were always besieging you at the palace gates and who always wanted to tell you about their quarrels?"

"And whom I always so enthusiastically agreed with. 'Yes, you poor fellow, you really have suffered great injustice! If I had to settle your case I would have decided at once in your favor. How my father will decide, unfortunately I do not know, or even whether he will make a decision at all. He is a great man, no one could ever take his place, but of late he has unfortunately aged and it all depends upon whether he has slept well or not . . .'"

Achitophel laughed. "Splendid, my prince, absolutely marvelous!"

"And then my charming affability," Absalom went on ironically. "Everyone who knelt before me I raised and embraced, even stinking peasants from the most outlandish villages. Day after day, friend, day after day! It's time for that to come to an end and for those stinking fellows to do something *for me*."

The king's councilor nodded. "It is time and everything is now ready. The only thing I regret is that your neighbor is not on our side—"

"Joab? Couldn't I win him over to us at the last moment?"

Achitophel shook his head. "The danger is too great. I seldom make a mistake when it comes to judging a man. Joab once said to me: 'Beyond the king's death I cannot and will not think.' That is enough for me; if he should so much as guess what we are up to he would immediately run to the king."

"The king's death," repeated Absalom frowning. "We abide by our agreement, Achitophel? I am not a pious man like my respected father, but I think it would bring me little luck to begin my rule with such a crime. If it is at all possible, my father must live. He must sign his own abdication, and he will then be taken to Bethlehem, where in peace and safety he can write his songs and play his harp. Closely guarded, of course! He is already a little weak with age now. Soon he will not even want anything better, and then I shall be the legitimate ruler—no rebel and no usurper."

217

Achitophel bowed silently.

"As for Joab, you are probably quite right," Absalom went on thoughtfully. "Fortunately friend Amasa is just as good a general as he. And he has one advantage over Joab—he has the army behind him. Influencing and winning over the individual commanders was a master stroke."

"It was not difficult after we had won Amasa himself. Soldiers always trust a general more than a statesman."

The prince's major-domo reported that a man had arrived with a message for Achitophel.

"Let him come in," commanded Absalom.

The man entered. He was dressed in peasant's clothes.

"Speak freely," Achitophel urged him. "What is your message?"

"Hebron sends you this word: We await the blare of the trumpets," the man reported.

Achitophel nodded. "Let them give you food, then rest and come back early in the morning. You may go."

As soon as the man had disappeared, Achitophel bowed low before the prince. He was smiling. "That was the news I was waiting for," he said. "Now all is ready, my lord and king."

"At last!" cried Absalom, and he drew a deep breath.

17

THE NEXT MORNING Prince Absalom appeared before the king.

"Give me permission to make a journey to Hebron."

"What will you do in Hebron, my son?"

Absalom's handsome face was very solemn. "When I was living in exile in Gessur, I made a vow that, should the Lord our God and the king's mercy permit me to return to Jerusalem, I would make a pilgrimage to the city where I was conceived and born and there sacrifice to the Lord. At first I dared not leave Jerusalem. But now that I have won your favor and your heart, I feel that I must not delay any longer."

David nodded. "You are right. A vow must be kept. Go in peace."

"Thank you, my dear father," and the prince knelt at David's feet. Then he rose and left the room. Two hours later he set out for Hebron, taking with him two hundred of his friends, not one of whom was aware of the prince's real plans. They were men whose loyalty to the king could not be easily shaken. But confronted with a *fait accompli,* they would either join the prince or they would be held prisoners.

In the middle of the night Huzal entered Jerusalem. Six miles before reaching the city, the ass he was riding had collapsed, and he had been forced to run the rest of the way. He was no longer young, and more than once he had had to stop, put his hand to his wildly beating heart, and gasp for breath. At the city gates he had shouted himself hoarse until a sleepy guard could be persuaded to call the officer of the watch, who knew the password. A further sprint from the gates to the royal palace and an angry exchange of words with a very young officer of the Cerethi —and then at last Ethai himself, commander of the bodyguards, appeared.

"Let the man in," he ordered. "Bring torches. I must see who it is."

"I am Huzal," gasped the spy. "I must see the king at once."

Ethai shook his head. "The king is asleep," he said indignantly. "Your news will have to wait till—"

"My news cannot wait one moment if you value the king's life, Ethai."

"What are you saying, man? Are you sick?"

"Not sick," Huzal managed to get out. "Only an arrow—in the left shoulder. Quick, Ethai, I implore you, don't waste time, man . . ."

The commander of the bodyguards shrugged his shoulders. "I'll have the king awakened," he yielded sullenly. "But your news had better be worthwhile or you'll wish you'd never been born."

"If you don't wake the king at once, we'll all wish we'd never been born," gasped Huzal. Now at last Ethai began to realize that the matter was urgent. "You'd better come along with me," he decided, and led the way.

A few minutes later David, rubbing the sleep out of his eyes, received them. "Where do you come from?"

"From Hebron, lord."

"By the living God! Has anything happened to my son Absalom?"

"He has allowed himself to be proclaimed king," Huzal blurted out.

"Have you lost your mind?" David stormed. "Or are you lying?"

"Lord, have I ever told you an untruth? It must be a well-planned plot. More than ten thousand armed men have cheered him, as well as all the people in Hebron. And just as I rode away, more detachments were arriving. Lord, all Judah has risen in revolt, and I heard the rebels say they expected troops from Israel, too."

Then it was as if the years suddenly fell from David like a cloak. He stood there, legs spread wide, hands clenched on his hips. "Huzal! You saw and heard that yourself?"

"By my life and by your life, lord, yes. And I heard them shout: 'Absalom is king! King Absalom reigns in Hebron!' And the prince—"

David stamped his foot. "Go on!"

"The prince cried, 'The whole country is behind me! My father has become a spineless old man. In two hours we set out—for Jerusalem, my capital.'" Huzal caught his breath. "I rode as fast as I could, but twice had to go a roundabout way or I would have been stopped by the outposts." The spy swayed.

"See to his wound," ordered the king. "Bring my weapons, my armor." Two frightened servants ran out. "Give the alarm signal. All available troops are to assemble before the palace. Not in the forecourt, Ethai! Wake the women and the young princes. In half an hour they must be ready to leave. No one is to take more than he can carry himself in case of need."

"What are you going to do, lord?" wailed an old servant.

"We must flee, Simeon," replied the king grimly.

From outside came the shrill notes of the alarm signal. The servants brought the armor and the weapons. "No greaves," the king ordered. "We have a long march before us. Fasten my buckler tighter."

Joab came in. "Lord, is what they are saying outside true?" he cried. The king nodded.

"By the living God," swore Joab. "May lightning strike me if I don't make the rebels pay for this!"

Abisai, already fully armed, rushed into the room. "I've got the first four hundred men together!" he reported breathlessly. "If it please the king: I'll be more useful outside than here. I must have the walls manned."

"No," said the king sharply. "We leave the city with all the troops."

"Are you going to flee before this boy?" Abisai shouted.

"Quiet, brother," Joab warned. "The king is no fool—like you. Are we to let ourselves be shut up here?"

"Remember Ceila," David admonished. "We must have freedom of movement."

Ethai appeared and reported: "The young princes and the women are making ready, lord."

"Ten concubines stay here to guard the palace," the king ordered ironically. "Let them decide among themselves which ones. All the others to the forecourt. No litters and no asses. We must keep together."

"It's like old times again," said Joab with a grim smile. "And King Saul was a more dangerous adversary than your young shaver . . ."

The forecourt was filled with excited, wailing, weeping people. Loud orders came from the street. Every now and then the alarm signal sounded again.

As the king, accompanied by Joab and a dozen younger officers, clattered down the main staircase, Abisai came running up to them. "The household troops are all here, lord, six hundred men."

"Out of the city," ordered the king. "And over the Cedron brook." When they came to the city gate, he halted and let the troops march past him. Meanwhile word that the king was leaving the city had spread; hundreds and hundreds of angry, frightened people crowded around him. "Lord, do not leave us!" they wailed. "Do not forsake us! Protect your city."

But the king's face was stony and he had no word of comfort for the wailing throng. Then the bodyguards marched past, the Cerethi and Phelethi from Gath. He beckoned to Ethai. "Do you really want to come with us?" he asked earnestly. "You and your men are foreigners and not long in the land. Return to your homeland and may all be well with you!"

Ethai pulled himself up to his full height. "As true as God lives and as true as my lord and king lives, we hold to you in life and in death."

David gave him his hand. "You teach me that there is still loyalty," he said quietly. "I thank you."

"Six hundred fighters more," thought Joab contentedly. "Two thousand two hundred men, all in all," he said half to himself. The king nodded.

"It isn't much," said Abisai, "but better than nothing."

The king made no comment. As the last rows of the body-guards and their supply columns marched past, he swung into line behind them with his retinue and passed through the gate. Behind him the lamentations of a city without its king gradually died away.

Shortly afterward the troops crossed the Cedron brook. The water was not deep. Joab and Abisai wanted to carry the king, but he waved them indignantly aside and trudged over like all the others. Through thick olive groves the road led up the slope of Mt. Olivet. The path was steep and stony and many stumbled in the dark. When the stars grew dim in the first pale light of dawn, Joab and Abisai saw that the king had drawn his cloak over his head. His back was bent and his shoulders shook. So far he had been calm and composed and had given his orders clearly and energetically. Now the inevitable reaction had set in.

"Absalom," thought Joab and his heart was filled with hatred. "May he die ten deaths!"

A messenger came stumbling up the heights. "The king," he gasped. "Where is the king?"

Joab gripped his shoulder with an iron hand. "Your report."

"Lord, troops are marching on the city. They are marching through the Valley of Hainnam, many thousands of them."

Joab and Abisai exchanged quick glances. "So he really did set out at night!" cried Abisai. "We got away just in time."

"What else?" asked Joab.

"The priests are coming behind us," the man said, "and they bring the holy Ark of the Covenant."

At that the king stopped and turned around. "Abiathar?" he asked. "And Sadoc?"

"Yes, lord," came a deep voice. "We are here."

It was the first joy since Ethai's declaration of loyalty. The Holy of Holies came with him; it had not fallen into the rebel's hands. But the next moment a second thought brought him up short. He waited until the priests had come up to him, Abiathar and Sadoc and their two sons, Jonathan and Achimaas. Then he held up his hand. "Put down the Ark," he commanded. "Listen to me. Do not follow me any farther. Turn and go back to the city. If I shall find grace in the sight of the Lord, He will bring me back again. But if not, then I submit to His holy will." Then taking Sadoc aside he repeated softly: "Go back. You are more useful to me in Jerusalem than here. I shall lie hid in the plains until I have word from you concerning matters in the city."

Sadoc nodded. "I understand, lord. But it will not be easy. Your enemy has secured the services of a man who thinks of everything—"

"Who is that?" asked the king, suddenly alert.

"A young priest approached us just as we were leaving the city," said Sadoc. "He came from Hebron. There he saw both men on whose help your son depends: General Amasa—"

"A good soldier but not a keen mind."

"And Achitophel."

The king bit his lip. "Are you certain?" he asked hoarsely. "Can you trust your informant?"

"I would stand surety for him," replied Sadoc sadly.

David put his hand to his forehead. Achitophel, his wisest councilor, on whom he had heaped honors! "All right," he said in a dull voice. If the son rose against the father, why not the friend against the friend? And Absalom had been his favorite, his joy, his pride, handsomer and more charming than all the others, the only one who had any resemblance to Jonathan, King Saul's son. But how could a faithless man look like the most faithful of the faithful?

"Go back, Sadoc, and see to it that you send me word soon—

in spite of Amasa and Achitophel." Sadoc kissed the king's hand and left.

David watched the priests take up the Ark of the Covenant again and begin to carry it slowly downhill. Then he pressed on. Never before had he felt so deserted—not even when he had been forced to flee from Gibeah, or when King Saul's enmity had driven him to the Philistines; not even when the news of Jonathan's death had reached him. Nathan's terrible prophecies were being fulfilled to the letter. And in the midst of his tribulation, the first lines of a new song began to form in the king's mind: "Why, O Lord, are they multiplied that afflict me? Many are they who rise up against me." But this was not the moment to give way to such a mood. He must act. He was still the king. And He whom the prophet Samuel had once called his only friend still lived. And David prayed: "Infatuate, O Lord, I beseech thee, the counsel of Achitophel!"

Then he saw on top of Mt. Olivet a shadowy outline. A man was standing there, an old man, and he was alone. A dozen steps more and David recognized him. It was Chusai. He had rent his clothes and strewn ashes on his head. "Lord," he said, "grant that your oldest friend go with you, no matter where you go."

The king embraced him. "Chusai has grown old and frail," he thought. "It must have exhausted him to come this far." "Yes, you are my oldest friend," he said, deeply touched, "but I cannot take you with me now. We must go into the desert as we did before when King Saul's wrath pursued me. You are not strong enough for such hardships." But even as he spoke the thought came to him that Chusai was the Lord's answer to his prayer. "You can do more for me, and better," he insisted. "Go back into the city and throw yourself at Absalom's feet. Offer your services to him. Tell him that you were his father's servant, now you will be the servant of his son. Then perhaps you can defeat Achitophel's councils."

"I *thought* that dog had gone over to the other side," cried Chusai, outraged. "Lord, it will be a pleasure to me to ruin his plans. For years I have longed for an opportunity—not just this sort, to be sure," he added quickly.

"Now listen to me," the king urged. "I sent Sadoc, Abiathar, and their sons back to the city with the Ark of the Covenant. Like you, they have remained loyal to me. You can always send word to me through them."

Chusai nodded, his face alight. "That is the King David I know! You have thought of everything, lord. I shall get to work at once. You are right: That is more in my line than climbing mountains and marching through the desert. I thank you and I shall not disappoint you." He placed both hands on his breast, laughed happily, turned, and began to limp downhill at a surprisingly swift pace.

He reached the city just as the vanguard of Absalom's army marched, unopposed, through the south gate.

The king's forces moved farther to the north away from the center of the rebellion. From time to time small groups of faithful adherents joined him, twenty or thirty, often only four or five. "Every sword counts," Joab declared. Huzal and other spies requisitioned a number of asses and rode ahead to look for more reinforcements. It was dangerous work, but they were used to it.

When they came to the ford over the Jordan, the royal troops made their first halt. Not only the king but even the soldiers needed a rest. Only Joab, Abisai, and a small number of their best men continued to work, rounding up all able-bodied men in the neighborhood and having the herds driven together to provide food for the little army in case they were obliged to go farther into the desert—a move that was inevitable if, as was to be expected, Absalom's powerful army set out at once in pursuit of the king. To be sure, in that case even those doubtful measures could scarcely save them. General Amasa had enough desert-trained troops at his command to challenge and destroy the king's little band.

"If they come in the next two days, we are lost," said Abisai quietly as he and Joab finally lay down to sleep for a few hours.

Joab shrugged. "Well, you die only once," he replied laconically. "But it would be a pity. I'd give a good deal for a chance to get at Absalom."

Abisai grinned. "You've never been able to stand being tricked. And that he did to perfection."

Joab's strong fingers played with his spear. "To think I did my best to bring him back from Gessur!" he said angrily. "But who knows—perhaps I'll be able to even the score, after all."

Abisai laughed. "I don't think he'll do us the favor of waiting before he comes after us, Brother."

"Perhaps he'll want to celebrate a victory," said Joab.

"Perhaps. But there's one man who won't consent to that."

"I know whom you mean—that accursed dog who always thinks out everything beforehand, Achitophel!"

"Long live the king!" shouted Chusai as he flung himself down at Absalom's feet. "Victory and triumph to the king!"

The young prince lolled back on the richly gilded throne in the banquet hall. "So you too, Chusai," he said with supercilious scorn. "Is that your loyalty to your old friend, my respected father? Why didn't you go with him?"

"My learned colleague Chusai prefers to sleep in a good bed rather than be plagued by sand fleas in the desert," said Achitophel disdainfully, and Absalom roared with laughter.

Chusai shook his head. "You are the chosen of Judah and Israel," he declared. "All the people are on your side—and so am I! And are you not the king's eldest son? I have served him faithfully. Now I shall serve you faithfully."

"Send the old chatterbox away, lord," cried Achitophel.

But Absalom knew that next to Achitophel Chusai had been the cleverest man in his father's Crown Council. It was not good for a ruler to put himself completely in the hands of one of his servants. The old man here could, under certain circumstances, be very useful to him. "I have my father's country behind me," he said. "I have seized his capital. The treasury and the Ark of the Covenant are in my hands. Now I shall take over the Crown Council. You, Achitophel, remain its chairman, the first man in the state after me. Chusai, too, remains a member of the Crown Council as before."

"The king is gracious and great," cried Chusai enthusiastically. "No wonder he has won the victory!"

"My first advice after the victory," Achitophel said in a resounding voice, and immediately he was the center of attention again. "The people must be made to recognize that the king has taken over all of his predecessor's rights. Therefore go to the women your father has left behind and take possession of them. Then everyone will know that there can never be a reconciliation between you and your father. That will encourage your followers, and no one will dare to side with the former king."

"Good advice," praised Absalom. "Let a tent be set up on the palace roof and the women brought there. I will go to them before the eyes of all."

Achitophel flung Chusai a triumphant glance. The old man smiled. "The king has no cleverer adviser than Achitophel."

"And here is my second piece of advice," Achitophel continued. "Let me choose twelve thousand men and set out immediately with them in pursuit of your predecessor."

Chusai had difficulty in concealing his alarm.

"He has at the most two thousand men with him," Achitophel went on. "We will overtake them in their flight and slaughter them. The former king will then fall into our hands, and as soon as I have him, any further resistance will cease. My lord and king—" he bowed low before Absalom—"my lord and king will realize that our original plan regarding his predecessor must now be revised. It is clear that through one traitor or another he was warned of our march on Jerusalem so that he could flee and escape us in time. Under these circumstances it is impossible to spare him any longer. Only his death can prevent him from becoming a center of unrest and a constant threat to the rule of my lord and king. As soon as his fate is settled, I shall easily win over the rest of the army for you and lead them to you. And then peace will reign throughout the whole land."

The dignitaries present dutifully applauded the speech. Only General Amasa and Chusai refrained—a point Absalom did not miss. "Amasa," he asked, "have you anything against this plan?"

The general stroked his well-kept white beard. "I did not know that the chairman of the Crown Council was also a military strategist," he said sarcastically. "And that is what he must be if he is to lead an army of twelve thousand men. But if my lord and king is satisfied, I have nothing to add."

"I'm afraid I have not made myself clear," said Achitophel quickly. "Of course I would never dare to lead these troops myself. It would be sheer folly when a commander of Amasa's stature is at hand. But I should like to accompany the troops—as the political representative of my lord and king."

Amasa nodded, only half appeased. But Chusai shook his head in concern and Absalom asked: "You apparently do not agree with that even now, Chusai. What is your opinion?"

The old man looked deeply worried. "Lord, a moment ago I called Achitophel the king's cleverest adviser, and that he is, too. But this time his advice is not good."

Achitophel was angry. "It is not only good, it is vitally important! Pay no attention to this man, lord!"

Now Absalom had never allowed anyone to dictate to him. "I wish to hear what he has to say," he said sharply. "Speak, Chusai."

"Lord," began the old man. "No one here has known your father so long and so well as I. There are people who think that in his old age he has become weak and irresolute. Nothing could be farther from the truth. And this I can prove to you. He did not wait for you to march on Jerusalem, either to defend himself here or to surrender. He anticipated you and slipped out. That means he is active and valiant. He took all his household troops with him. That means he has an army which, though small, is blindly devoted to him. And this army is under the supreme command of General Joab, who, as all Israel knows, is a first-rate leader who has never lost a battle. And you can imagine, lord, in what mood your father must be after all he has suffered in the last hours. I know what effect sudden danger has on him. I have seen it often enough. He becomes more courageous and bolder than ever, and each of his men becomes as bitter as a bear when her whelps are taken from her. Do not think, I beg of you, that you will have an easy time with him! It is true, you far outnumber him. But that was the case with King Saul—who could never lay hands on him. And why not? Because King David knows desert fighting better than any man alive. He has certainly hidden away in some cave or a ravine by this time and he could not help seeing an army of twelve thousand men. He will simply let them go by and then make a swift attack on the rear guard, or even only on stragglers. And what then? Then the rumor spreads that he has won, as he always did in the past. Perhaps you will have lost only two hundred men, but rumor immediately makes it thousands. The people remember the great heroes of the past; they begin to be afraid, they will desert you. And you, who have now practically won the victory, find yourself confronted with a bloody civil war, the outcome of which no one can foresee. No, lord, I have better advice for you!" Chusai paused. With deep relief he saw that his long speech had not failed to have an effect. The heads of tribes, the high officials, the commanders, all sat there looking perplexed and embarrassed.

Achitophel started to rise and speak, but Absalom waved him aside and he sat down again and stared straight before him, grim and scowling.

"What is your advice?" asked Absalom in a husky voice.

"Call out all Israel," cried Chusai. "The whole land from Dan to Beersheba. Gather together an army like the sands of the sea, that cannot be counted. And ride at the head of your troops *yourself*. Then when we find King David, we fall on him as dew falls on the earth, and of him and his men no one will remain alive. And if he should retreat to a fortress, then all Israel will place ropes on the walls, and we shall drag them down into the valley and leave no stone standing. Thus and thus only can we be sure that all danger is eliminated once and for all. That is my advice!"

"And it is good," declared Absalom.

"It is better than Achitophel's advice," Amasa agreed, delighted to be able to show that man who was always so superior that for once he was not indispensable. And immediately all those present voiced their approval.

Absalom stood up: "Amasa, order up all of Israel's reserves from Dan to Beersheeba!"

Achitophel gave Chusai a long, piercing look. But Chusai smiled goodnaturedly. "We are both old servants of the king," he said in a friendly tone. "This time it is my turn to be useful to him."

Achitophel nodded. "The question is *which* king you mean," he said very softly. His face was ashen.

"He has seen through me," thought Chusai, "but he can't prove it and neither can he refute my arguments. That means, he knows the game is up." And with reluctant pity he thought: "Too bad about the man!"

Achitophel, who was still looking at him, read him like a book. "I'm sorry I underestimated you, Chusai," he said softly. Then he turned away, bowed low before Absalom, and with his head high strode stiffly from the room. In the palace forecourt he ordered an ass saddled and he rode out of the city, alone. He rode to Gilon, the estate King David had given him. But long before he reached it he knew what he had to do. Chusai's victory in the council meant that the king now had plenty of time to take countermeasures. Joab and Abisai would get to work; probably their agents were already on the way to winning back the tribes in the north. If the king had only half—no, only a third of Absalom's forces, he would defeat Amasa, and with that, Absalom's fate would be sealed. "The king will let Absalom live," he thought coldly, "but certainly not me." It had been folly to believe that he could rule Israel through Absalom. And what shame to be defeated by Chusai!

Achitophel urged his animal on. When he arrived at his country estate he sat down and wrote his last will and testament, carefully and clearly. Then he hanged himself.

18

No one saw chusai go to the Ark of the Covenant to pray in the holy tent, and likewise to inform Sadoc of the result of the Council meeting. Sadoc and Abiathar had posted their sons at the Rogel fountain, south of the city of Jerusalem, where the Cedron brook flows into the Valley of Hainnam, and they sent an elderly maidservant there with a loaf of bread in which a letter was concealed. When the two young priests had read the letter, they set out immediately on their way north. In the village of Bahurim someone recognized them, informed a patrol of Absalom's men, and the two priests were obliged to hide in a well and wait until their pursuers had given up the search. Then they hurried on.

In this way, on the following day, David heard the comforting news that no attack was imminent. The old lion sighed with relief. He led his troops across the Jordan and moved farther to the northwest, to Mahanaim, where he set about organizing the resistance against the usurper. From all directions men streamed to his aid. Even the Ammonites, the kings of Rabbath-Ammon and Lodabar sent armed contingents, but especially beds, tapestries, earthen vessels, and the necessary provisions. By day Joab and Abisai worked tirelessly training the new royal army, and at night they drew up plans of battle. In this respect the neighborhood of Mahanaim offered great advantages. For not far from the city stood the dense forest of Ephraim.

"Woods!" cried the king with almost painful joy, "our dear old allies!" Again his troops practiced crawling and the various stratagems which he had taught his first victorious soldiers: swift attacks from the rear, nests of archers perched high in the branches of cork oaks, pits covered with brushwood and moss.

As soon as he heard that Absalom's army had set out for the north, the king kept their march constantly under the observation of his spies. But not until they had approached within a few miles did he order his troops to occupy their posts in the woods. He divided his force—even now only a little more than nine thousand men—into three groups under the generals, Joab, Abisai, and Ethai. "I myself will stand with Ethai's army group," he declared. But all three commanders urged him not to go into battle himself.

"You dare not expose yourself to this sort of war, lord," declared Joab frankly. "You are not young enough for it any more. Besides, if they kill me or Abisai or Ethai here, it doesn't matter. The others will go on fighting. But if you fall, the war is lost. You are worth more than ten thousand men. Stay here in Mahanaim. If we have to flee, you can come to our aid."

Though he protested at great length, the king finally gave in. He took up his position at the city gate and let the troops march past him. And as each commander came abreast he impressed on him: "No matter what happens, save the life of my son Absalom!" And he spoke in a very loud voice so that even the soldiers heard.

From the city's sacrificial mound David watched the long, long columns of the enemy draw near. Joab's weak forces swarmed out of the edge of the woods, rained a hail of arrows on them, and then quickly drew back into the green labyrinth. Now it depended upon which tactic Amasa would use. His army was so large that he could allow himself to encircle the whole woods and push forward toward the center. But either he was too impulsive or he hesitated to stretch his lines too far, for very soon it was evident that he had ordered the attack on the shorter front.

With anguish David saw that there seemed to be no end to the enemy's army. Absalom must have raised more than thirty thousand men—to be sure, not the entire army reserve of Israel and Judah, but nevertheless a tremendous force, three times greater than the king's army. The forest of Ephraim sucked them in. In there, under that innocent, peaceful, green shade, the fate of the whole land was being decided. There the flower of its youth was fighting, Israel against Israel, Judah against Judah, a ten-thousandfold fratricide. And the one who had brought this about was the king's favorite son.

David wept. It was impossible, it was unbelievable that Absalom himself, the most lovable of all his sons and the only one who reminded him of Jonathan the incomparable, that noblest of men, could have engineered this revolt himself. Someone had obviously tempted him, misled him, and it could only be one man—Achitophel. David vowed that Achitophel should die.

The forest of Ephraim swallowed one enemy column after the other; an ant hill swayed back and forth in there under the green treetops, or two ant hills trying to destroy each other. It was monstrous. God's people were tearing one another to pieces.

Once, in a brief moment of weakness, David had thought seriously of negotiating with Absalom, of abdicating the throne in his favor and withdrawing from all state affairs. But with the next breath he put aside the thought in horror. The crown was not his possession to dispose of as he pleased. The Lord Himself had entrusted it to him. Three times he had been anointed king, once in Bethlehem and twice in Hebron. He dared not surrender. He must defend the crown. He was the king—and that meant he was responsible to the Lord for the fate of his people. On him the Lord had conveyed this office and as long as his strength held out he dared not lay it down, especially not in favor of an inexperienced and faithless young man who had risen up in arms against his king and father. What was now happening in the forest of Ephraim was necessary. If only they spared the foolish young man whom Achitophel, and others too, probably, had goaded into this crime.

Amasa's last column disappeared into the woods. How peaceful it looked now, how untouched! The king clenched his teeth. "Wait," he thought. "All I can do is what old men do . . . wait . . . until the Lord makes known His decision."

Amasa was too young to have taken part in David's earlier campaigns. He expected, of course, that the woods would hold many traps, but he could not imagine that mere traps could check his mighty army. He believed in mass attacks. When the first hundred of his men disappeared in the gigantic pits Joab's men had so carefully dug, he commanded: "Onward! Crush all resistance!" Then he ordered the rear guard to make ladders of tree branches and pull out the men who lay in the pits. But there were many sharp stakes in the bottom of the pits and few of the men were still alive. Moreover the rear guard was so heavily attacked by Abisai's troops that they had difficulty in defending themselves and no time to bother about the men they had been sent to rescue.

Amasa himself, with his staff and ten thousand of his best soldiers, pursued Joab's fleeing troops, and Absalom, on a white mule, rode beside his general. But arrows shot from the tops of trees almost decimated the ranks, and so thick were the woods that Amasa lost all control over his men half an hour after the battle began. Not only were there archers in the tops of the trees, but also spies whose duty it was to watch the passage of the enemy columns and signal their direction and number to Joab's secret post. They waved a red cloth once for every hundred men they saw, and Joab immediately took countermeasures. So it happened that Amasa attacked again and again, but always in empty space! For more than two hours he pushed forward, first in this direction, then in that, but he never caught sight of the enemy and meanwhile he kept losing men in pits or from arrows. His rear guard—two thousand strong—was cut off, and it came within range of Ethai, who attacked vigorously with his entire force and wiped out every single man.

"These woods are murderous!" Amasa cried when he learned that his rear guard no longer existed. "We've got to get out. Then we'll set fire to them and smoke the enemy out of their damned hiding places."

But that was more easily said than done. Amasa did not know the region, and both leaders who had accompanied him and his columns had fallen victims to the archers at the very start. The woods were dense and big enough for men to get thoroughly lost in them. Four picked soldiers protected Prince Absalom and four protected Amasa. Within three hours they had had to be replaced five times, and Amasa was bleeding from a glancing blow on the cheek.

Absalom found the battle little to his liking. "By my life!" he exclaimed angrily, "if you can't lead us out of this woods soon, we shall all perish in it. This is not war—it's assassination by the thousands." He had scarcely spoken when a long arrow struck the mule he was riding. Though the thick saddlecloth softened the impact of the blow, the frightened animal arched its back, reared, knocked down two soldiers, and bolted.

"After him!" shouted Amasa. "Catch that mule! Save the king!"

About twenty men dashed after the fleeing animal, but they were on foot, for the asses and mules had long since disappeared. Amasa's next impulse was to ride after the prince himself, but that would have left his army without a leader, and he had to save what still could be saved. A few minutes later another column came up, several thousand men, and he sighed with relief: "Do you know the quickest way out of this wood?" he asked the commander.

"No idea," gasped the officer. "But I myself . . . will . . . never . . . get out." He crashed to the ground; then Amasa saw the arrow sticking out of the man's back.

Furious, Amasa pointed in the opposite direction. "Go on—in there," he commanded. "These trees have to end sometime." Half an hour later he came to an opening. There on the edge of the woods he saw before him the closely packed shields of Abisai's men. He roared out commands, putting his men on the defensive, but no sooner had they obeyed his order than behind him other enemy shields and spears appeared. He recognized the weapons

of the royal bodyguards. With the courage of despair Amasa
raised his sword and gave the signal to attack.

The white mule bolted headlong through bushes and under-
brush. In vain Absalom tried to control the animal, but it had
gone wild with pain and terror. Several times the prince cried out
as thorns tore his arms and legs, and again and again he had to
lower his head when the mule tore under low-hanging branches.
He would have let himself fall to the ground, but he did not
dare. "I would break my neck," he thought. "Why doesn't someone come to my aid? Where are they all?"

Again he bent to avoid a gigantic bough, straightened up, and
saw too late a second bough before him. A terrible jerk, a sharp
pain, and everything went black before his eyes.

It was the pain that brought him back to consciousness, a piercing, unbearable pain in his breast, in his left shoulder, and in
both arms. But the worst was a sinister feeling of insecurity, of
being detached. Wildly he looked around him. He was hanging
in the branches af a gigantic tree. Both his arms were tightly
caught and the slightest attempt to move caused agony. One
bough lay across his chest, cutting off his breath. "Help!" he cried
weakly. "Help! Help!"

From far, far away came the clash of weapons and battle cries;
it all sounded unreal, as though it had nothing to do with him.
He hung between heaven and earth and was not part of either.
"Help!"

The bushes rustled and a soldier stepped out, a stocky little
man with a scrubby beard. The man stared at Absalom, turned
around, and disappeared.

Joab had led the pursuit of a strong division of rebels who
were now fleeing to the west, which was exactly what he had
wanted them to do. Abisai's messengers had reported that he
and Ethai had slaughtered Amasa's column. Amasa himself, with
his staff, had escaped to the north. The entire enemy army was
scattered. It was good, clean work. "Keep on their heels," Joab
ordered. "Don't let them make a stand."

Someone tugged at his sleeve—an ordinary soldier, a Cushite from the Arabian desert. Had the fellow lost his mind?

"What do you want?" Joab roared at him.

"Lord, I have seen the prince," the man managed to stammer.

"What? Prince Absalom? Where?"

"Not a thousand paces from here, lord. He is hanging in a tree."

"He—is hanging?"

"He's caught in it," stammered the soldier. "His mule is grazing nearby. Perhaps it threw him off."

"Is he still alive?"

"Yes, lord, I saw his eyes move."

"And you didn't run your spear through his belly?" thundered Joab. "You fool! I would have given you ten pieces of silver and a belt."

The man shook his head in fear. "No, lord—not even if you paid me a thousand pieces of silver would I lay a hand on the king's son. I was there when the king commanded you and Abisai and Ethai to spare him. If I had killed him, the king would never have forgiven me. And would you have protected me from his anger?"

Joab stared at the man's face, which was distorted with fear. "You shall see what I myself do with him," he roared. "Here, armorbearer! Ten of you follow me! Lead us, man. You've probably got courage enough for that. Hurry!"

A few minutes later they stood before the tree in which Absalom was hanging.

"Truly, it is he!" Joab cried triumphantly. He raised his spear and plunged it through Absalom's heart. Then he pulled two more spears out of the nearest armorbearers' hands and thrust a second and a third time. The prince's body jerked convulsively, and his eyes bulged. "Tear him down from the tree," roared Joab, "and strike him, each of you! So shall he die ten times!" The men obeyed. Joab grabbed the trumpet from one of the men's girdles, put it to his lips, and blew with all his might the signal to assemble.

"The war is over," he said to the soldiers. "There's no use fight-

238

ing any more." He flung a last hate-filled look at Absalom's body. "Over there is one of our pits," he said. "Fling him into it and pile stones on him, as many stones as you can find!"

Troops now came from all sides. An hour later Joab knew that no more than half of the rebels had escaped. He sent a messenger and Absalom's white cloak to Amasa. "Tell him the prince is dead. There is only one king in Israel."

Achimaas, the son of the priest Sadoc, had asked permission to take the message of victory to the king. Joab gave the young man a wry look. Then he said dryly: "Your message will not be an unmitigated joy to the king. Prince Absalom is dead." He beckoned to the Cushite who had first found the prince. "You shall have the honor of telling the king what you saw."

The man looked at him uncertainly and stood first on one foot then the other.

"Run, man, run!" Joab shouted at him. "You don't keep a king waiting."

The man ran.

"You have not chosen a very worthy messenger," said Achimaas indignantly. "I shall run to the king, too."

"You fool," growled Joab. "Don't think it will get you any reward."

"That makes no difference to me."

Shrugging his shoulders, Joab turned away. "Do what you have to do," he said sullenly, and Achimaas ran. He was a swift runner and in a few moments he had overtaken the Cushite. The latter let him get ahead. He had a feeling that the honor Joab had reserved for him would not prove to be altogether to his advantage.

The king had let them put a chair for him between the two gates of the city, so that each of the officers he had posted above on the watchtower would be within call. Many hours he had sat there and waited; his attendants had tried again and again to persuade him to move into the shade of the little house that served in Mahanaim as the royal palace, but he would not leave. At last the call for which he had waited came.

"A messenger comes, lord. He is running very fast."

"Only one?" the king exclaimed joyfully. "Then he brings good news."

"He is not the only one, lord," called the officer on guard. "I see a second messenger now."

"He brings good news too," said the king. "If the battle were going badly, there would be hundreds of fugitives."

After a while the man on the tower called: "The one in front looks like Achimaas, the son of Sadoc."

The king smiled happily. "Nothing bad will ever come from him," he said.

"Victory!" cried Achimaas from afar. "Great victory!"

"Open the gate!" the king ordered. "Let him in." A moment later young Achimaas flung himself at the king's feet. "Praised be the Lord! He has destroyed the rebels who rose against my king!"

But the king asked anxiously: "How is it with my son, Absalom? Is he safe?"

Achimaas turned pale. "Lord," he stuttered, "all I saw as your servant Joab gave me this message was a great tumult. I—I—know nothing else."

The king nodded impatiently. "It is well. Stand aside; here comes the second messenger."

The Cushite had run as fast as he could. He did not mind letting Achimaas get there before him—let him put his foot in it if he wanted to—but the space between them must not be so great that he himself would not get the messenger's fee—if there really was to be one. He, too, flung himself down and touched his forehead to the ground. "I bring good news," he cried. "The Lord has given you victory over your enemies."

"Have you seen my son, Absalom?" asked the king.

The Cushite began to tremble and raised both hands. "Let all the enemies of my lord, the king, be as the young man is," he stammered in fear.

The king leaped up. "Does that mean that he . . . is he no longer alive?"

The Cushite dared not answer.

Then David cried aloud: "Absalom! My son Absalom!"

Around him was dead silence. He looked about him with eyes that did not see, and tears streamed down his lined face. It was as though he had aged ten years in the last moments, as though only the stiff royal robes held him upright. Achimaas and two officers rushed forward to support him. He thrust them aside as though they were enemies and tottered with short steps like an old man toward the house. "My son . . ." he wailed incessantly. "Would to God that I had died for you! Absalom, my son, my son . . ."

Two hours later the victorious army returned to Mahanaim. Instead of a reception as befitted the hour of triumph, they found an atmosphere of heavy mourning. The king did not appear. The soldiers stole into the city as though they had been ignominiously defeated. No one came to greet them. The women and girls of Mahanaim did not sing and dance in their honor, but stayed behind closed doors.

That was too much for Joab. In full armor he clattered into the house of mourning and demanded peremptorily to be taken to the king.

The servants before the royal bedchamber looked at each other in embarrassment. "The king will not see anyone," explained one, but a blow from the angry general's fist flung him against the wall, along which he slid helplessly to the ground.

"That does not mean *me*," cried Joab. "And don't you forget it, you lout!" and he strode into the room.

The man on the bed had covered his face and was weeping. With legs widespread, his muscular arms planted firmly on his hips, Joab stood before the king. "Never has such a thing happened since the world began," he said in a loud voice. "You have shamed this day the faces of all your servants that have saved your life, and not only yours, but the lives of your sons and of your daughters, and the lives of your wives and of your concubines."

The king did not move.

"You love them that hate you and hate them that love you," Joab went on in an even louder voice. "And you have shown that you care nothing for your generals and your soldiers who have presented you with the greatest of your victories. If the rebel Absalom had lived and we all had been slain, then it would have pleased you, wouldn't it? You lie there now and mourn and wail for the dead criminal who plotted against your throne and your life while he feigned love for you, and to you, those who fell today for your cause, for the holy cause of the anointed of the Lord, are not worth a thought!"

The king sat up slowly. He did not speak, but even Joab felt sudden pity at sight of his nameless grief. "Get up," he said more softly. "You must, lord, there is no other way. Put on the royal garments, go out and speak to the satisfaction of your people."

"I cannot," David groaned.

Joab's pity vanished. "I swear to you by the Lord, that if you will not, there will not tarry with you so much as one man this night," he said brutally. "Then see who will protect your throne and the life of your family."

David nodded mechanically. "I will come," he said. But when Joab would have helped him rise, he drew back from him as if he did not want to touch him.

"He doesn't know I killed Absalom," thought Joab. "But he senses it." And he knew that the king would never forgive him. In silence he left the room.

Half an hour later the king appeared in full regalia at the gate, spoke to the troops, and ordered rewards distributed.

The news of the king's victory spread like the wind. The tribes of the north immediately pledged their loyalty. The king sent the priests Sadoc and Abiathar to Hebron with the question: "Do you really wish to be the last to lead the king back to his house, you my brothers, my bone and my flesh?"

From the south came the message: "Forgive us, lord, and come back to us."

General Amasa surrendered with the rest of the rebel army. "Can you forgive me, lord?"

"You shall see how I forgive you," replied the king. "From now on you are my chief captain of the army in the place of Joab."

Joab was present. He did not move a muscle. Later Abisai raged: "It seems to be more profitable to lose a battle for the king than to win it!"

"Amasa didn't run three spears through Absalom's breast," replied Joab calmly. "Don't take it to heart, Brother. Once before there was a man the king preferred to both of us—or rather, he wanted to."

"Whom do you mean?"

"Abner. And where is he now?"

Absalom's revolt had shaken the kingdom to its foundations. The old jealousy between north and south, between Israel and Judah, flared up again. At the first great gathering of the tribes in Galgal it came to open strife. An ambitious adventurer, named Seba took advantage of the tension. "Those people in Judah have stolen our king!" he cried. "We have no part in David. Return to your dwellings, O Israel!"

His words inflamed the people of Israel and they walked out of the meeting. A second and even crueler civil war threatened. David ordered his new commander-in-chief Amasa to put down the rebellion, but Amasa proved to be slow and ponderous. The king, impatient, sent out his household troops, not under Joab— but under Abisai. Joab himself was allowed to command only a section, but even this last demotion seemed not to disturb him. A few days later Amasa was finally ready, and the two royal armies met and joined forces at Mt. Gabaon.

Joab went up to Amasa. "Are you feeling well, my dear brother?" he asked in a friendly tone—and thrust his dagger so deep into the unsuspecting man's body that his intestines spilled out. It was exactly the same stroke that had ended Absalom's life. Amasa died within a few minutes.

Joab's men, each of whom would have gone through fire for the grim old soldier, shouted: "Here to us, whoever is for Joab and the king!" And Amasa's army went over as one man to Joab. On his own authority Joab took over the supreme command and pursued Seba, who fled to Abela; he surrounded the city, had Seba murdered, and returned to Jerusalem, the victor once again.

And now, too, as after the death of Absalom, David did not venture to punish the guilty man. That could easily have led to a third civil war and would have meant the end of the kingdom.

"Joab was Absalom's friend before he killed him," Bathsheba said thoughtfully. "Now he will curry favor with Adonais."

The king gave the clever woman a long look. "Adonais is not of the caliber to rule," he said slowly. "He would be a second Amnon. My son Solomon shall succeed me."

Bathsheba's still beautiful face glowed with joy.

"Lord, lord . . . is that your firm will?"

"I swear it by the name of the Lord," said the king, and Bathsheba, radiant with happiness, bowed down at his feet.

19

Peace reigned in the kingdom many long years. Chusai, Achitophel's successor as chairman of the Crown Council and the king's first councilor, had reorganized the administration and long before his death had recommended to the king men to hold the highest posts. After Ethai, the commander of the bodyguards was Banaias, a man of Herculean build, of whom it was said that he could cut off the head of an ox with one stroke of his sword. The recorder Josaphat, the scribe Siva, and minister of labor Aduram, a gifted organizer, were trustworthy and incorruptible servants. The priesthood was still in the hands of Sadoc and Abiathar. And the commander-in-chief was still Joab, whose energy seemed to be inexhaustible. The people were contented, although they saw their king less and less frequently, the recorder now replacing him as administrator of justice. Receptions and audiences at the palace were given only at rare intervals, and finally they ceased altogether.

The people shouted and cheered as Prince Adonias drove through the fruit market in his magnificent chariot. The prince, a handsome young man, standing erect and dignified beside the charioteer, was a dashing figure in his mantle of Phoenician purple as he flung pieces of silver to the crowd. The two white mules that drew the chariot had silver reins and purple caparisons, and a bodyguard of fifty men ran before, behind, and beside the chariot.

"A generous young lord," remarked a man who had managed to pick up three silver pieces and had quickly put his right foot on a fourth. "He will be a good king one day."

"He won't have to wait much longer for that," said Ishac, the weaver. "King David . . ." he shrugged expressively.

"I've heard, too, that the king is dying," murmured another man. "Those people in the palace are probably keeping it secret so the sons don't get to quarreling."

"Why should they?" cried Ishac excitedly. "Prince Amnon is dead, Prince Absalom is dead—so, then, Prince Adonias is next in line."

"Maybe so and maybe not," said Baruch, the fruit merchant. "I heard that the king has named Prince Solomon as heir to the throne."

"Impossible!" Ishac protested.

"Quite possible," contradicted Baruch. "According to the law the king may choose anyone he wishes as his heir."

"Who knows—perhaps the king is already dead."

Baruch shook his head. "If the king were dead, there would have been an anointing. No, no, he is still alive. But he is old and weak and ill. He's over seventy anyway—"

"Of course the king is still alive!" cried an old woman in exasperation.

"How do you know that, mother?" Ishac jeered.

"I know it because my brother is a servant in the palace," said the old woman proudly. "Only yesterday he was at my house and he told me the king has written a new song, so beautiful that everyone will weep when he hears it."

"Yes, that he can do better than anyone else," nodded Baruch. "My little Joel knows many of his songs by heart. How does he do that—the king, I mean?"

"The Lord Himself has given him the gift," said Ishac.

"It's true," said the old woman. "And the Lord always tells him when he must write a new song."

This was a surprise to all. "How is that? What do you mean?"

"The king's little harp hangs above his bed," said the old woman. "It is the same harp he played when he tended his father's sheep and it has gone with him everywhere, in his exile and on all his campaigns. When the Lord wishes the king to write a song again, He sends a breeze through the window and that makes the old harp tinkle miraculously—and at once the king takes it from the wall and begins to compose the song that later on your little Joel learns by heart."

"Do you really believe that?" asked Baruch, scratching his head.

"Yes, of course. Everyone in the palace knows about it."

Meanwhile Prince Adonias was driving toward the city gate. The charioteer raised the trumpet to his lips and blew a fanfare, whereupon the officer of the guard hastily ordered the gate opened and the prince and his retinue dashed through. "Close the gate!" commanded the officer, wiping the perspiration from his forehead. The prince could be very unpleasant if he even had to slow down, and the gate had opened just in time.

The magnificent chariot drove towards the Rogel fountain. Not far from the fountain lay a sacrificial mound which the people called the stone of Zoheleth. There Abiathar the priest waited, and with him a select company of the great of the land. In a long, solemn ceremony, oxen, fatted calves, and sheep were sacrificed to the Lord. Then those preesnt withdrew to a large tent that had been pitched nearby, where they sat down to a sumptuous banquet.

No one paid any attention to the tall, gaunt man whose face was completely hidden by the mantle he had pulled over his head. They probably took him for one of the servants or for a cattle driver. He had attended the sacrifice and had then walked slowly to the entrance of the tent, where the celebration was in full swing. He stood there for almost half an hour before he walked slowly away to the Rogel fountain, where his mule was pegged. He untied the thongs, mounted, and rode back to the city. Halting in front of the royal palace, he sent for the controller of the women's quarters, to whom he whispered a few words.

The controller looked at him in amazement. "Who are you, anyway?" he asked haughtily.

The man threw back his mantle, disclosing a worn, deeply lined face with a white tuft of hair and short white beard.

Everyone in Jerusalem, even in all Judah and Israel, knew the prophet Nathan. The controller bowed low, let him in, and led him into an antechamber. A few minutes later Bathsheba entered.

The king, weak and listless, lay on his broad couch, motionless as he had lain now for many weeks. Beside him Abisag, a young girl of unusual beauty, knelt and rubbed his feet, as they were shivering with cold. This shivering and the slow rise and fall of his thin chest were the only signs that the old lion still lived. High above his bed hung a little harp, but no sound came from its strings. No breeze made its way through the narrow window into the twilight of the sickroom. A servant appeared at the entrance and beckoned to Abisag. She rose and let him give her the message, then, kneeling beside the couch again, she whispered to the sick man: "The noble Bathsheba begs to be received. It is very urgent."

The king was silent for so long that she thought he had not heard her. But just as she was about to repeat the message, he said softly: "She shall come in." Abisag nodded to the servant and immediately afterward Bathsheba entered and bowed low before the king.

"What do you want?" asked David wearily.

Bathsheba waited until Abisag had left the room. "Lord," she said, "you swore to your handmaiden in God's name that your son Solomon should be king after you. But now Adonias will be king without your knowledge. He has conspired with the other royal princes, and the priest Abiathar and your commander-in-chief Joab have joined him. Not only I, but all Israel is waiting to know your decision. I implore you, make known your intention! For otherwise we are lost, your son Solomon and I."

Then Abisag came in again. "Lord, the prophet Nathan desires to see you."

Immediately Bathsheba withdrew. After the king, the prophet Nathan was the highest authority in the land, and any other audience must be broken off when he appeared. But Nathan had told Bathsheba in advance that he would go to the king himself, and she waited in the antechamber.

Nathan, too, threw himself down before the king. "Lord, have you ordained that Adonias is to be your successor? He, the royal princes, Abiathar, Joab, and many others have offered sacrifices and are now celebrating in a great tent at the Rogel fountain. Every man present addressed the prince as 'my lord and king,' and wished him a long reign. Only the priest Sadoc, Banaias, Prince Solomon, and I were not invited. If this really is your will, why have you not sent me word?"

The king clenched his hands, the thin chest rose and fell more rapidly, and suddenly David sat upright with a strength that not even Nathan had expected.

"Bathsheba," the king exclaimed. "Bathsheba shall come in!" Nathan motioned to her and she entered the room.

"As true as the Lord liveth," said David and his voice rang clear and firm, "I have sworn to you by His holy name that your son Solomon shall be king after me. This very day I shall fulfill my oath." She fell on her knees.

"Bring Sadoc here," ordered the king. "And Banaias."

Both men were in the room within a few minutes. "Banaias," said the king, "order the household troops out at once. Sadoc! My son Solomon is to mount my own mule and ride with you, Banaias, and the bodyguards to the Gibon fountain. There you and Nathan shall anoint him king over Israel and Judah. Then let the trumpets blare their loudest and proclaim: 'God save King Solomon!' Return here and let him sit upon my throne. For he and no other shall be king in my stead."

In the huge tent at the Rogel fountain the celebration was still in full force and wine had already loosened many tongues.

"The High Priest Abiathar will now speak," announced Prince Adonias. "Quiet please, friends."

"Everyone knows," began Abiathar, "that I have been a loyal servant to King David from the earliest days and that I have always stood by him in many tribulations and dangers. And many who do not know the true facts of the case will wonder why now, in my old age, I turn from him and advocate that the heir immediately seize power and rule." He looked around him defiantly. "I do that because it is necessary," he declared. "King David is now only a shadow of his former self. He cannot lead the government much longer. Perhaps I should have gone to him and openly demanded that he give up the crown to his eldest son. But of what use is it to talk to a sick man, who is no longer capable of grasping what you say?"

"Old swindler," murmured Joab and made no effort to hide his broad grin. "You didn't dare!"

"So then I had no other course," Abiathar continued, "but to join a group of noble men to whom the future of Israel is more important than the fate of an individual, even though that man is the king. King David has done a great deal for the kingdom and the people of Israel. But it is now time for another, a younger and stronger man to seize the reins. I warn you of one thing only: There must be no bloodshed. I have made that my special condition."

"Of course, of course," growled Joab and drained his cup. "Only unfortunately he doesn't tell us how we are going to manage that." But the majority of the men present agreed—more out of politeness than conviction, as Joab thought he could detect.

"It is to be hoped that all goes well," said Prince Adonias. "Nevertheless we may possibly have trouble with Banaias. Too bad we couldn't win him over, but he is suddenly quite impervious to anything new, and therefore we could not even try. The same goes for friend Abiathar's priestly colleague Sadoc, and of course also for one of my younger brothers—he is not present, I see." The gathering laughed politely. "But I fear he would not have been allowed to come even if I had invited him," the prince went on sarcastically. "His mother is said to be very strict with him." More laughter. But Joab did not join them.

"It is not advisable to mention young Prince Solomon too lightly," Joab warned. "He has kept much in the background—that means he is cautious; but he has followers among the people, and the clan from which he comes has many connections. I advocate no further hesitation, or we shall have exactly what my worthy friend Abiathar is so anxious to avoid—bloodshed." With his mighty forearm he shoved plates and beakers aside. "We have eaten a lot, drunk a lot, and talked a lot," he said bluntly. "Now it is time to talk seriously about what has brought us together. We cannot afford to wait any longer. My lord and king—when will you give me the order to surround the palace with my troops? It can be done this very night."

Adonias fingered the gold chain around his neck. "Are you sure you can rely on your troops?"

Joab laughed. "They will only be told something about a conspiracy of the bodyguards, lord. That's enough—for the present. All we need do is to let them surround the palace and disarm the guards if they don't surrender. Then I go in with a few officers—there are enough here in this tent—to the king's room, and get him to sign his abdication. That will then be read out to the troops. They will swear fealty to king Adonias, and then friend Abiathar here can come with his anointing horn."

"Friends!" cried Adonias. "Our great general is right."

Joab's eyes sparkled. "I thank you, lord. I would therefore immediately—"

From the nearby city came the blare of trumpets. "The king's fanfare!" he exclaimed incredulously. Then they heard the confused and endless roar of the multitude, and again the trumpets blared.

"It's unbelievable!" cried Joab. "If I did not know it was impossible, I'd say the king is riding through the streets of Jerusalem."

At that moment a slender young man appeared at the entrance to the tent. It was Jonathan, son of Abiathar, pale and exhausted.

251

Adonias waved jovially to him. "Come in, my good fellow, and tell us what the good news is."

"Nothing good!" Jonathan managed to say wearily. "Our lord— I mean—King David—has proclaimed Prince Solomon king."

"How? What?" shouted Adonias. "Impossible!"

"They took him to the Gibon fountain and there Sadoc and the prophet Nathan anointed him," Jonathan went on. "On the king's own mule he rode into the city, accompanied by all the household troops under Banaias—and everywhere they proclaimed him king."

"And the people?" Adonias cried.

"The people cheered him," replied Jonathan. "And when I saw him last, he was entering the palace."

Adonias looked around him. There were already empty seats at the banquet table, and they quickly grew in number as more and more of the guests silently hurried away.

"Joab," whispered the prince. "What does this mean? Do you think—"

Joab gave a short laugh. "The old fox has got ahead of us," he said. "By my life, I would not have thought it possible."

"But what do we do now? What can we do?"

"Nothing at all," said Joab brutally, "except try to save what we can of our lives. It's too late now for anything else."

"You—you don't think Prince Solomon did this of his own accord? That _he_ should seize the reins of government—"

"Wake up, lord! He rode King David's mule. And Banaias has command of the household troops. That is not Solomon's hand, that is the claw of the old lion himself. Get out as fast as you can, lord, before they come for you."

The banquet table was now almost empty. Only Abiathar still sat there. He hid his face in his hands and wept.

"Put on plain clothes, lord," Joab warned the prince. "I shall do so too. Then we can go into the city and mingle with the crowd. But I'm afraid we'll have to shout 'God save King Solomon' if we don't want to be beaten to death."

"I'll shout," Adonias assured him. "But then? What then?"

Joab shrugged. "There are a few things King David has never

forgiven me for. Moreover, several of your guests who have just left in such a hurry will certainly tell him the plan I proposed a little while ago. It's all over with me. King David will no doubt spare you—he wanted his son Absalom to live. I doubt, though, whether King Solomon loves his brother as much as King David loves his son. Farewell, lord. I can be of no further use to you!" Calmly and without haste Joab walked out of the tent.

Nathan, the priest Sadoc, the gigantic Banaias, and many of Israel's leaders were gathered in the audience chamber. The doors opened and the young king entered solemnly. Drums rolled and trumpets blared. Solomon, slender, graceful, and still very young, wore his father's crown and had buckled on his father's sword. Slowly he walked past the deeply bowed backs of the courtiers, mounted the steps, and seated himself on the richly gilded throne. Immediately Banaias stepped to his side and one hundred picked bodyguards formed a half circle around the throne.

Sadoc, the priest, raised his arm. The great door to the king's private apartments opened for the second time and four servants carried a litter into the room. A murmur ran through the mighty gathering. On the litter—worn, hollow-eyed, his hair completely white—lay the king of yesterday. The servants carried him to the foot of the throne. Sadoc the priest cried in a loud voice: "May God make the name of Solomon greater than thy name, and make his throne greater than thy throne."

Then slowly, with a tremendous effort, but alone and unaided, David sat up on his couch. He crossed his almost fleshless arms and bowed before his son, who was now the king. And for the last time the great of the court heard the unforgettable voice, which could tame even King Saul's demon, which had challenged Goliath to fight, and had hundreds of times inspired the army to victory.

"Blessed be the Lord, the God of Israel," said David, "who has given that this day with my own eyes I may see my son sitting on my throne."

Solomon did not move. But when the servants picked up the

litter again and carried his father out, tears rolled down the young king's cheeks.

King Solomon visited his father daily and gave him a report of all his acts of government. David lay there, weak and almost always with eyes closed, and he questioned him.

"Have you found Adonias?"

"Yes, father. He had fled in disguise to the sacrificial stone in front of the holy tent."

"There a man cannot be harmed."

"Yes. And he refused to leave the place until I promised to spare his life."

"Did you do that?"

"Yes—with the condition that he would live quietly. He flung himself at my feet."

"You raised him?"

"No, father. I ordered him to go to his house and not to leave it."

"You have done right. And Abiathar?"

"He is and remains a priest of the Lord. I have exiled him to Anathoth."

"It is good. And . . . Joab?"

The young king sighed. "I do not know what I should do with him, Father. He has been your loyal servant for so many years. And he is still the best general we have."

David was silent for a while. Then he said: "Lean closer, my son. What I have to say to you not even the wind must hear." And he whispered to him: "A king must sometimes do things that no one else dare do and go unpunished. Joab has shed blood, and not only that of my enemies. He murdered Abner, the son of Ner, and Amasa, Jethra's son. Since then I have always hated his presence. And now? To end with, he has risen against me. Do not let him go unpunished, my son. And note carefully the names of my other enemies, who are now yours also . . ." As he went on whispering, Solomon listened gravely and nodded. Finally David said: "I shall soon go the way of all flesh. Take courage and be a man! Above all, keep to the law of the Lord

God, for only then will you be fortunate in everything you do. Now I am tired. Come back tomorrow morning. I still have the most important things of all to tell you."

The next day David spoke only of one matter: "When I made Jerusalem my capital and built this palace, my heart was sore. How could I live here in pomp and splendor—when the Lord our God had only a miserable tent for shelter? And I wanted to build Him a palace too, more beautiful and magnificent than my own. Then the prophet Nathan spoke to me in the name of the Lord, saying that not I, but one of my sons, was called to that task. And the Lord spoke through Nathan: 'I shall be his father: he shall be my son. And his throne shall endure forever.'"

Solomon was deeply moved.

"Perhaps you are the one," David whispered, "or perhaps it will be your son or your grandson . . . I do not know, I do not know . . ." His voice faded and for a second Solomon was frightened, thinking it was the end. But David was still breathing. He had only fallen asleep.

Day after day Solomon came, and David always spoke of the house of God. From time to time his thoughts wandered and he sang softly to himself, verse after verse of his songs. "The Lord is my rock, and my strength, and my savior. God is my strong one, in him will I trust: my shield, and the horn of my salvation. He lifteth me up, and is my refuge. My savior, thou will deliver me from iniquity. I will call on the Lord . . . and I shall be saved from my enemies . . ."

Then David's thoughts were again of building the temple, and he spoke of the cedar wood he had sent for from Phoenicia, of the precious and semiprecious jewels he had collected, and the treasures of gold and silver that were to pay for the work.

"If the Lord so will, I shall build the temple, Father."

David nodded, a slight smile on his bloodless lips. "The Phoenicians . . . will . . . help," he whispered.

Two days later the sick man lost the power of speech, and it was clear that he was nearing the end.

In the antechamber the royal princes and the great of the land were gathered; in the old king's chamber were only the young king, his mother Bathsheba, and the priest Sadoc. David saw them as if through a thin gray veil. But his eyes bade farewell to the wife who had been his great love, to the loyal priest, and to his son, the king. In the land between life and death the air was so thin that his thoughts could no longer take wing, and thoughts that had not come from him hovered in space. Where did they come from? Suddenly he knew why the temple of the Lord could not be his own work. Only the purest hands could build it, and there was blood on his hands. He was not worthy—but the Lord could make him worthy through his son . . .

Was it Solomon?

The figures by his bedside faded to mere shadows, and were extinguished. Solomon, too, would one day shed the blood of his enemies. He, too, would fail to build the true temple. Only when one of his descendants was innocent of bloodshed—except his own, sacrificed for others—only then could the temple be built.

Suddenly a great light, brighter and more radiant than the sun, came to him, the knowledge that the thoughts of the Lord were not the thoughts of men. The Lord did not think in terms of cedar wood, precious jewels, gold and silver. All the treasures of the earth would not suffice to build His temple as He wished it —greater than Jerusalem, greater than all Israel and all Judah. For its stones were the hearts of men. It was so clear, so simple— why had he not known this long ago?

Sadoc, the priest, closed David's eyes. And on the dead king's face there was a gentle, happy smile.